An Angel's Heart

by

Annette Miller

An Angel Haven Romance, Book 3

An Angel's Heart

Cover Art by *Angela Anderson*

The Wild Rose Press, Inc.
PO Box 708
Adams Basin, NY 14410-0708
Visit us at www.thewildrosepress.com

Publishing History
First Fantasy Rose Edition, 2016
Print ISBN 978-1-5092-1018-3
Digital ISBN 978-1-5092-1019-0

An Angel Haven Romance, Book 3
Published in the United States of America

Dedication

For my hubby, Brian, and my boys, Scot and Alex,
who always believed I could achieve my dreams.

"What are you doing?"

He stood in the doorway, wearing only jeans. His hair was in more disarray than usual. The early afternoon sun shone in, making him almost glow in the light. Magic flowed from him, filling her heart with joy at his presence. She could see bright light dance across his skin. Could that be his aura, and if so, how did she learn to see it? She'd carry the memory of how he looked right now for the rest of her life.

She held up the music box. "I was listening to it. I hope you don't mind."

"Not at all." He laid his left arm across the middle of his back and held out his right hand. "Shall we?"

Winding the music box and letting it play, she stood and took his hand. His steps were easy to follow, even though she'd never waltzed in her life. They twirled around the living room, the music seeming to get larger and fuller the longer he held her. As the music box wound down, they slowed and eventually stopped.

"That's such a beautiful melody. First the lullaby, then the music box. Your family knows the prettiest, and yet somehow incredibly haunting, tunes."

"It's part of our charm."

Praise for Annette Miller

"[*NIGHT ANGEL*] is the first book of Ms. Miller's Angel Haven series, and I'm hoping she will come up with a bunch more."

~*Annetta Sweetko, Fresh Fiction Review*

Chapter One

It's all my fault, Rachael thought. Tension radiated from the Angels team, and they'd avoided her all the way to the dark blue van that now carried them home. She'd tried to apologize several times, but the heaviness in her chest choked the breath from her, and the words wouldn't come. Heat blasted from the vents, trying to dispel the frigid January temperatures but couldn't warm the coldness she felt coming from Kristin.

She glanced at her team leader. As Kristin drove, her hands clenched the steering wheel, her back, ramrod straight, her gaze never wavering from the road stretching out into the descending darkness before them. Rachael had wanted to say something, anything, to ease the edginess around them but didn't know how or even where to start.

The gray bark of bare trees and dull, green bushes all blurred together as they sped back to Angel Haven, their home on the outskirts of Westchester, NY. She rubbed her right palm. These strange mood swings and slow loss of control began when an elderly man the Angels had saved shook her hand, holding it tightly. Pulling her gloves off, she absently scratched at it while continuing to stare out the window.

She thought back to the night's battle. *How could I have been so careless?*

Kristin turned up the long drive to the mansion

they shared and parked in the garage on the side. The Angels climbed out and hurried inside, never looking back. They were tired and dirty and knew there was a discussion coming. A private discussion held behind closed doors between Rachael and Kristin.

Kristin laid her hand on Rachael's shoulder. "Come to my study. We need to talk about what happened tonight."

Rachael followed her through the kitchen and family room, down the hall to where Kristin could usually be found when not working out. The long runner on the floor muted their steps, the framed pictures on the walls, barely reflecting their passage as they headed toward the last door on the right. She sat in the chair in front of Kristin's modest desk, the queasiness in her stomach reminding her of her days as a child being called to the principal's office.

"Before you say anything, I don't know what happened to me out there," she said, her Irish brogue more pronounced when she was upset.

Kristin folded her hands on her desk. "You put us all in jeopardy. We have a specific code in place, and we don't break it. Ever."

"I'm sorry. When that flunky for Dagger took aim at you, I lost it. My temper got the better of me."

Kristin stood and leaned forward. "We are heroes. The power in us can be devastating. We cannot afford to 'lose it.' You're lucky the villain in question has a high healing factor and it was Jack's ULTRA team that responded to the call. I don't want to see you hauled away for murder. Our team *does not* kill."

Rachael jumped to her feet. "I know, Kristin. I'm not five. My power sometimes makes it hard for me to control my emotions. Don't you dare lecture me on our team's regulations. I know them all. You're going to have to be a little more understanding about what I go through when I shift. Every animal has a different temperament. There are times when I have a hard time controlling the various urges that run through me."

Kristin was silent for a few minutes. "Karen called me a couple of nights ago. She indicated a confrontation was coming."

"How would she know? Ever since she married Randall, we hardly see her anymore."

"The northeast clan's oracle knew what was going to happen, and Karen wanted to let me know. She thinks you may need help. She says the fairy court can feel your power growing. The magic attached to your shapeshifting is getting stronger. You need to learn how to get a handle on it."

Rachael laughed. "So now you think I can't control my own abilities?"

"I didn't say that. I believe your power is growing, so I made a phone call. Someone will be coming to talk to you. After that, it'll be your decision. You can accept his help or not. But Rachael, you need to get a grip on the changes in your powers. If you don't, the next time, you may actually kill someone."

"Fine. I'll talk to him. But after that, you all need to stay out of my business."

Rachael stalked from Kristin's office, stomping up to the second story and down the hall to her room. As much as she hated to admit it, everything Kristin said was true. She was losing control, and it scared her. Lately, she'd sensed an outside power following her. It was strong, dictating her actions at times. She sometimes felt her mind wasn't her own. Maybe, whoever was coming to see her, would be able to figure out what was going on in her life.

****

Joe opened a portal behind the scaly abomination as Damen fired more rounds into it, forcing it back. The blessed ammunition ripped jagged holes through the tough, gray hide, its black blood dripping on the ground. Roaring in pain, it swiped at Joe, the breeze from its thick hand making his hair wave from its passing.

He dove to the ground, rolling out of its grasp. "Chrissy, now!"

A thin, dark-haired woman stepped forward, purple light emanating from her hands. She thrust her hands outward, the light rushing forth, slamming the other-worldly beast in its shoulder and pushing it through the portal. Joe waved his arms in a wide arc, shutting the doorway before the thing could recover and charge back through.

Sweat rolled down his face despite the fact the temperature was in the twenties. He walked over to where he'd thrown his jacket and grabbed it, brushing the snow from it. He shrugged into it, zipping it halfway. He pushed his hair back and wiped his forehead with the back of his hand.

Joe turned to his friends. "Is it me, or are these lower level demons getting tougher?"

"You might be right," Damen said. "I don't think we've ever had such a hard time with one before."

Chrissy dusted off her pants. "How's your hand?"

Damen pulled out a small vial of clear liquid. "Nothing a little holy water can't fix. I still have some of Gizel's salve left, too. Joe, you okay?"

Joe touched his temple and flinched. "I'm all right. I just need an ice pack and some aspirin. Chrissy, how about you?"

She laughed. "It never touched me. I let you guys take the beating."

The two men looked at each other. "Figures," Joe said.

Damen checked his watch. "It's after seven, and we all have somewhere we need to be. I've got a meeting for a baptism. Joe, didn't the Angels team call you for some help with a situation?"

He nodded. "Yeah and I'm already running late. Chrissy, when you find out how the level one escaped its realm, let us know. We may be getting into something bigger than we think."

"Sure. Later, guys."

As she drove off, Joe and Damen headed for their own cars. Damen stopped and turned. "Joe, something about what you're checking into feels bad. Watch yourself."

"All the time. Keep the faith."

The priest smiled. "I always do. It's how I earn my paycheck."

He headed north out of the city to the more upscale community in Westchester, wishing he'd had time to get cleaned up first. A little hot water would do wonders for his aches and pains right about now. He did wonder why the Angels had called him and how they'd gotten his number. He'd have answers soon enough, and he was curious to meet them.

The Angels had been in the news more and more frequently over the past eight months. After the hidden cabal had been broken at ULTRA, it seemed the public and other, more popular hero teams, were accepting them. It probably didn't hurt they had the best ULTRA field commander in the organization's history vouch for them, either.

A chill worked its way into his bones as the night got blacker. The closer he got to Angel Haven, the more unsettled he became. He pulled over and, getting out, called up his mage site. As a teen, he'd mastered the ability quickly, grateful on many occasions he'd done so. Moonlight lit the woods with silver light, his mage sight showing only the creatures that belonged there. Nothing appeared out of the ordinary, but still, the whole area felt a little off. A trickle of blood leaked from his nose. He sniffed hard and wiped it off.

Something evil was out there, watching him, waiting for its moment. He frowned. He didn't believe in coincidences. The slight nosebleed told him that much. There was a being with a lot of power that didn't want him to get to his destination. The strangest part was the familiarity of it, like a memory he just couldn't put his finger on.

When nothing moved or charged to kill him, he started again, breathing a sigh of relief when the entrance appeared on his right. Saying his name into the speaker, the gates swung wide, beckoning him up the long drive to the mansion looming at the end. The tires crunched on some loose gravel and snow laying on the concrete as the car rolled to a slow stop.

He parked directly across from the front door, taking small comfort from the solitary light burning there. Stepping out, he stayed next to the car as he looked up at the second story. A dark miasma hung over the far corner of the house. It didn't feel like a haunting. It felt like magic. Dark, ancient, forbidden magic wizards throughout the centuries had tried to destroy. He took a deep breath and wrapped his fingers around the pendant around his neck while muttering a short, protection spell, then slammed the car door shut.

Jumping over the two, low, concrete steps, he rang the doorbell and waited. Long minutes passed, making him check over his shoulder. The hair on the back of his neck stood up, and a shiver that had nothing to do with the temperature crawled down his spine. When the door opened, a tall woman stood there. Chestnut brown hair brushed her shoulders and, from her grip as she shook his hand, she had more muscle than her slim build indicated.

"I'm Kristin, the Angels' team leader. The northeast werewolf pack told me I can trust you."

He nodded. "Joseph Caine. Sorry I didn't have time to get cleaned up. Had to take care of something before coming here tonight." He smiled a little. "And I know the pack well, so yes, you can trust me. How can I help you?"

"It's not me. It's one of my teammates. Her name is Rachael. She's a shapeshifter."

"I know who you mean," he said. "She's the member that can change into any of the earth's natural animals."

Kristin led him to her study. "Yes. We've known her power has magic at its base, but lately, her abilities appear to be getting out of control. We were wondering if you could help her figure out what was changing."

He shrugged. "I'm not sure what I can do, but I'll try."

"Wait here. I'll get her."

Joe studied the room as the door clicked shut. Dark brown paneling matched the desk and bookcases lining the wall to either side of a small fireplace. From what he could see, all the volumes were reference materials. There was a long filing cabinet, each drawer meticulously labeled. Three small plants were on a decorative, white, metal stand in front of a window covered by a sheer, off-white curtain.

He walked over to them, rubbing a leaf from each one between his thumb and forefinger. The plants let their fear bleed into him, and he fought the coldness trying to seep into his heart. He knew they could feel things more acutely than any human and tried to visualize what they were sensing. He shook his head, the images too incoherent to sort out. But now he knew for certain, something evil was here.

"You guys feel it, don't you? There's something here, and we've got to get it out, or the whole team is doomed."

Shadows danced to the flickering of the fire and instead of warm and cozy, the room held a sense of danger, of something started and cruising quickly to a bad conclusion. Joe shrugged his jacket up a little higher on his shoulders and rubbed his pendant between his thumb and forefinger. The sooner he could find out what was going on and fix it, the better.

Chapter Two

The door opened and Joe turned. Rachael stopped just inside, and he stared at her. She was shorter than him by a good five inches. Loose ringlets the color of obsidian framed her heart-shaped face. In the middle, on top of her head, a shock of white hair hung over her violet eyes. Her natural defensive stance showed the toned muscles in her body.

His gaze moved down her body, from her perfect breasts to the tips of her tiny feet. The flare of her hips looked like they'd fit perfectly in his hands. She may be petite, but her strength of spirit filled the room and washed over him, letting him know, in no uncertain terms, she was no pushover. She was a fighter and an incredibly fierce one. He sensed her connection to the planet, and the underlying magic called to him, filling his senses with the sweet, yet spicy aroma of earth magic.

He frowned, picking up a taint in her abilities, a corruption in the early stages before showing itself. He shoved the feeling to the back of his mind and opened up his senses to try and find the reason why the magic in her powers was changing.

He stuck his hand out. "Joseph Caine. I'm guessing you're Rachael?"

Walking over to stand in front of him, she shook his hand. "You'd guess right. Rachael McCafferty."

He gestured to the chairs in front of the desk. "I was asked to come here to talk to you. Your team is concerned your powers may be getting stronger."

"Yes," she said, scratching at her right hand.

He waited. "Can you elaborate on that?"

She shrugged. "When I shift, I feel like I'm tapping into the earth itself. Like I'm not just becoming any of the animals that live here, but that I'm becoming the earth. It's a new feeling for me."

"I see." He was silent for a few minutes. "It sounds like a natural progression of your abilities. I'm not sure why your team called me. I'm a wizard, not a geneticist."

Rachael leaned a little closer to him, making him fight not to inhale her light perfume. It mingled together with the calming scent of lavender soap and shampoo, and the tangy, sweet scent of magic. With the floral perfume swirling around too, he didn't think anything would smell more wonderful than the woman in front of him.

"I think something is trying to control me. Tonight, we were called to a situation, and I seriously hurt one of the people we were trying to stop. That's not like me. I feel like I'm losing more of myself when I change."

Someone trying to control her would explain why her powers felt strange to him. "It's possible an outside force could be at work." Joe glanced at the ceiling. "What's in the upper story on the left side of the house?"

Rachael hesitated. "My room."

"With your permission, I'd like to check it out."

She smiled. "Is this a come on?"

His gaze shot to her face. Her slight smile showed

dimples, and her eyes, an odd light violet he'd never seen before, twinkled with mischief, making him falter. "What? No. I picked up some bad vibes. I'd like to check it out and see if something permanent is here or not."

She stood. "Well, let's go."

He followed her out and up the stairs, admiring the way her hips swayed as she walked. And that unblemished white hair tapered down to the middle of all those curls. He loved the Irish brogue in her voice, and the pixie-like quality it gave her. As they walked down the hall, getting closer to her room, the air became heavier and more fetid. He struggled to draw a decent breath and forced all thoughts of Rachael out of his head.

When she reached out to open the door, he stopped her. "Wait. Don't go in."

Staring at him, she withdrew her hand and stepped back. "If you say so. I'll wait here if you need me."

Joe eased her door open and shut it behind him when he was in. He almost gagged from the smell of decay. How could she be in here and not notice it? Something was after her all right, and that corruption was most certainly throwing her powers out of whack. He took a deep breath and pulled up his mage sight.

He scanned the room, looking for anything out of the ordinary. Everything appeared normal, but something had left its mark here. Studying every piece of furniture, every item, he found nothing that could be the cause of her lost control. His mage sight showed him everything was clear, except an area by the window.

He walked over and inspected the glass and the

frame around it. He stared out the window at the grounds. There. A spot by the large, oak tree. A portal had been opened. He opened the window and leaned out, the portal coercing him to come to it. His left hand came down on ice, the cold shocking him back to his senses. He slammed the window shut and turned.

Pressure began to build around him and making him back toward the door. He turned the knob, and when nothing happened, Joe turned to face whatever it was in there with him. Something crawled over his hand, and he jerked it up. Nothing was there. Starting at his feet and working its way up was the feeling of tiny legs, tickling his skin, trying to get inside him as pressure built in his mind, his sinuses aching so bad, he felt they would explode. Blood began to run from his nose.

"It's just an illusion. That's all. An illusion and nothing more. Nothing here can hurt me."

A deep laugh reverberated through him, and Joe grabbed his head, dropping to the floor. "And now you come to me," a deep voice said. "I am not an illusion. Leave the little shifter to me, wizard. Your ancestors couldn't stop me, and neither will you."

His gaze darted around the room, and he saw a black mass loosely form the shape of a man. A very large man. "How do you know me?" Joe gasped out.

"I know more about you than you know yourself. You will have only one warning. I will destroy you if you interfere."

"Then I guess I'll see you on the battlefield."

"So be it."

The voice faded away, and Joe wiped at the blood on his lip. Whoever was after her was more powerful than he, powerful enough to give him a serious nosebleed. The last time that happened, he, Damen, and Chrissy had fought a level three demon, and the thing had been incredibly powerful and evil. He clutched his pendant again, murmuring a quick prayer. He was going to need all the help he could get.

****

Rachael waited in the hallway and leaned against the wall. She didn't know what he could be doing in there. She had to wonder just what he was searching for in her room. She chuckled. Was he going through her closet? Or maybe he was looking through her dresser to see what she wore underneath. That thought gave her a quick shiver, letting her know fighting bad guys hadn't totally killed her libido, just dampened it a little.

When she first saw him, she had misgivings. He was covered in dirt and dust, and a large lump was forming on his temple. She saw a thin braided leather cord around his neck that disappeared under his T-shirt and wondered what sort of talisman he wore for protection. Was it a symbol of the power he wielded? And if she pulled it out, would it be warm from his skin? Would her hands tingle from touching him?

Rachael took a deep breath. She'd tried hard not to notice the way his shoulders filled out his worn, brown, leather jacket or the way his T-shirt accentuated the lines of his chest. His too long jeans hugged his hips, and the wrinkled layers dragged off the back of his sneakers. He was trim, in a muscular, sports fitness kind of way.

Weariness flowed from him, but his spring green eyes were sharp, missing nothing. He was handsome and ordinary, powerful and, at the same time, she felt a vulnerability in him. She crossed her arms and shook her head. She shouldn't be having these kinds of thoughts. She glanced at the door and smiled a little. Then again, why not?

Reddish-brown hair had lost the battle being parted down the middle, instead sticking out in all different directions, like he'd been in a tornado. Long bangs hung to either side of his face, the back just barely skimming the collar of his jacket. His jaw was covered with short, light brown, stubble and even though she didn't really care for beards, on him, it looked good.

A loud thump jerked her to a defensive stance as she stared at the door, waiting for something dark and unspeakable to emerge. It opened, and she relaxed when Joe walked out, pinching his nose. She looked over his shoulder into her room. It all looked the same except for the lamp near the door was on the floor.

"What happened?" she asked.

He held his hand up and didn't say anything for a few minutes. He let go of his nose and sniffed. He pressed the back of his hand underneath it, and it came away clean. "Let's go downstairs."

She could see the tightness in his shoulders as he walked stiffly down the stairs. She took a deep breath, his butt looking like it'd been made for jeans. She almost smiled as she realized he was a perfect candidate to be added to "The List" on the refrigerator door. She had a quick thought of slipping her hands into his back pockets. You'd better start concentrating on the situation, not on the person here to help with said situation, she told herself.

They went back to Kristin's office and sat in the same chairs. Rachael watched as he sat back and his lips moved silently. She waited until he was ready and then sat forward.

"Has anything strange or different happened recently? Have you been given anything or bought anything you wouldn't normally pick up?"

"No. What would that have to do with my powers?"

"There's someone or something incredibly powerful after you. It spoke to me, and I think it wanted to get rid of me right then, but for whatever reason, couldn't. Whoever it is, it's evil." He stared at her. "The entity has to be attached to something. Now think. Is anything different?"

"There's nothing different. I can't think of anything I've bought or gotten lately that could have something so evil in it. But—"

"But?"

"A couple of weeks ago, we saved an old man and he shook my hand. He didn't give me anything, he didn't do anything, just shook my hand and said how grateful he was we were there."

He held his hand out to her. "May I?"

She put her right hand in his and trembled as the warmth of his hand traveled up her arm to spread through the rest of her body. She fought to not curl her fingers around his and yank him forward to kiss him. Her skin felt every light touch, every trace he did. His fingers were calloused, rough against hers.

"Why is your skin so red?"

"I keep scratching it," she said. "It's been itching like crazy for the past week."

He just stared at it before reaching in his pocket and pulling out a business card. "You can call that number any time, and you'll get me. It's my cell phone. I've got a few ideas I want to check out with my partners."

She stared at the card in her hand. "Is there anything I should be doing until I hear from you?"

"Change rooms," he said. "And try not to use your powers any more than absolutely necessary."

She nodded and stepped a little closer to him. "Will you call soon?"

He reached out and brushed her hair back. "How about tomorrow? I'm not sure what time, though."

"Sounds perfect."

The door opened, and Kristin came in. "Can you help her?"

Joe shrugged. "I'm not sure. There's something involved here I don't know about. I think once I have all the answers, I'll know how to proceed. I'm going to call sometime tomorrow and find out how the night went. If you can leave Rachael out of any missions for a little while, it would be good. I don't want her tempted to lose control."

Kristin nodded. "I'll do what's necessary to keep her safe. We look forward to hearing from you."

Joe let himself out as Rachael turned to Kristin. "'*We*' look forward to hearing from you? It's my problem, Kristin."

"I know. I just wanted to let him know we're going to work together to help you."

Rachael sighed, her shoulders drooping. "I'm sorry. I think you're right about something being off with me. I've been snapping at you a lot lately. It's like I can't help it."

"It's all right. Joseph Caine will be able to figure

out what's going on. I'm sure of it."

Rachael looked toward the front door. She knew in her heart he'd know what to do. The fact that he was really hot didn't hurt. She was looking forward to working with him. She wondered. Did he feel the same?

****

Joe drove home and thought about the meeting. Rachael had told him all she knew, he was certain. He needed to find the old man the team had saved and talk to him. Maybe he'd have more answers afterward. He turned into his parking lot and got out as the motion sensor light clicked on. He hurried to his ground floor apartment, lowered the wards on the entry way, and was inside before the light went out.

"How'd it go?" Chrissy called from the kitchen.

Joe took his jacket off, dropping it on the back of the couch. He sat down and laid his head back, closing his eyes. "The whole situation is strange. Powers don't suddenly get all wonky just from shaking hands with some old guy." He paused and rubbed his eyes. "The magic fueling her powers feels off, like it's been tainted somehow."

"The old guy may not be what he seems. He's probably marked her. I can check if I meet her." Chrissy walked out, wiping her hands on a dish towel. "Is it something you can fix?"

"I don't know." He opened his eyes and turned to look at his friend. "Oh, he did mark her, I'm sure of it, and it's in her hand. Her powers are being forced to evolve by some being that's got a heck of a lot more power than I do."

She studied him, seeing blood in his slight

17

mustache and followed the trail through the stubble down to his chin. "Did whoever it was give you the nosebleed?"

He nodded. "And I'm getting a killer headache. Whoever it is, knows me. Knows my family."

"I saw revelations were going to be made to you, but I didn't know what they would be. Go wash your face, then come get something to eat," she said. "I knew you'd need something not too heavy tonight."

The small dining room table had seen better days, the spindly, metal legs getting more unsteady all the time. It shifted when Chrissy brought in a pot of thick, vegetable soup and some fresh baked rolls, setting them down in the center. She put a cup of hot tea on the table, then took her usual seat across from him.

Joe took a bite and closed his eyes. "Delicious as always. Did you find out anything about the increase in creatures we've been seeing lately?"

"Not too much." She grabbed a roll and buttered it. "It seems they're all being controlled, but I can't find out by who. I don't think it's a coincidence these creatures are roaming more freely at the same time a shapeshifter is losing control of her abilities."

They ate for a few minutes before she spoke again. "I've seen a vision of a warlock breaking chains holding him in a dark place. He might be the one behind everything."

"You're probably right. Your visions haven't led us wrong yet. One of the first questions we need to answer is, who helped him? The second is, how did they do it?"

"That's going to be hard to find out."

He looked up at Chrissy. "If he's trying to control

Rachael, his power may be allowing her to develop some kind of telepathic link to the magical creatures we've been encountering. If that's true, things could go from bad to worse." He wrapped his hands around the cup of tea, trying to ward off the internal cold slowly chilling his soul. "Something big is coming, Chris. I'm afraid by the time we find out what's going on, it's going to be way too late."

Chapter Three

The next morning, Joe sat at his computer staring at the screen, the blinking cursor waiting for a command. He'd been through his reference books the night before, after Chrissy left, but wasn't any closer to finding out the warlock's identity in his friend's vision.

"Who are you and why do you want Rachael so badly?" he said in a low voice.

His usual websites turned up nothing. He even checked some sites run by wannabe spell-casters and still had no luck. He'd messaged some of the people around the city he thought might know, but so far, no replies had come in.

However, many in the magic community had noticed the rise in portals being opened, giving demons and nether beasts access to their world. Concerns for novices had most of the masters pulling them off the street to keep them safe after some disappearances had been reported. Joe sat back, staring at the screen. It all had to be connected. But how? And who had that kind of power?

The hair on the back of his neck stood up as the increasingly familiar internal chill froze the blood in his veins. Easing out of the desk chair, he turned seeing no one, but he sensed a presence. Someone had blown past his wards and protections like they weren't even there. He sensed they were still intact, but power had been syphoned out of them, weakening them.

"Your wards are nothing to me, wizard. Your skills are laughable and you are not as powerful as you believe you are," a deep voice thundered in his mind. *"They should not have called you. The little shifter is mine, body and soul. You will be easier to destroy than I originally thought."*

Blood streamed down Joe's face, dripping off his chin onto his T-shirt. *"You won't claim her as long as I'm here to stop you. Identify yourself. Tell me your name."*

A shadow figure appeared before him. A bolt of pure force shot from his hand dropping Joe to his knees and making him clutch his head in both hands. *"I don't think so. I am more powerful than you. Do not try your pitiful tricks on me. Consider carefully, wizard, before you plan to make me your enemy."*

"You were my enemy before we even met," Joe said. He pushed himself to his feet, ignoring the pounding in his skull from the telepathic invasion. *"I will not surrender and let you claim an innocent soul."* He forced his hand to his pendant and curled his fingers around it, smiling when the speaker bellowed with rage in his mind. *"And you will not defeat me!"*

Bright, white light exploded out in a circle around him, sending the warlock screaming from his home. When he no longer detected the dark presence, he allowed himself to drop to the floor, pressing the back of his hand to his nose. He closed his eyes, saying a short prayer of thanks he hadn't been splattered where he stood. Everything just got a whole lot more complicated, he thought.

"Okay, so you just confirmed you're definitely

after Rachael." He pulled himself to his feet. "But why am I on your hit list?"

He staggered to the bathroom, pinching his nose shut, and jumped in the shower. He still needed to clean the previous day's fight from his skin and get the blood off his face. The warm water worked wonders, making him feel almost human by the time he stepped out. Now he had to call the Angels. After yanking on clothes he scooped up from his bedroom floor, he grabbed his cell phone and dialed Damen.

"Hey, I need a favor."

He could hear dishes clinking in the background. "What can I do?"

"I was just attacked in the psychic plane." Joe hurried to the kitchen and grabbed the carton of orange juice from the refrigerator. "A shadow figure appeared in my apartment. It completely ignored my wards as if I was a novice. I need to know who has that kind of power and how I can fight it. I know he's incredibly evil because of how often my nose bleeds. I need to know more about him and how he knows me."

"Maybe you should call your mother."

"No. It's bad enough he's after me. If I call my family, he might find them. They haven't called me about any attacks. As long as he stays focused on me, they should be safe. And I'm not going to risk them being found, just in case. I just need information. As soon as I know who he is, I can take him down. Of course, I may need a little help from my friends. We're stronger together. So the sooner you can tell me who we're up against, the better off we'll be. I'm going to get Chrissy in on it, too. Her intuition will be helpful."

"Let me do some research. Come by later and we'll

discuss the problem at length."

"Will do."

Joe hung up and stuffed his phone in his pocket. After taking a few gulps out of the carton, he put it back in the refrigerator and walked across to Chrissy's apartment. He banged on the door, smiling at her frown of disapproval when she answered.

"Orange juice is not a good breakfast," she said, holding the door wider. "And you've apparently left your clean clothes on the floor again."

"So you've said and yes, I did. I was just attacked. Whoever he is, he blew by my wards like they weren't even there. He did the same thing to my mental defenses last night. Have you discovered anything, no matter how insignificant, that might help me figure out what's going on?"

"Not with the Angels case. Was I supposed to be looking into that, too?"

He sat on her couch and shook his head. "I just want to know who is after Rachael and now me. He's already getting on my nerves."

Chrissy sat next to him and curled her legs under her. "One of my friends on WitchNet said there was a rumor floating around about a powerful warlock who broke a binding spell placed on him about a hundred years ago and is now free."

"When did you hear this?"

"It was a little after midnight. I checked your apartment, but your lights were out. I thought you went to bed early." She smoothed the afghan draped over the back of the couch. "I think he's the one after Rachael. It can't be a coincidence her abilities went haywire the same time he got free."

He nodded. "I agree. He got a name?"

"Ezra Barghest. The name is familiar, but I don't really know that much about him. My contacts are trying to dig up some more information for me. If I hit a dead end, I might call my dad. He knows a lot of history. He may have some idea of who we're up against."

"Good idea. I've got Damen checking, too." He got up and pulled out his cell phone. "I'm going to call the Angels and tell them what we know. I need to talk to Rachael again and see if she remembered anything else."

"Good luck," she called as he headed out the door.

****

Rachael spent a restless night. She'd refused to leave her room and crawled into bed. The longer the night went on, the more she thought maybe Joe had been right about her changing rooms. Shadows danced on the walls, and she heard every little sound in the great house. Grabbing the Celtic cross necklace her mother had given her, she held it tightly as she finally fell asleep.

She thought about the old man who had shaken her hand. He hadn't seemed sinister, but the more she tried to recall him, the fuzzier the memory got. Could he be responsible for the surge in her powers? As much as she wanted to say no, it looked like the answer was probably yes.

She'd told Joe about him and now couldn't remember why she'd thought such useless information was valid. He'd probably laughed at her all the way home. Some harmless old man was not the cause of her current problems...or was he? Things were getting complicated and completely out of control.

Sitting up, she felt she'd dreamed of someone all night. A tall man dressed in Victorian era clothes smiled at her and beckoned her to go with him. At first it had been a pleasant dream, but when she'd sensed a darkness in him, an evil that made her want to run as fast and as far as possible, the dream had turned frightening. She'd shrunk away from him, angering him, and his rage terrified her. She'd fled, not caring where she went as long as she was away from him. When he'd chased her, Joe appeared and defended her. Whatever was going on, her heart told her Joseph Caine was going to be her own personal savior.

Sunlight pushed its way into her room, banishing the fear from the night before. She stretched slowly, easing the cramps in her legs and the aches in her shoulders. Rubbing the back of her neck, she moved her head from side to side, trying to loosen her muscles. She dragged herself to the shower, reveling in the hot water splashing her face and easing the tension from her body. In no time, she began to feel like herself.

She'd finished dressing and was brushing her hair when there was a brief knock before Kristin entered. "Joseph Caine just called. He said he was sorry he didn't call earlier. He wants to meet you for lunch at a small café near St. Michael's church."

The thought of seeing him again made her heart flutter and her breath come a little quicker. She worried when he didn't call earlier and she almost sighed with relief.

"What time?"

"Around noon."

She nodded. "I'll be there."

After Kristin left, Rachael thought about Joe. She hadn't stopped thinking about him since he left the night before. It was more than how he looked. She couldn't ignore the connection between them, like they were two of a kind. The animal side of her detected his ties to the earth and it bound him to her. She was sure his powers gave her the same link, as well.

She'd thought of him before falling asleep. She would be a damsel in distress, and he would ride in to save her. She smiled. Not that she ever needed saving in real life, but it was nice to let him take charge in her dream. Would she let him take control in other ways, too? She'd like to find out.

She headed downstairs, snapping her mother's necklace around her neck. A small chill started and soon clamped itself around her heart. Joe's concern for her made her anxious to see him again. She gripped the Celtic cross tightly and prayed he would have the answers to stop whatever evil was after her.

****

The small eatery was filled with business people on their lunch hour. Rock music played a little too loud from speakers in the ceiling. Clinking of plates and the clanging of silverware mingled with voices of the patrons, making the noise level rise with every new customer. The air was warm from the grill and all the bodies waiting in line or sitting at tables. Bright lights banished every shadow from the corners.

Red, vinyl tablecloths stood out against the black and white linoleum floor, hanging over tables with thin, metal legs. The "to go" menu was posted on a large, backlit board behind the counter. Laminated double-sided menus graced every table for those eating there.

Joe sat across from Rachael at a two-person, back table. Delicious aromas rose from their plates. He turned a glass of water around in a small circle as he watched her. She was as beautiful as he remembered. She'd pulled up her long, black hair with a large clip, making the white patch on top more pronounced.

She looked up. "What?"

He reached out and lifted a lock of her hair. "In the middle ages, you would have been branded a witch with that shock of white on top."

She sat back and smiled. "You have any more pick-up lines as good as that one?"

"Tons." He watched her as the waitress refilled their glasses. "Where in Ireland is your family from?"

"Cork. I still have family there. I came to the States to study with a friend of my father's. He helped me understand and control my powers."

Joe drank some of his water. "Anyone I know?"

"Kristin's father. He keeps a low profile and is away on business a lot. He's involved with something political right now. It could be big."

"I stay out of real world politics," he said. "I have enough trouble keeping up with magical politics, which seem to change every day."

"A friend of mine married a guardian of the fairy world. She says the same thing."

He stared at her for a few minutes. "Your friend wouldn't be the one nicknamed the Dragon Angel, would she?"

Rachael smiled and laughed. "Yes, she would."

Joe sat back and nodded at the waitress who came to get their plates. He stayed quiet so long, he watched as she began to fidget in her seat. "Did she tell you something evil is trying to control you?"

"No," Rachael said. She stared hard at him. "All I have is your word something is after me. It could very well be you. You know what they say. Evil wears a pretty face."

"Thanks, but it's not me."

She leaned forward, her arms folded in front of her. "Prove it."

Tugging on the leather braid around his neck, Joe pulled out a small, dark brown, wooden cross. "Evil doesn't have faith."

"True." She held the cross between her fingers. The wood was warm, and she swore she heard it humming. "It's almost vibrating."

"An ancestor carved it from the fallen twig of a rowan tree. Every generation adds its own spells of protection to it. I added a layer when I first began studying, and I've continued to add to it every year." He grinned. "You aren't the only one with an Irish lineage. My mother's family is from the southern coast."

"I guess it is a small world."

He nodded. "Her family have been spell-casters for generations. I'm the current one. My mother taught me a lot of what I know and helps me figure out the rest. I also got some help from the fairy realm. I've added a lot of their spells to my own arsenal."

"You must be very powerful."

He shrugged. "That's what they tell me."

She gazed at him, leaning closer. "You don't usually find a spell-caster with faith. You're quite unusual, aren't you?"

"They tell me that, too."

The closer she got to him, the more he could smell her. The subtle perfume and the sensation of her magic wrapping around him sent sensual, invisible fingers tickling parts of him that would be better left alone until he knew what was happening. He couldn't help taking a deep breath and holding her scent inside him. Before he got too distracted, he paid their check, escorted her out, in the direction of St. Michael's. He watched Rachael look around.

Unlike the recent days full of dark gray, rolling clouds, the sky was a clear, bright blue, and the sun was shining, trying its best to warm things up. Snow lay piled against buildings and curbs. Dirt from cars and every day pollution had turned the top an ugly brownish black, but Joe knew underneath the superficial color, was the original pure white that fell from the sky. He glanced at Rachael. It was a perfect comparison to her. He could sense the darkness beginning to surround her, but felt the purity of her spirit deep within.

"I love January," she finally said.

"Why?"

"The holidays are over and things are returning to normal. The trees are bare, and it's still way too cold, but there's something in the air. Even with the snow covering the ground." She smiled as she looked around. "Stores are getting ready for Valentine's Day and Easter. Pastel colors are everywhere, and you just know warm weather will be here soon."

He stuffed his hands in his pockets, sure if he didn't he'd be holding hers in mere moments. "Well, spring is always hovering. It's got to be what you sense. You can feel it if you let yourself and if you know how."

She glanced at him. "And you know how?"

He nodded. "Of course. I'm an earth wizard. I'm tuned into the world. I can feel things, like when the seasons change." He spied a small tree near the church. "Come here."

People hurried by them as they stood in front of the tree. The sounds of traffic faded to the background when Joe put his hands on her shoulders. Normal city noise always seemed to mute when he tapped into the earth. He tuned to the power running beneath his feet, filling his heart and soul with the joy of being part of the wonder of nature. In turn, he could sense her connection to the planet and the living creatures who lived there. His power automatically began to seek out hers in a magical, connected wave.

Pushing those thoughts down, he said, "Think about how the tree will look in the spring. Because of the nature of your powers, you're tied to the earth. It shouldn't be hard."

She nodded and stared at the tree. "Now what?"

"You have enhanced senses. Take a deep breath, but concentrate on the tree. Close your eyes and picture it."

He watched her face scrunch up in concentration, feeling the exact moment when she made the connection, delighting in the instant when she sensed what he could without thinking.

"I can smell new leaves waiting to come out."

He knelt and brushed the snow away, revealing a small patch of frozen mud. "Put your hand on the ground." She did what he asked. "What do you feel?"

"I feel the roots taking a firmer hold in the dirt. I can feel the strength and the life in it." She turned to him, a brilliant smile lighting her face. Her eyes were bright with the new found knowledge of what she could do. "Wow."

He glanced up in the tree and a squirrel watched them. "Check it out."

Holding his hand up, the animal scurried down the trunk and jumped into his palm. He reached in his jacket pocket, pulling out a shelled peanut. The squirrel took it, cracking it open while Joe stroked its tiny, gray head. It chirped before running back up to the branch it had been sitting on.

He turned to Rachael as they rose to their feet. "How did you do that?" she asked

"Because my magic ties me to the earth, talking to animals is easy. That little guy was waiting for something to fall so he could grab it. I always have something for any critters that might be looking for a handout."

She wrapped her arms around him, and Joe didn't even try to stop himself from draping an arm around her shoulders, pulling her tightly against him.

"As an animal shifter, you're tied to the earth, body and soul. The warlock who's after you, this is what he wants to take from you. Don't let him."

"I won't." She glanced up at him and smiled. "I have you to protect me."

Chapter Four

St. Michael's church stood silent and stoic in front of them, making Rachael shiver as the shadow covered her. "Is it getting colder?"

He closed his eyes. "No, the temperature hasn't dropped. It probably just feels colder because of the shadow." He guided her toward the rectory door. "I want you to meet a friend of mine. He's trying to help me figure out what's happening with you and printed out some information for me."

The solid, wooden door had a small window with a frosted flower etched into the middle of it. The building itself was made of light tan brick, large windows on the ground floor, smaller ones on the second story. Five concrete steps led to a small porch with an iron railing on each side, scrolled bars anchoring it. Large, empty flower pots sat to either side of the door.

She nodded. They walked to the steps, and she stopped, not wanting to go in to the church. She rubbed the back of her neck, feeling a weight settle on her shoulders. "Something doesn't want me to go in there. I can't understand it. I've never not been able to enter a church before.

Joe stared at her, his eyes narrowing. He passed his hand in front of her. He could "see" a dark force trying to compel her to turn away. "It's the warlock who's after you. He knows you'll be beyond his reach in there.

We have to go in."

They turned as the door opened, and Damen walked out. "I thought I saw someone out here. Are you two coming in?"

Joe glanced at him. "That's what we're trying to decide."

She'd gone to church her whole life. Why was she hesitating now? Her mind turned again to the old man. She'd felt different ever since he touched her. Who was he, and why would he want to harm her? That was the real question.

Joe glanced at her and took her hand. "Take it one step at a time. Don't let him stop you."

She nodded and took a deep breath, letting her fingers curl around the iron railing in a tight grip. The cold chilled her hand, and she held it there, letting her palm warm the metal. She put one foot on the steps and hesitated, hearing someone roar in anger in her mind. Another step, then another. She concentrated on her feet, forcing them to move until she was inside.

As soon as the door shut behind her, she felt better. It was as if the outside world and all its problems and, yes, its evils couldn't touch her here. She stood in a small entryway, a worn welcome mat under her feet. The expected religious pictures hung on the walls. On a small, wooden table was a glass bowl with keys in it and some mail scattered across the top.

The walls were painted a cheery, light yellow, giving the whole house a welcoming glow. A doorway to her right showed a small dining room, with a kitchen at the back. To her left was a living room and next to that, a few steps down, was a closed door. At the end of the short hallway, a staircase curved up and to the left.

Next to it and directly ahead was another closed door.

Clattering came from the kitchen, and Damen carried three small plates with slices of pie to the dining room table. Joe swept his right arm out in front while his left curled around her waist. He guided her to the dining room, held a chair out for her, and hung her coat on the back, before throwing his on an empty seat.

As he slid into the seat across from her, he said, "Damen started doing some research for me about your situation."

"Joe said you haven't gotten anything new, correct?" Damen asked, bringing in three cups of tea. "No new trinkets, books, jewelry, anything like that?"

She scratched her palm. "There's nothing new. I haven't picked up anything different lately. A couple of weeks ago, an old man shook my hand. That's all. Is it possible my powers have just taken a bizarre, random turn? If so, as soon as I learn how to control the new abilities and urges, I'll be fine."

She studied the priest in the warm light of the afternoon sun. He was thin, but his arms showed strength under his rolled up sleeves. His age was indeterminate as his dirty blonde hair had the beginnings of gray threaded through it. His narrow face was angular with worry lines around his eyes and mouth. He looked like he had a permanent five o'clock shadow, yet his eyes were bright blue, with a gentleness to them that put her at ease. She could feel, just by being close to him, he was a good man.

Damen took her hand and turned it over, looking at her palm. It was red from her scratching it. He finally looked up. "I think it's more than that. Something has been planted on you with or without your knowledge. It could be something small, something you'd never suspect of being a conduit for a stronger force."

"I'm sorry, but I haven't found anything on me" she said. "There's nothing."

"As red as your palm is, I think it may have been imbedded under the skin."

She shuddered as Joe glanced at the priest. "Chrissy and I had that same thought."

Damen handed him some computer print outs. "Here are a few things I've found. Something in here should help you get started."

Rachael watched Joe as he thumbed through the papers. He underlined a few things, mumbling to himself. His hair hung over his eyes, but he kept studying the printouts. She stared at his mouth, his lips moving as he read. His long fingers tapped the table while he studied the papers. Scars covered his knuckles, the white, healed skin standing out against the tanned flesh.

The stubble on his jaw appeared to be more from the fact he'd forgotten to shave than trying to fit in with the so-called "hipsters" of the day. He gave her the impression he'd shave if he remembered, but didn't seem to matter to him as much as other things. She smiled a little. And it was that attitude that was another big attraction for her. She'd brushed off more dates than she wanted to think about because each one always looked like he was trying to be the next GQ cover model.

Another glance in Joe's direction. The tanned skin on his hands traveled up his arms, and she couldn't help wonder if he was that tan all over. What about his chest and back? What about his legs and, saints above, the butt that begged for her touch every time she walked behind him?

His leather jacket came to just below the top of his jeans, leaving her view unobscured. Handsome, sexy, and a body that made her mouth water every time she saw him made her conclude he had to be magical. No mere mortal could ever look so good. She silently reminded herself to make sure to add his name to "The List" when she got home.

As she gazed at him, she propped her head up on her hand. How would it feel to have him move those lips against her skin? To have his fingers trail over the sensitive areas of her body, making her beg for more. Was his stubble as soft as it looked? She licked her lips, suddenly mortified at the thoughts dancing in her mind as she sat in a *priest's* home. Oh, what the heck, she decided. Watching Joe was worth the risk of going to hell.

A clink of a fork on a plate snapped her out of her musings. She snuck a glance at Damen, who smiled while he ate. She nibbled a little of the pie he'd brought out for her. Her cheeks burned as she realized the priest had to know what had been going through her mind.

She cleared her throat. "Find anything interesting?"

"A few things that need to be checked out. It's a lot more than I hoped for when I got up."

Rachael tore her gaze away from him and turned to Damen. "Do you believe we can stop whoever it is that's after me? Do we even know why he's after me?"

Damen stood and began to clear the table. "We're not sure why he's picked you. Yet. He's probably got some plan that involves a shifter with your abilities. But, yes, given enough information, power, luck, and a little bit of faith, I know we can beat him."

The clock ticked loudly as Joe continued to flip through the papers. Soon, he sat back and threw the pen on the table. Rubbing his eyes, he stood. "I don't know what to do with most of what's here. I'll have to sort it out and see if it correlates with anything else in my files."

"Has Chrissy had any luck?"

"She said one of her contacts on WitchNet told her a warlock has freed himself from a dimensional prison. Don't know if he had outside help or is powerful enough to break the bonds himself. Considering the attacks lately, it could be the latter. We'd better get going so you can get to the homeless shelter. I'll call you later in the week."

They left St. Michael's and headed back to where they had lunch, walking in silence. Racheal started to say something several times, deciding against it at the last possible moment. Her hand began to itch, and she scratched it as they walked back to where they parked. It felt like the irritation went all the way through to her bones. She'd have to put something on it when she got home.

They got back to their cars and stopped, just looking at each other. "I can't protect you if I don't know who or what is after you," he said. "Are you sure you told me everything?"

"I know and I did. The only different thing was the old man." She scratched her palm again. "I hope he didn't have anything. My hand has been itching since he shook it."

Joe turned her hand over and stared at it. He saw the same thing Damen had—red, irritated skin. "It's pretty obvious the old man marked you. Irritation always springs up around a marked area. Where did your team meet him?"

"A tiny shop on the outskirts of the city. I can show you where, if you want," she said, forcing the words out.

He nodded. "That's a good idea." He caressed her palm. "I just don't know who would have so much power. I've got to go farther back in the histories. Something may be hidden in all the other stuff that's in there. The old man is tied in somehow." He reached out and pulled her close. "I'll call you later, if you want."

She nodded. "I want. Do you think I'll see you again soon?"

"Of course. How about if I come get you for dinner about six thirtyish." He smiled. "That soon enough?"

She stepped closer to him. "It'll do for now."

His gaze drifted to her mouth and she felt her body quiver. He traced her lower lip with his thumb and she slid her arms around his waist under his coat. She didn't know how long they stood like that, but she felt colder when he finally stepped back. "Until tonight, then."

He held her car door open for her. "Until tonight."

She pulled out, glancing behind her as he got in his own car. She sped toward Angel Haven, Joe never leaving her thoughts. She'd told him about the irritation in her hand but not how bad it was getting. She didn't know why she didn't, just that something felt weird in telling him.

She arrived home and hung her coat in the hallway closet, stopping by the kitchen to add Joe's name to the ever expanding piece of paper hanging on the refrigerator. She hurried to her room and stood in the middle of the floor, turning around slowly. The atmosphere felt different. She scrutinized every inch before crossing to the window and looking out. The yard looked the same. The afternoon sun cast long shadows. What had changed while she was out?

She shook her head and was about to drop the curtain into place when she thought she saw movement in the yard by the big tree. She leaned closer to the window, narrowing her eyes. There is was again. A shadow glided out from behind the tree—large, man-shaped and blacker than onyx—it stood there staring at her window. She forced her breath out in short gasps as if she'd forgotten how to breathe.

She stepped closer to the window, placing her palm against the glass. The shadow man raised his hand, matching hers. Even from far away, she could feel his touch against her skin, the frigid glass no barrier at all. Her palm tingled, and she leaned closer to the window, trying to see him better. As he stepped back, she knew he smiled, even though he was only shadow and she couldn't see his face.

As he disappeared, a chill settled in her heart and she missed his presence. She opened the window, leaning out to find out which direction he'd gone. Not seeing any obvious evidence as to his direction, she banged the window shut. She practically ran down the steps. Grabbing her coat, she rushed outside and ran to the large tree, her feet barely touching the ground. she searched the area for any sign of the mysterious visitor.

Nothing. No sign he'd ever been there. Her shoulders slumped as she walked around the tree a little slower, and her hand dragging around the trunk. Something crinkled, bringing her to a halt. She stepped back and there, tucked into a tiny crevice in the bark was a note. She plucked it out, stuffed it in her coat pocket, and hurried back to the house.

She took the stairs two at a time, slamming the door shut to her room before sitting down to read the note she knew was meant for her. Her fingers trembled as she opened the two folds. It was indeed addressed to her.

My dear Rachael,

One of my followers has given you my mark, letting me know you are the one. I shall come to you again soon. Tell no one we have been in contact. I am being hunted by people who wish ill upon me.

Until then,

Ezra

Rachael held the note close to her heart. Her instincts screamed danger, but her curiosity told them to take a hike. A mysterious stranger apparently needed her help. She shook herself and threw the note on her nightstand. Joe had to be told right away. He'd told her to be on the lookout for anything, no matter how small. She backed away from the small paper sitting there so innocently. Maybe she should see if she could find out who left her the note before telling Joe.

Her combat sense kicked into overdrive at that point, making her fingers massage her temples. Her mind was muddled and the air in her room weighed heavily on her, suffocating her with dark, dank, oppressive vibes. She stuffed the note in her pocket. She would tell Joe when he came for her.

In the back of her mind, someone laughed, a dark, malicious sound that invaded every fiber of her being. And the sound froze her soul.

****

Kristin called upstairs when Joe arrived. Rachael took one last look at herself in the mirror and nodded with satisfaction. She chose a simple outfit, just in case she needed to shift. One never knew what might happen. Reaching into her pocket, she verified the note was still there and hadn't done one of those horror movie vanishing acts.

She descended the staircase, smiling when Joe's eyes lit with appreciation. "Six-thirtyish, just like you said. I guess that makes you right on time."

He pulled her arm through his. "I never give a definite time so I'm always punctual. It's my well-kept secret."

She laughed. "I knew it had to be something like that. Where are we going for dinner?"

He held the car door for her before going around to get in. "No place fancy, but some place that's got good food and a nice atmosphere."

"Sounds wonderful."

They drove in silence for almost thirty minutes until Joe parked and they strolled the short distance to the restaurant. As they were shown to their table, Joe nodded to a few people Rachael assumed he knew. She watched him flip open the menu and scan the contents, then he looked up and their gazes met.

They sat like that for a few moments before he spoke. "Do you know what you want?"

She nodded as she continued to look at him.

He grinned. "I meant from the menu."

"Oh. Yes, I think I know what I'm going to order."

She told him what she wanted and could feel her cheeks grow warm. Was she really that brazen? Not usually, but there was something about him that appealed to her on a level she didn't even know she had. He drank some of his water, and she watched the muscles in his throat move. She followed his arm as he set the glass on the table. It was all she could do not to squirm in her seat.

"Has anything else happened?"

She stared at her water glass, suddenly not wanting to tell him about the note. "Not really. I have to confess I stayed in my room and then I wished I hadn't."

Leaning forward, he stared at her. "Did something else happen?" he repeated.

"It was just more of a feeling. I kept seeing shadows move and hearing things. The air felt so heavy, I thought I would choke on it."

"Anything else?"

She shook her head. "No. Everything is the same as it was the first time we talked."

I need to tell him about the note, she thought. Their food came and as they ate, she tried again. "I found something around the large tree on the grounds at Angel Haven."

He looked up. "What?"

"It was…" She stopped. "It was…never mind. It's not important."

"Are you sure? The littlest thing could be important."

She took another bite of her dinner, wishing he'd stop staring at her. "I'll show you next time you come to the house."

"All right. How about tonight?"

Rachael couldn't think of any reason to deny him, so she agreed. When he took her home, she'd show him what she found.

She sat a little straighter and stared at the back corner. "Is something back there?"

Joe waved the waiter over and got the check. "Yep. It showed up about ten minutes ago. It's a hunter. It stays in shadow form in the light, then solidifies into something large and nasty. I picked it up when it first came in."

"I never seen one of these things before. Have they always been around?"

Joe nodded as he signed the check and stood. "They've been hunting people since there were people to hunt. We're going to have to run for the car. Don't stop." He handed her the keys. "I might be able to slow it down for a few minutes. Just get in the car and get it started."

She took the keys, noticing her hand tremble a little. "What does it want?"

They pulled their coats on and headed for the door. "I think it's here for me. I've been after these things for a long time. We're going to head for St. Michael's. I need Damen's help to banish it."

The other patrons were oblivious to the thing's presence, laughing, talking, and eating their dinners. "How do they not see it?" she asked.

"You've got to have some magical ability to be able to pick them up," Joe said, pulling his coat on. "Ready?"

She nodded, and they hurried outside. Rachael clamped her lips together so she wouldn't scream as a long, black shadow oozed down the wall and slithered along the floor after them.

Chapter Five

Outside, the shadow coalesced into a large beast, its front legs longer than the back, giving it a hunched appearance. The muscles in its chest moved fluidly as it stalked toward them, claws scraping the sidewalk. Its hide seemed to continually alternate between gray, black, and deep green as glare from windows shined on it. Its murky green eyes watched their every movement and it snarled, showing large teeth.

Rachael glanced behind them as they alternated between walking and running to Joe's car. "It's gaining."

"Don't look at it. Just do what I told you."

Rachael unlocked the driver side door and jumped in. She rammed the key in the ignition, and the car roared to life as she hit the gas a little too hard. Joe turned and a bright light flared from his fingers, making the thing stop in its tracks and scream in pain before Joe tumbled into the passenger side.

He slammed the door shut and lowered the window. "Hit it. Turn right at the corner."

The hunter shook off the effects of the light burst, ambling into a run after them. It roared as Joe leaned out the window, flicking tiny darts of light at it, smiling grimly when they struck the hunter's hide with little explosions, leaving smoking holes where they hit.

"At the light, turn left and go straight for three

blocks. The church will be on your right. Pull into the parking lot and head for the rectory." He fished his cell phone out of his pocket. "Damen, we've got a problem." He fired more tiny missiles at it before slamming his head against the car as Rachael made the turn.

Cold wind filled the car as she sped down the street, whipping her hair around her face. "The church is coming up."

"We're here. Get outside now."

Joe ducked back inside the car, jumping out as soon as she stopped. Damen came running out of the rectory, his gun aimed right at the hunter lumbering in behind them. Joe grabbed Rachael's hand and pulled her toward the building. He heard Damen hit the hunter, but it didn't slow down.

Joe pushed Rachael away from him as he turned to make a stand against the hunter. "Rachael, head to the church."

The hunter leapt, knocking Joe to the side with its giant paws. Jaws, dripping with saliva, snapped just above his head as he scurried backward. The hunter took another swipe, sending Joe rolling along the ground. It growled at Damen, then turned its attention back to Joe. It swiped at him again, tearing through his jacket and shirt, all the way to his skin.

Joe scrambled to his feet, swinging his arm across his body and up. Leaves flew from the ground, swirling around the hunter, confusing it. He turned his palms upward and stabbed his arms straight up in the air. Gravel and small pebbles zinged toward the hunter, pelting its side and making it growl louder. He held one palm above the other, orange light building between them.

The hunter slowed and lowered itself to a crouch as it watched them. Menace rumbled from its chest deep enough to vibrate the ground. Its massive, black head swung in Rachael's direction, its pond scum colored eyes missing nothing. Joe brought his hands together, releasing the fire bolt he summoned. Damen fired again, the blessed ammunition tore holes in its side, making it howl.

Rachael stopped as the beast gazed at her, a piteous noise working its way up from its massive throat. "Stop firing."

Joe and Damen watched as she walked slowly toward the hunter. It laid down and waited for her, not moving. Rachael stopped in front of it and just stared. "Why do I feel your pain?" she murmured. She put her hands in her coat pockets and the note from Ezra crinkled as her hand brushed it.

She reached out, laying her right hand on the slimy, cold muzzle, and the burning in her palm flared before dying to a tiny itch. "You poor thing," she murmured.

Joe opened a portal underneath it, sending it back to its home world. As soon as it was gone, Joe and Damen breathed a sigh of relief. Joe walked over to Rachael. "How did you do that?"

"I don't know. All of a sudden, I could see what it saw, feel what it felt. It wanted me to help, and I didn't know how."

Joe put his arm around her and held her close. "Let's go inside and see if we can find some answers."

When Joe took his jacket off, he shook his head at the torn leather. He closed his eyes and pale, green light formed around his hand. He passed over the tears in his jacket, and they wove together, repairing themselves. He smiled as he handed it to Damen.

The priest hung up their coats before leading them down to the dining room. "You fixed your jacket again, but how are you? You okay?"

"I'll live, but I'm going to feel this tomorrow," he groaned, easing slowly into a chair.

Damen grabbed a bottle of ibuprofen and set it on the table with three mugs. "Tea or coffee?"

"Tea for me," Joe said, his gaze never leaving Rachael's face as he reached for the bottle.

Rachael looked everywhere but at the man in front of her. "Tea for me, too, please."

No one said anything, and Rachael knew what they wanted to ask. "I don't know how I could talk to it," she finally said. "It's like the two of you are blaming me for something."

"We're not blaming you for anything," Joe said. "It's got to be your animal connection that allowed you to understand it."

"That seems the most likely explanation," she said. "But I've never been able to talk to magical creatures before. Why now?"

"It's probably the influence of the warlock we suspect of trying to control you." Joe stood. "I'm going to clean up these scratches. You still got some holy water in the medicine cabinet?"

"Always. There's some salve left, too. Make sure you get everything cleaned out."

Joe nodded. "I'll be back in a few minutes."

Rachael watched Damen. He went back to fixing tea for them and didn't say anything. "Why do you think I could talk to that thing?" she asked.

"As a priest, I'm really not supposed to make judgements."

She leaned forward. "Please. There's something going on with me, and I don't know what it is. Frankly, it's a lot scarier than I want to admit."

He turned around and folded his arms. "Fine. I know you've received something recently, and you're hiding it. It's a particular talent of mine. I also know now, you're afraid of me, and if you could, you'd be out of here in a second. You're only staying because you're beginning to have feelings for Joe. If what you're hiding is influencing these changes your powers are going through, we can't help you unless you tell us what it is."

The note, she thought. He knows about the note. She would tell Joe about it when they were alone. She didn't want Damen to know. Even if the priest did suspect something, she refused to be the one to tell him. She felt so different from the last time Joe brought her here. The note. She didn't have it then.

She finally sighed. "And now we're back to that. I am not hiding anything. How many times do I have to say the same thing?"

"Until you believe it. Keep in mind, you may be saying that because whoever is in charge of whatever you're not hiding may be wanting you to say that."

Rachael sat back and played with her spoon. "I don't even know how to respond to that." She glanced down the hallway, wishing Joe would come back.

Damen went back to fixing the tea, the silence around them getting longer and more uneasy. Rachael wanted to be anywhere but where she was, and she wanted Joe to be with her. She rubbed the back of her neck, trying to work the tightness out.

Joe came back in. "What happened?"

Damen handed him a mug. "We were just talking. Let's go to the living room. It's a little more comfortable."

The three of them walked across the small hallway to the living room. Damen turned on a few lamps, making the room feel warm and homey. Joe sat on the couch, smiling when Rachael sat next to him. "Could the warlock be wanting to control Rachael for some reason? Could his influence be what let her talk to the hunter?"

Damen shrugged. "Rachael and I were talking about that possibility. I think the warlock has a specific plan. We need to find out what it is before he does something to implement it."

She set her mug on the table and curled up next to Joe, taking a deep breath and releasing it when his arm went around her. "Is there any way we can find out?" she asked. "I'd like to know for certain if someone is trying to control me."

"I want you to meet a friend of mine," Joe said. "Her name's Christine Ford. Her magic is more intuitive than mine."

Rachael smiled. "Apparently, you've got a lot of attacks in your arsenal."

He chuckled. "I can blow stuff up, but the more delicate magic is not my forte. I've mastered the power driven spells, Damen's magic lets him find hidden things and he's also got his faith, and Chrissy is a type of clairvoyant. She's no slouch in the power department, but that's not really who she is."

She looked up at him. "And who is she?"

"She's the anchor that keeps us grounded in a fight." He held Rachael a little tighter. "If you want, you can stay with me tonight. I'd like to keep you under better protection and close in case something happens."

"I'll be fine," she said. "I'm more comfortable at home, but I may take you up on that offer in the future."

"It's always open, and maybe Chrissy will cook. She makes the best food."

It sounded like he had feelings for Chrissy and that was unacceptable. She wanted to be his anchor. Yes, she'd meet her. Then she'd let her know she was no longer welcome in Joe's life.

Rachael frowned. Where that had come from, she had no idea. It wasn't like her, and she definitely didn't care for what kept rolling through her mind. I'll tell Joe soon, she silently promised. About the note and these hateful thoughts. There really is something bad going on with me.

****

Joe drove her toward Angel Haven. She'd been different ever since the battle with the hunter. "Are you sure you don't want to stay with me tonight?"

"I'm sure. I feel better when I'm in familiar surroundings." She smiled at him. "Thanks for the offer, though."

They soon pulled up to the front of her home. Joe suppressed a shudder as he looked at the great house. Something felt more off than it had the day before. He glanced at her. She gave no outward sign that she felt anything wrong.

"I'll be by in the morning. I want you to talk to Chrissy as soon as possible."

She gazed him for a moment. "Should I be jealous?

50

It sounds like you have feelings for her."

Joe laughed. "We're just very good friends."

"And does she feel that way, too?"

"Yes. We had that conversation. Our friends thought we'd get together, but those types of feelings aren't there." He took Rachael's hand and held it tight. "We really are just good friends."

She glanced at his hand holding hers. "And what are we? Am I just some person who needs your help?"

He slowly raised her hand to his lips. "I'm hoping there's a chance we'll be something more."

Joe pressed his lips against the back of her hand and smiled a little when she shuddered. He looked up to see her gazing at him in a way Chrissy vowed never to look at him. Feelings were there, but he could see coldness in the depths of her eyes. He swore whoever was after her would not have her while he was alive to prevent it.

She got out, and he watched her walk to the front door. Her hand went in her pocket for just a moment, before she pulled it back out. Yes, she was hiding something. He hoped she'd tell him soon.

Somewhere in the black shadows, something laughed, making his magic cringe and a trickle of blood run from his nose.

Chapter Six

Power. She could feel it pound through her veins, sing in her blood, and wrap around her from the woods circling her. Rachael looked up through the trees and smiled when the moon's light spilled over her. She didn't recognize where she was, but didn't care. She was out of the house and free.

"You are free, little shifter."

She spun around and stepped back. "Who are you? I warn you, I won't be easy to take down. And where are we?"

Holding his hands up, he walked toward her. "I'm not here to harm you. I'm the one who left you the note. I wanted to finally meet you face to face. We are in the woods near my home, but only in a dream state. You are still in your bed."

"Oh. What did you mean in the note when you said I have your mark? I don't understand."

"I need help opening a portal so I can return to the earth. I've been locked in a nether dimension for so long." He closed the gap and took her hand. "I need someone with abilities like yours. Someone special. Someone who I know will do the right thing."

Rachael couldn't look away from his eyes. They were dark, almost black, hiding things she was sure she didn't want to know about. "You scare me. I don't know you. I don't know anything about you. I don't know if you need help or if it's just another take over the world scheme."

He laughed the same dark laugh she'd heard in the back of her mind when she read the note. "I have no illusions of grandeur. I just want to end my exile. I've completed the first step. I need help with the rest of it. And that is where you come in."

They began walking deeper into the woods surrounding them. Cold seeped into every part of her, making her teeth chatter. She wanted to be out of here. "You're not going to sacrifice me or something are you?"

"No. There's no sacrificing of *you* involved." He smiled. "Don't worry. I will always be watching and will protect you if you need it. You mustn't let anyone know about me. There are forces, wizards, at work that will try to stop me from returning."

Rachael thought for a moment. "You're talking about Joe and Damen, aren't you?"

He linked her arm through his and patted her hand. "Yes, among others. All you need to do is keep my presence a secret. If you do, you will have more power than you've ever dreamed of."

"I don't want power," she whispered.

"You will, once you realize what you can do with it." He stopped suddenly and turned her to face him. He cupped her chin, gazing at her. "I know you are beginning to have feelings for the wizard, and I can't stop you. Just remember me when you two are together, and all will be well."

Rachael stared at him. "Will he try something?"

"It's possible. Don't let him. I know his family. I've fought them for generations. They are deceivers."

"I'll be careful," she promised.

He lifted her hand to his lips. "Time is growing short. I can only maintain a presence on the dream plane for a short time. Think of me, Rachael. Dream of me. I will come to you again soon. I promise."

She smiled and he faded away. She turned to the trees, and Joe stepped out. She ran to him, and he pulled her into a tight embrace. She snuggled against his chest. "I missed you," she whispered.

"Liar. You meet with the enemy and try to soothe me with pretty words," he growled.

Rachael stepped back, and Joe's features had changed. A deformed abomination stood before her, reaching out to grab her. Rachael used her power to shift into a large grizzly bear and swiped her massive paw at him, raking his stomach. He fell to the ground, his blood soaking the area around him.

He morphed back into himself and looked up at her, a tear welling before spilling down his face. "Why did you kill me?" he whispered. The light left his eyes as his chest slowed to quit rising all together.

Rachael stumbled back and screamed. She shot straight up in bed, covered in sweat, her chest heaving as she struggled to make her lungs remember how to work. That dream was a bad omen if ever there was one.

****

Joe tossed and turned, before giving up and swinging his legs over the side of the bed. The skin across his midsection was on fire. He rubbed it and sucked in a breath when it felt like he'd dragged sandpaper across a sunburn. He shuffled to the bathroom, yawning. Even when he had to be, he hated being awake at two in the morning.

He flipped on the bathroom light, blinking furiously. His mouth hung open, and his eyes widened. What the heck happened? Three bloody stripes went downward from the bottom of his chest, tapering off on his side. It looked like he'd be attacked by a wild animal while he slept. If he wasn't awake before, he was now. And blood dripped from his nose.

Wild animal. He pinched his nostrils together and walked to the living room. Rachael shifted into earth's natural animals. No fantasy beasts, just creatures you'd find every day. He'd just flipped on the kitchen light when there was a knock on his front door.

He dropped the wards and opened it, knowing who was there before he even checked the peephole. "Hey, Chrissy, come on in. I was getting ready to put the kettle on for some tea."

"I knew you were going to need me. I've been up for the past thirty minutes waiting for you."

Joe put two mugs on the counter and started the kettle. "I'm having orange mint. You?"

Chrissy slid into one of the dining room chairs. "The same. What happened and who'd you lose a fight to?" she said, pointing at the scratches on his torso.

"I don't know. I had a nightmare that I don't remember. I woke up and discovered the marks." He poured the water and brought the mugs in before sitting across from his friend. "I think, somehow, Rachael affected me on the dream plane."

Chrissy stared at him, her eyes wide. "How is that possible?"

"I don't know. Her powers don't work like that. She's a shifter. And while magic is at the base of her abilities, she's not a magic user."

"Then someone is messing with some serious power. Do you think you might have had a vision?"

Joe stared at the steaming mug in his hands. "I hope not. I thought I lost that ability a long time ago, and I don't want it back. Visions are your department. But the nosebleeds are getting more frequent and heavier."

He turned to look out the window. The blackness enveloped them like a constricting turtleneck, choking them until they couldn't draw a decent breath. "There's something out there. I just wish I could figure it out before it's too late. I mean, I get nosebleeds for two reasons."

"I know," she said. "Attacked by something powerful or in the presence of absolute evil."

He looked up. "I think it's both. Any warlock is bad news, but I think he's going to be the worst we've ever faced. I'm afraid for us. I'm pretty sure we've all been targeted."

"I think you're right." She stared at him. "And you know Rachael's at the heart of it."

He nodded. The whole situation seemed to revolve around her. They clinked mugs. "Here's hoping we live through it," Joe said.

****

Early the next morning, Joe was admitted to Angel Haven and Kristen led him down to her study. His eyes never stopped searching the house, and the miasma of darkness felt thicker and larger than it had the previous evening. He pulled his jacket tighter around his shoulders and sat in the chair facing Kristin's desk.

"Before you call Rachael down, I want to ask you a

few questions."

"All right. How can I help you?"

He sat back and hesitated. He was about to accuse her teammate of duplicity, of being secretive and lying. "Has Rachael been different in the past couple of weeks? I mean like hiding things, not being completely honest?"

Kristin leaned forward and folded her hands on top of her desk. "Exactly what are you saying? Are you accusing her of doing something illegal?"

"No. There's something different about her. Every time I see her, she's changed a little more. If I'm noticing changes in her, I'm sure you, as her teammate, have also seen things not quite right about her. I need information if I'm going to help her on any level. Is there anything at all you can tell me?"

"She's been staying in her room more. That's not like her. When she does go out to walk the grounds, she seems to have an obsession with the large oak tree out back. It's directly across from her window."

Joe stood. He'd noticed the oak his first night there. "Can you show me?"

Kristin nodded as she headed to the door. "Of course. Mr. Caine, what do you think is going on with her?"

"She's being possessed by someone that hates everything and wants to be free."

They headed out of the house, and she pointed out the large tree before going back inside. Joe walked closer to it and laid his hand on the trunk. He squeezed his eyes shut as images bombarded his mind. A large, shadowy figure, a small paper, Rachael coming out to the tree. He knelt and dug his fingers in the dirt at the base. The roots were getting sick from being near the shadow man.

"Someone has been here," he said, his voice hushed. "Multiple times. He's stood here, watching the house, watching her."

He rose slowly to his feet and turned to stare at an upper window. He could sense Rachael moving around in her room and feel the darkness pervading her area. He called up his mage sight and slowly looked around. He could see a black stain leaking out from around the tree and oozing in a straight line to the house. He followed it and could tell it was beginning to climb the side.

The whole area needed to be purified. He had to get Damen out here as soon as possible. Rachael was in danger and her teammates were too, just by being near her. The warlock wanted her. Badly. He was willing to destroy everything and everyone in his path to get her. Joe had to figure out how both he and Rachael fit into his plans, and soon. A sense of urgency made his hands tremble. The sooner he knew what they faced, the better.

He walked back into the great house and headed for Kristin's study. "Do you remember saving an old man a few weeks ago?"

"Yes," she murmured. "He thanked all of us and then grabbed Rachael's hand. He held it longer than I thought necessary, and she talked to him for a few minutes. Ever since then, when she thinks no one is watching, she scratches her palm like she's going to peel the skin off."

He sat back, gripping the cross around his neck. "I need the location. I've got to meet the old man. He's the catalyst that set everything in motion. I have to know what he did to Rachael so I can undo it."

Kristin pulled out her phone and sent the address to him. "I've sent the address to your phone. Plug it in to your GPS and it should take you right back to where we were that night."

He checked his phone and the message came through. He closed it and rubbed the back of his neck. A message slammed into his mind before he could stop it.

"You will not undo my work, wizard. I will destroy you if you try. Remember the scratches down your torso. I can attack you whenever and wherever I chose."

Joe grabbed his head and fell to his knees on the floor. His jaw ached from the force of his clenched teeth, and he felt blood drip off his chin and on to his legs. A light touch on his shoulder grounded him, and he came back to himself.

"Are you all right?"

Joe looked up into Kristin's face and nodded. "I'm okay. Psychic attack." He got his feet and wavered. Kristin grabbed his arm until he steadied himself. He pinched his nose and waited before letting it go and sniffing hard.

"Whoever it is after Rachael is a lot more powerful than I am." He closed his eyes and could "feel" Rachael headed for the study. "She knows I'm here. You got a tissue?"

****

Rachael watched Joe out of her bedroom window and frowned. Kristin showed Joe the tree, her tree. Why would he ask her for help? Kristin wasn't the one having problems. Joe was supposed to be there for her. Rachael's fingers curled into a tight fist. Was he the type of man to try and hook up with two women at once? At first, she would've said no.

She rubbed the back of her neck. He'd made no physical contact with Kristin. She only pointed out the tree, then had gone back inside. Rachael thought about the way her body tingled every time she felt his gaze and knew he had no feelings for her team leader. Joe wore his feelings out in the open, and he was taken with her. She squeezed her eyes shut. Or was she just imagining things?

"I told you he was only leading you on," Ezra's voice whispered. *"When the time comes, you and I will destroy him together."*

Rachael hurried downstairs to meet him when he came in. The farther she got from her room, the more she started feeling like herself. She took a deep breath and smiled when they came in. "I saw you out by the tree. Find anything interesting?"

Joe glanced at her. She'd pulled her hair off to one side, and the outfit she wore was loose, but having seen her in a more form fitting clothes, he remembered the curves she hid underneath. He pulled up his GPS and plugged the address in. "As a matter of fact, yes. Grab your coat. We've got some errands to run."

She gathered her things and followed Joe to his car. They got in, and he sped down the drive to the main road as fast as he could. He didn't slow down until his GPS said they had reached their destination.

Rachael laid her hand on his arm. "What did you and Kristin talk about before I came down?"

"I asked her about you." He turned in his seat and

looked at her, searching her face for any sign of the black entity he kept feeling skulking around her. "I needed to know if you had changed any from when the old man touched you."

"I haven't."

"According to Kristin, you have."

Rachael stared out the windshield and crossed her arms. "I'm telling you I haven't."

"Would you know if you did?"

She slowly turned in her seat. "What do you mean?"

"I mean, a lot of people I help don't know when something is controlling their actions. I'm beginning to think that might be the case with you. These changes in your powers came on too quickly for natural progression. I think someone is forcing your abilities to evolve and taking you along for the ride."

She chuckled. "That's a lot of supposition."

He got out and walked around to her side of the car and opened her door. "And that's why we're here. I need something concrete, or I can't fight whoever is behind it all."

Chapter Seven

Rachael stared at the building. "This can't be the same place," she said, walking forward. "It looks like it hasn't been lived in for years."

The building in question had broken boards across the windows and doors. A huge padlock hung from a rusted metal hinge, and the condemned notice had ripped away from one of the nails and flipped around in the slight breeze. Tall weeds waved, the spindly stems almost bending in half. The walkway to the door could barely be seen because of the thick mounds of grass filling the cracks.

The roof sagged over the warped porch, the wooden siding weathered to a faded gray, warping in many places. Windows that had once been impressive, looked like they had been the object of a lot of target practice from the neighborhood kids. Flapping could be heard inside and Joe was certain there was more than one hole in the roof. He checked the address on his GPS again and they were at the right place.

He laid his hands on Rachael's shoulders and led her back to the car. "Stay here. There's something wrong."

"But I can help."

"If it's clear, I'll call you in." He pulled her close for a moment. "I don't want you tempted to lose control. Trust me." He grinned. "Next spooky location is all yours, all right?"

She nodded and wrapped her arms around herself. He watched her lean against the car before he headed back to the building. He put his hands together with his palms turned outward toward the door and slowly moved them apart. As he did, a portal opened, and he stepped through.

He shut the doorway he'd created, making sure Rachael couldn't follow him in. He stepped over debris, trash, and other things he really didn't want to know what they were or even what they were supposed to be. Scrabbling in the other room made him look up. It could just be some animal, but he needed to make sure.

The sound came from behind a partially closed door, and he laid his hand against the rough wood, pushing it wider. The same musty smell of decay hit him square in the face. He coughed and stepped farther in, kicking things out of the way. Dark corners held secrets he knew he didn't want revealed, but nothing moved. Taking a deep breath, he walked to the middle of the room and turned in a slow circle. Evil was present in the whole place, and he knew he wasn't alone here. Some thing or someone lurked just out of sight.

Thump! Thump! Thump!

An object bounced down stairs, drawing Joe's attention back the way he came. He stepped back out to the front door and saw a narrow staircase tucked in the far corner of the hall. A small red, rubber ball rolled to a gentle stop in the middle of the floor. "Well, a spooky cliché for a spooky house," he murmured. "Good times."

Carefully ascending the stairs and never taking his

eyes off the upper floor, he wasn't surprised when his nose began to bleed again. "At this rate, I'm going to need a transfusion just to replace what I'm losing."

A soft creaking sound drew him down the hallway to the bedroom at the end. Joe blew the doors open with a blast of cold air and walked inside. A short, squat, hairy man stood there, his toothy smile anything but pleasant. His gray skin was dirty and slime seemed to have coagulated in all the creases on his face. Beady, black piggy eyes glared out from beneath an over large brow. "Welcome, Wizard Caine," he hissed. "The master has been expecting you."

"Kerrick," Joe growled. "Where's your master? I've come to have a few words with him about an 'old man' that apparently used to live here."

A sound like a deflating balloon escaped the goblin's lips, and Joe knew it was trying to laugh. "The master was the old man."

"Like I didn't realize that the moment I walked in here. Where is he?"

Kerrick's fingers curled and uncurled all while he stared at Joe's neck. "The master is in his home. He said if you want to talk, that is where you need to be."

"Terrific."

The goblin took several steps toward him. "Leave my master be. He is going to be more powerful than you when the warlock returns. Let me end your suffering before it begins."

Joe held his hand up, and a wall of force erupted in front of him. "I don't think so. Tell your master I'll be there to see him tomorrow."

Joe flung the goblin against the far wall and hurried out to Rachael and his car. "Get in," he said and sped away as soon as they were buckled in.

"Was the old man in there? Why did the building look so bad?"

"There was no old man," Joe said. "It was just someone disguised as an old man to get your trust long enough for him to mark you. I'm going to see him at his home tomorrow. And the building didn't look bad because, when your team was there, there was an illusion on it. Behold, its true appearance."

Out of the corner of his eye, he watched Rachael's mouth frown. Her chest rose and fell with every breath she took, and her hands were folded in her lap. They were laying right at the most distracting point on her slim body. Right where he wanted to have his hands. He swallowed hard. And other parts. He made a sharp right and hit the gas.

"Where are we going?"

He finally glanced at her. "I'm taking you home."

"I don't understand. Aren't there other things you said we needed to do today?"

Joe pulled into a parking lot and put the car in park. He turned in his seat and stared at her. "Let me put it another way. If I don't take you home now, something might happen I'm not sure would be good for either of us."

She smiled. "You mean the way you keep staring at me when you think I'm not looking? The way you were just gazing at my lap?"

"Yeah. Like that. You're the most beautiful woman I've ever met, but with your bad situation hanging over you, it makes me afraid."

"Of me?"

He nodded once. "I've had a vision, and it wasn't a

good one. Rachael, I think you're going to kill me."

She stared at him. "Seriously?" He looked away. "Joe, I've had my thoughts about you, too. And there a lot of things I want to do to you, but killing you isn't one of them. Take me to your place. You said it's safe because you have wards and protections and things, right?"

"Yeah." He put the car in gear. "But it might not be the best idea."

Her smile was back and her eyes twinkled with mischief. "That depends on what you think is a best idea."

Pulling out into traffic, he headed for his home with a black-haired Irish beauty that may or may not cause his death sometime in the future.

****

Rachael stared at the neat two story building they parked in front of when they pulled into the parking lot. Joe led her to his door, and lowering the wards, he ushered her inside, his hand at the small of her back. He shut and locked the door and raised the wards again. He dropped his jacket on the back of the couch and helped her off with hers.

She looked around at his apartment. She thought it'd be smaller and messy with magical talismans laying around everywhere. What she saw was not what she expected at all. The whole place was neat and orderly. There was a desk near the door, and a closed laptop on top with a coffee mug stuffed with pencils to the left by a small lamp. A picture of a couple that looked like they might be his parents was off to the right with a Celtic cross next to it.

Bookcases lined almost every wall. From what she

could see, they were all double stacked with some volumes laying on top. She walked over to check out some of the titles. Apparently, he had wide and varied tastes. Biographies, reference materials, fiction, non-fiction, sports, fantasy, science fiction, any genre she could name was there. "Have you actually read all these?"

He walked over and ran his fingers along the spines. "Most of them, yes. I brought some when I moved from Nebraska, but the rest I've been accumulating since I've been here."

"How do you find the time?"

"Once you look around a little more, you'll figure it out."

She frowned as she walked slowly around the living room. The couch sat in the middle of the wall across from the door with French doors off to her right. End tables with slim lamps sat at either end and a low coffee table was clear except for a small candle. A small dining room table with four chairs was off to her left, close to the kitchen doorway. Alongside of the kitchen was a short hallway that led to the bedroom.

"Where's your bathroom?" she asked.

He nodded down the hallway. "It's just off the bedroom. I really don't like that setup, but I can live with it because it's a nice place with reasonable rent. I don't have a lot of visitors anyway, so it's not a problem."

On either side of the French doors were plants. There were large ones in pots, small ones on stands, and shelves lined with them. Every single one was deep green with health and several had long vines tacked up over the doors. She went over to them and rubbed a shiny, large leaf between her fingers.

"These are beautiful," she exclaimed. "I've never seen such healthy houseplants before. What's your secret?"

He grinned. "I'm an earth wizard, remember? I can sense what they need, when they need it. I can also feel when they sense something wrong with the earth. It's part of who I am. I could no more deny them than you could deny helping the hunter the other night. We are who we are."

She scowled. She couldn't believe he'd brought up that incident again. "Are you trying to say something?"

"No," he said, shaking his head. "Because you could communicate with it, I figured out it was being used like the rest of us. I'm not happy with that. I'm glad you were there."

His words caressed her, and she wanted to run to him and feel his arms around her, but he went to the kitchen. "You know the hunter wasn't evil, right? He was commanded to hurt you, and their race has to follow any command they're given."

He came back with two sodas and handed her one. "I didn't know that. I can't read them like I can the creatures from our plane."

"I didn't know I could talk to dimensional creatures either. My new ability might come in handy for the next one we meet."

He stepped closer to her. "It might."

Her heart began to pound in her chest, sending her blood racing through her veins. She could smell the earth magic in him and felt it call to her. The green of his eyes captivated her and made her feel as if she could see the life blood of the world they were part of

An Angel's Heart

swirling in their depths.

"Like what you see?" he whispered.

"Very much."

He leaned forward a little more, taking her mouth in a gentle kiss without touching the rest of her body. Rachael's eyes drifted closed, and she stepped a tiny bit closer. She deepened the kiss, laying her hand on his arm, more to steady her trembling body than anything else. When his free hand went around her waist, and he opened her mouth to taste her, it was as if her spirit fled her body to circle the moon.

Every nerve, every fiber, every molecule exploded and reformed, doing so over and over again. Their souls intertwined, flew apart, and then bonded together again. His magic took her flying on a cloud of ultimate sensation she'd never thought possible. She could feel the heat of his body shoot up, and she pressed her hips to his, trying with all her heart to pull him into her, to keep the feeling going. How could she feel all of that from one single kiss?

A knock on the door broke them apart. Joe stared at her for a moment. "If that's what it's like kissing you, doing more will probably cause me to explode."

He put his soda down and went and opened the door. Rachael touched her lips and wondered what he meant. If he had felt the same things she did, he was right. Doing more would be more wonderful than anything she'd ever felt in her life.

A thin woman with short, dark, spikey hair came in and smiled at her. Rachael could still feel the heat from Joe's kiss and turned away. The woman extended her hand.

"Hi. I'm Chrissy."

Rachael looked back at her and stared. She must be Joe's friend, the one he said kept him grounded in a fight. She detected nothing out of the ordinary, and she could sense Chrissy and Joe really were just good friends. "Rachael. Joe's told me a lot about you."

"Really? It's all lies, unless what he said were good things. Then it's all true."

"They were good things," Rachael said. She couldn't help smiling. Chrissy was likeable, more so now that she'd had her world turned inside out by Joe's kiss. "He said you're kind of a clairvoyant, and you might be able to see if something is controlling me."

"Anything's worth a try. We'll give it a shot after lunch. Did he tell you I'm the most awesome cook on the planet?"

"Yes."

Chrissy laughed. "Well, I am. Did you figure how he has time to read yet?"

Rachael's gaze shot to her. "Not yet, but I think I'm close." She looked around a little more. "I've got it. You don't own a television."

"That's it."

"Isn't it against the law not to have a television?"

He chuckled. "Sometimes, I think so."

****

Ezra paced in his dimensional home. He snorted. More like prison. When the Circle of Nine banished him here over a hundred years before, he vowed he would get out and take his revenge. The leader of the Nine had been Joseph Caine's ancestor. And now the wizard plotted to take the shifter from his grasp.

The kiss they shared was only the beginning. That was the last thing the oracle had told him before he

70

snapped her neck. Rachael would be his to do as he bid. He would take full control of her mind, body, and soul, bending her to his will. Then, when she no longer questioned him, he would have her kill Caine. With the wizard's blood, he'd open a permanent portal to the earth and bring his minions through to wreak the havoc he so craved.

If he could get to their world, it would be so much easier, but the binding spell placed around him stymied him at every turn. The best he could do was send his shadow self, and that drained him more than he wanted to admit. He was lucky he could do that much and get to the dream plane. Again he cursed the Circle.

Ithick would do what was necessary to make sure the next part of the plan went flawlessly. He'd already marked the shifter, so now it was time to do the same to Caine. Ezra smiled. All was coming together, just as it should.

Chapter Eight

Rachael looked at Joe and sighed. "How do you not weigh five-hundred pounds? You were right. Chrissy is an amazing cook."

"Magic use burns a lot of calories. Think back. Have you ever even seen a picture of a fat wizard?"

She thought for a minute. "Now that you mention it, no."

Chrissy came out and sat with them. She laid her hands on the table and stared at Rachael. "Let me see your hand. I'm going to try and see if I can tell what kind of mark has been imbedded in you."

Imbedded? Gross. She held her hand out, and Chrissy took it, turning it palm down on the table. She covered the back with her own hand while staring in Rachael's eyes. After a few minutes, she flipped Rachael's hand over and laid her palm over the other woman's.

Rachael watched Chrissy sit up straighter and her fingers curled around her wrist. "What do you see?"

"The man who marked you wasn't a man at all. He is working for a warlock of incredible power. The warlock's name is Ezra Barghest. The mark you bear is like a homing beacon for him. He needs you for a dark purpose. If he succeeds, the whole world will burn. The mark can be removed, but only if you are willing to give it up."

Chrissy let her go and sat back. She closed her eyes and rubbed her temples. They were all silent for several minutes. Joe got up, bringing Chrissy a mug of tea. He sat down and waited for her to speak.

When she looked up, she stared at Rachael. "Are you willing to have the mark removed?"

"Of course. I don't want something in me that will mean destruction to the world."

Joe pulled out his cell phone. "We need Damen. He's going to have to bless the item and lock it away so it can't do any more harm."

Before he could dial, his phone rang. "Hello?"

He didn't say anything else, just nodded and listened to whatever the person on the end was saying. He finally hung up and looked at the two women. "We're going to have to put it off. I've got to go across the bridge into New Jersey. Someone has some information for me. I wanted to go tomorrow, but he wants me there today."

"You can't trust him," Chrissy said. "You're not going to be able to bribe him. His master is pulling his strings now."

"If I can't bribe him," Joe said, pulling on his jacket, "then I'll destroy him. That's not a road I want to take, but I'll do what needs to be done."

Rachael jumped up. "Let me come with you. Maybe I can help reason with him."

He laughed. "There's no reasoning with him. He's not even human."

"She can stay with me," Chrissy said. "Maybe we can pull up some more information on the warlock."

"Sounds good." He saw Rachael open her mouth to protest. "Stay here and be safe. I'm trusting you to backup Chrissy if something happens."

She hesitated, then nodded. "You can count on me. But please be careful."

"All the time. I should be back before dark."

He rode in silence until he crossed the state line, then turned toward the western rural area of the Garden State. The GPS lay on the seat next to him, its dark screen reflecting the light coming in. He didn't need to have it telling him directions. It was only a forty-five-minute drive, and he'd made far too many trips here. He snorted. It wasn't one he wanted to make now, either. Doppelgangers were untrustworthy, and Ithick was absolutely the worst of all the ones he'd had the displeasure to meet.

As soon as he turned into a driveway that led to a moderately large house, he sensed an air of discordance surrounding the well-kept grounds. A lumbering man-shaped thing with grayish black skin stepped in his way, making Joe hit the brakes. When had Ithick started hiring trolls?

"The master says you park here and walk to the house," it rumbled.

"Figures," Joe mumbled. "He's still predictable."

The house and grounds were pretty, in a stately sort of way. This whole part of the Garden State quickly made one forget the traffic and industry over near the coast in cities like Newark and East Rutherford. Again, Joe wondered how Ithick managed to live out here without any humans nearby to feed on.

Gravel crunched under his shoes, and snow was piled high on both sides of the driveway, as he walked up the long hill. He kept glancing over his shoulder to his car, getting farther and farther away. The troll stood in front of it with his arms crossed, glaring at him until he reached the house. He held his cross and prayed he'd get out of there mostly intact and hopefully alive. Pressure built in his sinuses, but Ithick had never made his nose bleed. He just made them hurt.

Joe stepped up to the door and pounded hard on the light colored wood. He stepped back when he heard footsteps thumping down the hallway. The door was flung open, and Kerrick scowled at him. "The master said to expect you."

"Great. Where is he?"

Kerrick grinned, saying nothing.

Joe scowled and summoned a wind gust, blowing Kerrick aside like a dry, autumn leaf. He closed his eyes and turned in a slow circle. "The study it is."

Standing in front of the door were two more of Ithick's servants. Their brown-gray skin resembled Kerrick's, and their beady black eyes narrowed as he approached. "The master said you were to wait until he summoned you," the goblin said.

"Seriously? I don't have time for your idiocy."

He pointed at the one on his left and small, green balls of light flew from his fingertips, knocking him away from the door. Joe gestured toward the other guard and a wave of clear energy rippled outward, pushing the goblin down the hall. Flinging open the door, he saw the house's owner by the window, swirling red, suspiciously thick liquid in a large brandy snifter.

His skin was gray, almost corpse-like, but not dry. A film of something shiny covered his face and hands. His eyes were black and too large, his lips too thin on a too wide mouth. His hair was combed and neat, but the winter sun revealed a greasy sheen. Fingers much too long, with nails too thick and claw-like to be a normal human's, beckoned him closer.

"I'm glad you came, Caine. I know you're looking for information, and I can give you something to help you." His voice was soft, coiling around Joe's mind like a poisonous viper.

"Stop with the mind control. It didn't work last time, and it's not going to work now. Why did you want me to come here?"

Ithick laughed, a horrible sound that made fingernails on chalkboard preferable. "You are trying to protect a shifter. A very special shifter." He glided toward him on feet that never seemed to touch the floor. "She's very important to my master. I gave her his mark so he could find her."

"Why? What did you do?"

"You'll find out soon enough." Ithick glanced to the door, and Kerrick charged in, knocking Joe off his feet. "Keep him there, Kerrick. The wizard needs to be given a present."

"Tackling somebody makes them not want to get anything, you know."

He turned to Joe and grinned, making sure he saw the pointy teeth in his mouth. "I could tear the flesh from your bones in mere moments."

Joe struggled against the weight of the goblin. "Not the best way to treat a guest, either. Especially one you invited here."

Ithick studied his nails as he stood over him. "That is true. Hospitality shall be observed for now, or until I tire of you."

"Nothing goes on in here that doesn't escape your

notice. Who is your master? Why is he after me?"

"Very good questions, wizard. My master is the warlock Ezra Barghest. He was defeated over one hundred years ago. A binding spell was placed on him, and he was locked away in the void, but I discovered how to find him. I helped him open portals to your world."

Joe had started checking out Ezra as soon as he'd heard his name. He was a warlock without scruples or conscience. All that mattered to him was power and control. He'd almost taken control of leaders of several countries until the Circle of Nine stopped him. Locking him in the void limited his access to magic, even stopping him from creating portals to let him back into their world. He now had no anchor and limited control over what he could do.

Ithick stared down at him. "The master has all but broken the binding. All he needs is a shifter of power with ties to the earth and the sacrifice of a wizard. The spell will be broken for all time, and he will be free to dominate the planet and take the souls of its people for his own."

He crouched next to Joe and grabbed his left hand. "And guess which wizard he has chosen to sacrifice. I shall enjoy your pain, wizard." Flexing his fingers, the nails extended like the claws they resembled. As he pierced the skin of Joe's left palm, Ithick shuddered as the blood welled around his nails.

Joe shoved at Kerrick, while trying to pull his hand free from Ithick's clammy grip. Blood ran down his arm and dripped on the floor. "I'll fight you," he gasped. "Both of you. Ezra Barghest can't have her."

"Your concern for her makes you weak," Ithick

said, releasing his hand. "The master's plan is to have her kill you. Then he'll have two souls for the price of one. Oh, and he will also be able to add your magic to his own. Think of it. My master will truly be ruler of the earth then."

"But why me?" Joe asked again, cradling his hand.

"Because, wizard, your family founded the Circle of Nine. It's only right your death open portals to the nether realms forever."

As Kerrick moved off, Joe climbed to his feet. "I really hope you washed your hands."

"Your sad attempts at humor still do not amuse me." Ithick waved his hand and opened a black doorway. "To give you some company on the road home, here's a present."

An unearthly screech echoed through the house. Claws ticked across the stone passageway and soon a great feline head flowed from the darkness, its fur so black, it appeared to absorb all the light touching it. Large green eyes with red pupils peered at him. Giant paws hid the rest of the claws that showed just from the tips of its toes. Joe knew the shaggy fur covering its body hid taut muscles, giving it the power to rip a person in two.

As he took several steps back, he realized he'd forgotten how big witch-cats were as it looked him in the eye. "Uh oh."

The witch-cat crouched low, its haunches readying to spring as a low growl filled the room. Joe turned and ran toward the window, crossing his arms in front of his face. He dove through, rolled to his feet, and began the long run to his car, hoping he wouldn't get eaten before he got there.

The witch-cat screeched again, loping after its prey. It swiped at him, catching him on the side of the head. He slammed into the ground, scrabbling on his hands and knees, trying to get his feet under him. Claws raked his back, and he cried out, rolling to the side as sharp teeth snapped in the air where his head had been.

He clambered to his feet, spinning around, swinging his arm as hard as he could. The punch landed squarely on the beast's nose. The cat reared, roaring in surprise as it backed up a few paces. Joe summoned a blast of wind, blowing the piles of snow at the cat, blinding it momentarily. It rubbed its eyes as Joe ran for his car, slipping on gravel and ice before jumping in and gunning the engine.

He grabbed his cell phone off the center console and speed-dialed Chrissy. "Is Rachael still with you?" he shouted as soon as she answered. Checking the rearview, he saw the witch-cat had disappeared.

"We've got a big problem. Get to St. Michael's. I'm going to be there as soon as I can. Tell Damen there could be a witch-cat following me." He paused. "Yes, I know how rare they are. Just get to Damen."

He threw the cell phone on the passenger seat. "I can't believe he was dumb enough to summon a witch-cat." He snorted. "I can't believe I was dumb enough not to expect him to pull something so incredibly bad. I'm old enough to know better."

He drove as fast as he dared, taking mostly back roads instead of the highways, speeding across the bridge into the city just before rush hour started. All the time, simultaneously checking for the beast, and praying Rachael and Chrissy were all right. They were each powerful, but neither had ever fought a witch-cat, and Joe was afraid they wouldn't survive the encounter.

He pulled into the parking lot, tires screeching and smoking as he slammed on the brakes. Relief flooded him as he jumped out, seeing Chrissy's car near the church. As he ran for the door, he was slammed into from behind and a sharp pain on the back of his neck had him yelling and swatting at the attacker.

Burning pain in four spots on his back had him wriggling to get away from the cat. The more he struggled, the deeper he felt the claws go in. Hot, fetid breath moistened the back of his neck, and he felt liquid run down. Whether it was blood or the witch-cat's saliva, he didn't know and wasn't sure he wanted to know. The cat rumbled, and Joe felt it vibrate all his internal organs. It hissed and reared up, then it was suddenly gone.

"Grab him!" Damen shouted, firing at the witch-cat.

Chrissy and Rachael each took an arm and dragged him to the church steps. "Stay here," Rachael said.

The two women ran back to the fight, Chrissy pulling a dirk from a sheath on each leg as Rachael shifted to a large tiger. Damen shot the cat in the shoulder while Chrissy plunged each dirk into its back. The beast roared, rearing on its hind legs. Tiger Rachael rushed forward with her head down, bashing it in its rib cage.

The snapping and cracking of bone echoed in the early twilight. Joe staggered up and opened a portal under it, cursing as it jumped to its right. Chrissy weaved the blades back and forth, drawing its attention while Rachael circled around and charged, shoving it through the doorway. The portal winked shut, and they all breathed a sigh of relief.

Rachael shifted back to human and walked over to Joe. "Can I borrow your jacket?" she asked, her voice husky.

He stared at her, the struggle to breathe not caused by his wounds. Bits of her body peeked out from her shredded clothing, teasing him. "How can one woman be so perfect?"

She shivered. "And I'm perfectly freezing. It's January, and I ruined what I was wearing to save you. I need something to wear."

"I'm sorry." He smiled. "I guess I got a bit distracted there for a minute." He took his jacket off, crying out when it opened the drying scratches on his back.

Rachael turned him around. "Your back is a bloody mess. Damen, I think Joe needs your help."

"I'm not surprised." He looked at Joe's back. "That thing ripped gouges out of you."

"Figures."

Rachael and Chrissy helped him inside to the spare bedroom while Damen gathered what he needed to clean the scratches. They got him undressed and covered him to his waist.

"Get some sleep," Rachael said. She kissed his head, making him smile as sleep overtook him.

Chapter Nine

Damen entered the kitchen about a half an hour later. He threw the bloody gauze in the trash and sat at the table, picking up a sandwich Chrissy had prepared for them. Rachael had dressed in some extra clothing Damen kept for people who came to him with nothing.

"What was that thing?" she asked.

"A witch-cat," Damen said. "They're incredibly rare, and it takes an inordinate amount of power to control one. They're highly intelligent and fiercely independent."

"Then why attack Joe?"

"He was probably promised as a reward." Chrissy leaned forward. "Witch-cats can't be affected by magic. Their main prey are witches and wizards from novices to grand masters. They don't care. They kill the wizard and absorb the magic that gets released at the time of death. They're like a giant sponge, except furry with teeth and claws."

"I'm glad I was here to help." Rachael turned to Damen. "Does Joe know how bad his back is torn up?"

"I'm going to tell him when he wakes. He should know by the amount of pain he's going to be in. I'd tell him he needs to be in a hospital, but I'd be wasting my breath. I should be able to get him healed in a day or two. Thank God witch-cat claws aren't poisonous like some other creatures. Just really nasty and incredibly sharp."

"But why him?" Rachael insisted. "Who could hate him so much?"

"Joe's been fighting dark forces for a long time," Chrissy said in a low voice. "He's made a lot of friends, but more enemies. The person he went to see is called Ithick."

Damen snorted. "Person." He looked at Rachael. "Ithick is a doppelganger. A long time ago, he killed a business man and took his place. Not sure how he can transform into different people now. Doppelgangers usually only take one identity. The warlock had to have magically increased his abilities. Ithick's as evil as they come, and he has ambitions. Big ambitions. He wants to move up the magical hierarchy. It's possible this warlock has made promises of power to any being who can deliver Joe to him."

"Why? I though he was after me?"

"He is," Joe said from the doorway.

They all turned, and Rachael hurried to him as Damen turned a chair so the back was against the table. Chrissy ran to the living room and grabbed the fleece blanket from the back of the couch and draped over the chair. Joe eased himself down and folded his arms across the top and leaned forward. He was pale, his arms and legs trembling.

Rachael looked at him as he made himself comfortable. Large, deep scratches marked his back and a large bump formed on his temple. That beautiful reddish-brown hair was matted on the back of his head, and he had a real shiner around one of those amazing green eyes. Her gaze slid back to the tight, toned muscles in his back, shoulders, and arms. She sighed inwardly. If only he wasn't wearing those jeans. What she wouldn't give to see all of him.

Stop getting distracted, she silently scolded herself. She cleared her throat. "Are you so powerful someone would send a beast that dangerous after you?"

"Ezra Barghest thinks I am."

Chrissy brought them all something to drink. "I've had a vision. If Joe joins with someone with as strong a connection to the earth as his, he would be incredibly powerful."

"He'd be almost unstoppable," Damen said.

Joe winced as he reached for a sandwich. "The operative word there is 'almost.' Right now, I'm pretty stoppable."

Rachael sat back and looked at the company of wizards in front of her. "It makes sense. If the warlock can possess me, he'd own me, and then Joe could be destroyed easily. He'd be trying to protect me and not himself."

"I'm pretty sure it's why Ezra Barghest is after you. Ithick said the warlock needs a shapeshifter with a lot of power to break the chains on the portal from his dimension to ours," Joe said. "Knowing that confirms I need you to stay with me. You can't be alone. One of us should always be with you."

Rachael took a deep breath and slowly released it. She frowned a little and did it again. What was that smell? It tickled her senses and her animal side struggled to be set free. She sniffed again and turned her head.

Joe's jacket. She'd hung it on the back of her chair. That was the source. It was his blood on his jacket. The delicious, coppery scent underscored with the rich outdoors aroma of earth magic mingled with the smell of his shampoo and soap.

"Damen, I have to go home. I had to shift and my clothes got ruined." She gestured at what she was wearing. "These will do for now, but I can't live in them until everything is over. I need some more to wear."

"Not a good idea," Joe said.

She walked over to him and smoothed his hair back. "How about if I take Chrissy with me? Then we can either come back here or go to her apartment."

Joe and Damen looked at each other. "All right, but be quick. I don't want you gone any longer than necessary."

"Will do."

Chrissy laid a hand on his arm. "I'll protect her. You just heal up. We'll be back soon."

Joe watched them leave. "Famous last words," he muttered under his breath.

****

Damen got Joe settled back in the bed and checked the dressings on his back. "Looks like the salve is working, but slowly."

Joe nodded, knowing that witch-cat wounds always took longer to heal. "I never want to face one of these things again."

"That's what you said the last time you faced a witch-cat. And a demon hound. And the skrill bat. And…"

"Yeah, all right. Enough. I get it."

Damen sat in the chair and leaned forward. "Why didn't you tell me you were going to see Ithick? I would've gone with you."

"Because, my friend," Joe said, grinning, "the last time you went with me to see him, you shouted some very un-priest-like things at him, and then you shot him."

"Little bastard deserved it."

"He said he had information. I had to go. He knows everything that happens, big or small."

Damen sat back and ran his hand through his hair. "I know. At least he confirmed the warlock's identity." He stood and walked to the door. "Get some rest. I'll poke around to see what else I can find."

****

Chrissy pulled up in front of Angel Haven, parking close to the porch. She stared at the house and shivered. "Something evil is here."

"Joe said the same thing." Rachael looked at her home. "I wish I could feel what you two feel."

They got out of the car and walked inside. "Hurry and get what you need," Chrissy said. She glanced up the staircase. "Do you want me to come with you?"

"No. I shouldn't be long." She gestured to a room on her right. "That's the family room. You can wait there."

She stripped out of the borrowed clothes and threw on her robe. Pulling her overnight bag from her closet, she packed quickly, shoving clothes inside, not really worrying about how they would look when she pulled them out. The air in her room seemed thicker than the last time she'd been there, and she just wanted to be gone.

A shadow passed in front of her window, grabbing her attention. She walked over and peered out into the darkness. The shadow man stood by the tree and beckoned her to join him. She yanked the curtains together, squeezing her eyes shut.

"I'm not listening," she mumbled. "You can't control me. Go away."

Tendrils of darkness leeched into her room, wrapping around her legs. They climbed her body, stealing her will and sapping her strength. Her hands dropped to her side and she stood straight, turning to the window.

I see you, little shifter, came a familiar voice. *Come to me now, just as you are.*

Without a second thought, she hurried down the back steps and out the kitchen door. She ran to the oak tree where he'd left the note. "I'm here," she whispered.

He stepped out from the shadows, larger and more impressive than he'd been in her dreams. He lowered the robe from her shoulders, allowing it to pool at her feet. The cold January air whispered over her naked skin, making her shiver.

"This is how you were meant to be," he said walking in a slow circle around her. "Unfettered, free from the garb of man. You are a force of nature. Feel the power sing in your veins. You are far above the humans who try to control you."

She closed her eyes and, yes, she could feel her power build in her. She felt it in every nerve, every cell. She felt his hands on her shoulders as her power charged through her. Her chest rose and fell in time to the rapid beating of her heart.

"Just let go," he whispered in her ear.

His breath tickled her skin, and she gripped his arm. The sensations running through her burned her flesh and turned her bones to rubber. She whimpered, feeling her body straining to hold the energies inside her. Finally, she could feel the crescendo hit, and her power exploded from her.

She sagged against the man behind her, finally coming back to her senses. He still held her shoulders, now to keep her upright. "What did you do to me?" she asked.

"I helped you unchain your abilities. You had clamped them away, kept them in a bottle. I just helped you open the lid and set them free."

She turned and stared at him. "I kept them suppressed for a reason. Without limits, I could seriously hurt someone."

He smiled. "I know." He turned her right hand over and kissed her palm. "I created a special link between the mark I've given you and one of my enemies. It will not harm you, but it will drain power from him and add it to yours. I know you'll like it. What you've just experienced is but a sample of what I can do for you." He picked up her robe and handed it to her.

Ezra leaned closer and whispered, "Soon, you will be able to take power from the wizard Caine. You must make him want you. Seduce him. Get him to love you. Then, when the time is right, his life will be yours to take." He slipped her robe around her shoulders. "Go, and tell no one we have spoken."

Rachael shivered as she pictured it and nodded, before returning to the house.

****

The sound of footsteps made Chrissy turn around. "There you are. I was getting ready to come look for you."

"It took a little longer than I expected to get

everything I thought I might need."

Chrissy stared at her. "You look different. You weren't attacked, were you?"

"No. I mean, I don't think so." She frowned. "It's fuzzy."

Chrissy picked up her bag. "Let's get you out of here. We'll go back to the church first and check on Joe. You can decide then where you want to stay."

"Sounds good."

They had only been on the road for around ten minutes, when Chrissy suddenly pulled over. Rachael watched as her eyes glazed over and her hands fell from the steering wheel. She sat quietly until Chrissy shook herself and glanced at her.

"Are you all right?" Rachael asked.

She nodded. "I just had a vision. Thank goodness I get some warning when it's about to happen," she said, then grinned. "I don't want to crash while having a vision that I crash."

"That would be a little too ironic."

Chrissy put the car in drive. "Let's get to Damen and Joe. All of a sudden, being outside is not the best place for us."

Rachael nodded, glancing at the blackness surrounding them. Someone out there wanted to get at them. She'd never been so afraid. Now, fear danced along her spine, agitating her nerves. She clamped her hands together and prayed for a quick trip.

****

The two women hurried into the rectory, both breathing a sigh of relief when the door was shut and locked behind them. Damen came down the stairs and stopped, nodding to them before hurrying to the kitchen.

"Damen, what's happened?" Rachael asked.

"I don't know. He was sleeping, then it was like something attacked him. It came on so quickly, I didn't have time to block it. Then, just like that, it was gone. He's weak right now."

"Can I see him?"

"He's been asking about you. Go on up. I'll bring up some tea," he said, setting out cups while Chrissy helped him.

Rachael hurried up the steps and threw open the door to Joe's room. He was on his side, blood seeping through the bandages. His hair was stuck to his forehead, his arm hanging listlessly off the edge of the bed. His color worried her. His skin was pale, almost to the point of gray. Blood had dried under his nose.

She went over and knelt by the bed. "What happened to you?"

"Not sure. On the dream plane, something hit me. It felt like it was draining my magic. I tried to stop it by connecting to the earth, but I couldn't. I think the warlock now has the ability to block me and pull power out of me."

His eyes drifted closed, like speaking had taken more energy than he had to spare. Damen came in and set the tray on the small dresser. He went over and checked Joe, shaking his head. He turned to Rachael. "Did anything unusual happen to you while you were getting your things?"

"I think someone spoke to me, but the more I try to remember, the fuzzier it gets. It wasn't an attack, just conversation. Nothing happened to me."

"Someone is playing with a lot of power on the

dream plane." Damen nodded toward Joe. "And he's their target."

Rachael reached out and stroked his hair. She took his hand and pressed her lips to the back of it. "I wish whoever it is would just attack me and be done with it. There's no reason to keep going after him."

"There are plenty of reasons, just no obvious ones that we know of right now."

Joe's eyes opened, and he rolled over, taking a deep breath. He suddenly sat up and looked around. "What the heck?"

As the two of them watched, his color improved immediately and he swung his legs over the bed. Damen frowned. "What happened? How are you feeling?"

Joe looked at Rachael. "When she touched me. I felt my energy returning. It was like I suddenly got re-connected to the earth and my magic."

"Rachael, would you please wait for us downstairs. I need to check him out."

She nodded and left. At the foot of the stairs, she turned and narrowed her eyes. They were going to talk about her. She just knew it. She headed for the living room and sat on the loveseat across from Chrissy. Her head began to buzz, and she rubbed the back of her neck. She glanced over her shoulder. Joe's friends were in danger.

She looked at her hands. But were they in danger from the warlock trying to control her or from Rachael herself? She didn't know, and that fact scared her. No, not scared. Terrified. She was terrified of herself. She shivered, praying they would figure out what was going on with her.

Chapter Ten

"There's something off about her," Damen said while he checked to see how his friend's wounds were healing.

Joe flinched when his friend dabbed more of the salve on his back. "We shouldn't have let her go back to Angel Haven. I think the warlock activated the mark in her hand."

Damen got up and started putting things away. "I picked up on the mark the other day while you two were here. When were you going to remove it?" He threw a set of Joe's clothes at him.

"Earlier. I was going to call you to come help us, but Ithick called me and said he had information." He pulled his shirt over his head. "I really should've taken you with me so you could've shot him again."

Damen grinned. "You may not have gotten the information he had, but we would've felt better. Did Ithick do anything to you? It's strange that everything started after you get back from seeing him." He paused. "Rachael said her memories are fuzzy. Could you have been marked, and now yours is connected to hers?"

Joe pulled his pants up and grabbed his socks and shoes. "He dug his nails in my left palm. Whether there's a mark there now connecting me to Rachael is anyone's guess."

They walked downstairs and found Rachael and

Chrissy in the living room. Chrissy sat, flipping through a magazine, while Rachael stood staring out the window. She turned when they came in. "So, are you done talking about me? I didn't hurt him, you know."

Joe sat next to her. "We know. Try to think. Can you remember anything about your dream?"

"It was something about power and how mine needed to be set free." Her delicate brows drew down. "There was a man. I couldn't see him clearly but he touched me and next thing I knew, it was like my body exploded. I was so weak afterward, but at the same time, I felt energized, invigorated. It was almost—sexual."

Joe and Damen looked at each other. "It was probably the warlock," Joe said. "Did he do anything to you physically?"

"I think all he did was lay his hands on my shoulders. I don't remember the rest of it." She stared at the two of them. "You think he did something to me to make me hurt Joe, don't you?"

Joe crossed the room and took her hands. "Not at all. We think he used your power to give him the boost *he* needed to hurt me. I don't think you have it in you to hurt me like that."

She gazed at his mouth and lick her lips. "Why?"

He brushed her hair back. "Because you have an angel's heart. Ithick dug his nails in my palm and drew a lot of blood. Did you feel anything around that same time? Like a connection or something?"

Rachael frowned as her brows drew down. "Maybe? I don't know." She hung her head. "I'm sorry. The more I try to think about it, the more it slips away."

"I think Rachael should stay here," Chrissy said.

93

"The warlock has already proven he can get through Joe's wards. Here would be safer."

They all nodded. "I think you're right." Joe said. "Until I can get my wards boosted, the rectory is the safest place besides the church."

Rachael hugged herself and glanced at Chrissy and Damen. "I think he wants me to hurt you two. I'm afraid of myself, of what I might do."

Laying a hand on her arm, Joe smiled. "It won't come to that. I'll keep you and everyone else safe. But you're going to have to trust me."

"I'm trying, but it's hard. I'm getting more confused the longer everything goes on."

Chrissy stood and grabbed her jacket. "I'm going to head home. It's almost sunset, and I want to be inside before dark. Call me if you need me."

"Will do," Joe said.

****

After Chrissy left, Joe took Rachael upstairs to the only other spare room the small rectory had available. He put her suitcase on the bed. "It's a little small, but comfy. You should be okay in here."

"You're not staying here with me?"

As Joe watched, her posture straightened, and he could sense a change in her. "Do you think that would be a good idea?"

"Yes. I do." She turned and took off her jacket. Her eyes had darkened to deep purple, and she let him stare at the loose blouse she wore. Her nipples poked the fabric, telling him she wore nothing underneath. "I know you want me," she whispered. "There's nothing on under my skirt either. I was hoping I would get you alone. I want you."

94

He stared at the skin above the opening of her shirt. "I want you, too. I've wanted you since I first laid eyes on you."

He stepped back as she moved closer. Her smile was almost malicious as she cornered him against the door. When she kissed him lightly, there was no explosion of light and color like there had been before. It felt tainted, like they weren't in control.

"See?" she whispered. "That wasn't so bad."

He cupped her chin and kissed her again, groaning when he felt her hands work their way under his shirt. "Your eyes are different. They're almost black."

"Does it really matter what color my eyes are?" she asked, dragging her nails lightly across his stomach.

A small noise came from his throat, and he finally shook his head, as she continued to run her hands over his skin,

"You know you want me, wizard," she purred softly.

"Yes." He began working the buttons of her shirt. "You're so incredible, so beautiful."

She took his left hand in her right and pressed their palms together. A shock jolted through him, and he staggered to the bed and fell back. She followed him down, not letting go. Lying next to him, she kept his hand firmly in her grip. His power bled into her, coursing hotly through her veins.

The same exaltation as when Ezra freed her power, rushed through her as she felt Joe's magic leech into her. His breathing came in short gasps while she clenched his hand tightly, feeling her nails cut into the back of his hand. His skin was pale, paler than it should be.

"The wizard is weak. Notice how he couldn't even handle the small amount of power you took from him."

Rachael smiled. *"It will be such a pleasure when we end him. How soon, master?"*

"I will tell you when the time is right. Wait for me. I will come to you again."

"Waiting will be hard. Take care, master. They plan to stop you."

Ezra laughed. *"You mean they will try to stop me."*

Joe's eyes fluttered open, and he gazed at her. "Rachael," he moaned quietly.

She smiled. "I'm here. Let me help you."

He rubbed his right hand over his eyes and tried to sit up. "I feel drained. What's happened to me?"

"Now that your eyes are open, I'll show you."

She grabbed his left hand again in her right and smiled as she pulled more of his magic out of him and into her. His back arched, and she knew he wouldn't be able to hold out much longer.

"You will be the perfect sacrifice for my master," she whispered.

****

In the descending darkness, a deep laugh made the night a little colder, forcing people to hurry inside and bolt their doors. The marks worked perfectly. Now, if only Rachael didn't kill him before he was ready to take the wizard's soul in sacrifice, his plan couldn't help but succeed.

Chapter Eleven

Rachael rubbed her temples, trying to get the cobwebs out of her brain. Her muscles ached, and she wondered what happened. She'd never blacked out before. Her small suitcase wasn't nearly heavy enough to make her arms hurt the way they were hurting now. She opened the door to her room and staggered down to where Joe was staying.

Stopping in front of the door, she knocked lightly. "Joe, are you in there? Something happened to me, and I can't remember."

Waiting a few more minutes, she knocked again. When he still didn't answer, she opened the door. Joe lay on his bed. His condition made her stumble back a few steps. His skin was too pale, he was sweating too much, and his breathing almost non-existent. She hurried to his side, laying her hand on his forehead. He was burning up with fever, and his hands were clammy.

Rachael flung open the door and ran downstairs. "Damen. Come quick. Something's wrong with Joe."

Damen came out of his study, took one look at her face and ran up the steps. "What happened?" he asked, opening the door and sitting on the bed, checking his friend over with careful precision.

"I don't know. I think I blacked out. I came to talk to him about it. I found him just as you see him. I checked to see if he had a fever, hoping he'd recover like the last time when I touched him, but he hasn't moved." She stepped to the end of the bed. "What do we do?"

Damen shook his head. "I'm not sure. It seemed to come out of the blue." A red splotch on the bedspread made him turn Joe's left hand over. "How did he get these cuts?"

"I don't know. I don't remember anything after he showed me the room I was going to be using."

"They look like they were made by fingernails."

"You think I hurt him on purpose," Rachael said, her eyes narrowing. "Why would I do that when I want to…" she let her voice trail off.

"The warlock must have a stronger hold on you than we originally thought. I think maybe he can affect you no matter where you are."

She straightened her shoulders. "Then I need to find some way of fighting him. I can't stay here. If I hurt him, Joe's in more danger from me than anyone else."

She fled the room and grabbed her coat before running out of the rectory. She shoved her hands in her pockets and stalked away from the church. A cold breeze fluttered her hair and skirt and she realized she wasn't wearing anything under it. She stopped and looked back at St. Michaels. A memory tickled her brain, and she closed her eyes, trying to summon it to the front of her mind.

She remembered feeling a rush when she took power from him. She'd wanted everything he had and took it, draining all she could. She felt as if she wasn't herself and Joe had mentioned her eyes were changed. Did she hurt him on purpose? Could she be that—evil?

She rubbed her head and trotted down the street, feeling better the farther she took herself from him.

A horn honked behind her. She turned and saw Chrissy. "Hey."

"I wanted to be in for the night, but I had a vision that you needed a friend right now." She pushed the passenger door open. "Hop in, it's freezing out there."

Rachael hesitated before getting in and letting the heater warm her. There wasn't enough heat anywhere to thaw her soul. The realization of what she'd done clung to her, making her chest tight.

"It wasn't your fault," Chrissy finally said.

Rachael gave a short laugh. "I was the only one there. Tell me, exactly, whose fault is it? I *hurt* him. How can you say I'm not to blame?"

"I see more than I tell people because, most of the time, what I see isn't good and no one needs to know the ugly part of my power." She glanced at Rachael. "I knew something was going to happen."

"Then you should have spoken up."

Chrissy shook her head. "I couldn't. I know it's hard for you, but it needed to happen, just like it did. Things may seem bad now, but it's going to have a huge impact later on. And before you ask, no, I haven't seen that far ahead. I just have a feeling what happened was incredibly important."

They rode in silence until they reached Chrissy's apartment. The young wizard held the door open for her. "You're welcome in my home. You're not the evil monster you believe yourself to be. However, the night is not kind to us, and it's definitely not your friend. We need to be inside, away from the beasts waiting to do their master's bidding."

Rachael walked slowly into Chrissy's home and jumped as she shut the door and locked it. Looking around, everything was pretty much the same as Joe's place. Bookcases lined the walls, but with less variety. A television was on a stand against the wall. "No plants?"

"I'm not as good with them as Joe is," Chrissy said. "He'll watch movies over here, but no broadcast television. He's funny like that." She took her coat off, hanging it in the closet. "His magic is tuned to the earth, and I'm more of an ethereal wizard."

"Like ghosts and mists and stuff?"

"Kind of. It's hard to explain. It's more like mind magic. I get visions and I can see auras, but I'm not one of those store front psychics who are in it for the money. Sometimes, I can read peoples' minds. But thoughts have to be strong for me to pick them up. It works well with my clairvoyance."

Rachael took off her coat and sat on the couch. "Auras, huh? What does mine look like?"

Chrissy sat next to her and stared. "It's duller than it should be, and there's something dark creeping around the edges. That's the warlock's influence."

"How do we stop him?"

"I don't know. Yet. But don't worry. There's always a solution." She stood. "I also know you haven't eaten anything today. You want some dinner?"

Rachael noticed the emptiness in her stomach and felt a slight rumble. "I could eat."

Chrissy went to the kitchen, and Rachael stayed on the couch. No. She hadn't eaten any physical food, but what she'd consumed from Joe had been filling and heady. She looked toward the door. What would happen if she went back to him and took more?

"You'd kill him," Chrissy said from the kitchen. "The warlock is trying to exert his control over you now. Don't let him. Concentrate on something else."

"Like what?"

"Tell me about your team. I've been a fan of the Angels for a long time. I knew you'd all be accepted eventually."

Rachael walked to the kitchen, nausea rolling through her as she tried to fight Ezra's influence. "My team leader is the one who called in Joe to see if he could help me. She's a genetic construct, highly intelligent, with a very small sense of humor.

"There's also a martial artist who, apparently, you guys know as the Dragon Angel." She grinned when Chrissy smiled at that. She was beginning to feel better. "One member is from another dimension, one is from the stars, one goes intangible, and then there's the telepath."

Chrissy turned to her. "You don't trust her and you barely like her. Why?"

"She started out as a criminal. She wormed her way into our house and onto our team. We had a lot of battles before she switched sides. I'm worried she may slip back."

She watched Chrissy gaze into space momentarily. "She won't. She will have to do some things you, and other heroes, won't like, but she's one of the good guys, through and through. Come get some food."

They ate in silence for a few minutes, and when Rachael finally looked up she asked, "Is Joe all right?"

"He's fine. Damen will figure out how to help him."

"I wish I had your confidence," Rachael said, pushing her food around on her plate. "How can he help me if I want to hurt him every time I'm near him?"

"It won't be every time. The next time you two are together, things will go in a different direction. It will be better for you then. You won't hurt him."

Rachael barely looked up as Chrissy cleared the table. She wished she could trust herself around him. Small shivers worked their way up her spine, becoming full blown tremors. She wrapped her arms around herself and huddled down on the chair. "I'm so tired of being afraid."

"Then don't be."

She looked up, and Chrissy stood there, smiling at her. "It's not that easy. I've never not been in control of myself. I've never been afraid."

"Oh, Rachael. You've been afraid ever since your powers manifested. You've been terrified you'll seriously hurt or kill someone."

"How do you know?" she whispered. "I've never told anyone that."

"Intuitive magic, remember? It's your fear the warlock preys on. It's what guided him and Ithick to you. That's why you currently bear the warlock's mark. It needs to be removed so his power over you will be less."

"I don't know how not to not be afraid. I've lived with fear for so long."

They moved to the couch and sat at opposite ends. "That's why what happened earlier today was important. Yes, you hurt him when you took power from him, but there was a part, a very small part, of you that was you. You need to find that piece and hold onto it. Joe can help you, but you have to tell him everything."

Rachael snorted. "I couldn't even tell him about the note I found. Ezra left it for me."

"Don't say his name. It gives him power over you."

"There's so much I don't know about all of you, about magic," Rachael said, burying her face in her hands. "I'm so tired."

"Come with me."

Chrissy led her down the short hallway to her room. "You can sleep in my room. There wards are stronger here than any other place in my home."

"Thank you." Rachael walked over to the bed and pulled the covers down. She turned to Chrissy. "There's just one more thing."

Chrissy turned and took a step back. "Your eyes. They're black."

A deep voice rumbled, coming from Rachael's mouth. *"That's because the little shifter is mine. And you have doomed yourself bringing her here."*

Rachael shifted into a creature not native to the Earth. Chrissy stepped back as Rachael loomed over her, swinging her now thickly muscled arm at Chrissy who crashed into the wall, pain exploding through her chest, choking off her air.

A clawed hand reached down, grabbing the front of Chrissy's shirt, and yanked her to her feet. She struggled as Rachael's teeth clamped down on her shoulder. She screamed and shot a large ball of purple energy at Rachael and hit her in the face.

Rachael roared as Chrissy dropped to the floor, her leg crumpling beneath her, and her arm sticky with her own blood. The large paw came down in a wide arc and

Chrissy threw her arm up to block the blow. Bones snapped as she lay on the floor summoning what strength she had left to conjure a shield spell between her and Rachael. Rachael hit it with both fists, making it flicker before collapsing. With her blood coating most of her body, Chrissy was losing strength fast.

The monster Rachael had become stood over her, saliva gripping from her fangs. "Look at her, master," she hissed. "Now you can feast."

Ezra's shadow form floated over. "If I had my body, I would take your soul. Instead, I will let Rachael destroy you." He turned to beast Rachael. "Would you like that, little shifter?"

Rachael nodded, swinging her large head toward the woman on the ground, her lips pulled back in a hideous grin.

Chrissy tried not to scream as the thing that used to be her friend closed in.

Chapter Twelve

"Feeling better?" Damen asked.

Joe sat up and groaned. "Kind of. I've had worse injuries that laid me out for longer, so why do I feel so wiped out?"

"You've had power forcibly taken from you. It's not natural for that to happen, so obviously, it's going to hurt."

"But what happened to me?"

Damen stood and helped his friend to his feet. They went downstairs and Damen made them a light dinner. "Near as I can figure, Rachael tried to seduce you, and the warlock helped her steal your power and weaken your connection to the earth. She didn't remember a thing about it." He nodded to Joe's left hand. "Her fingernails cut the back of your hand."

Joe turned his hand over and looked at the still fresh cuts. "I remember her eyes turning black. I remember kissing her, and she wasn't wearing anything under her clothes. After she touched me, everything is blank." He looked away. "If the desire wasn't there, I would've been stronger."

"The warlock took something that should be powerful and beautiful, and turned it into something ugly, something he could use against both of you."

"He keeps talking about my ancestors and the Circle of Nine. Could it be possible this is nothing more than revenge for something an ancestor of mine did a long time ago?"

The priest shrugged, putting two plates on the table. "In our business, anything's possible. You know that as well as I do. There hasn't been a Circle for a long time, so I don't think there's anyone we could ask about what's going on."

"When did Rachael take off?"

"Right after she called me to help you," Damen said. "She freaked out that she might have been the cause of your injuries and ran out the door before I could stop her."

"Where do you think she might have gone?"

Grabbing the salt shaker, Damen shook his head. "Not a clue. We'll call Chrissy after we eat and see if she knows something."

Joe nodded. Something felt wrong. While Damen fixed sandwiches, he wandered around the rectory, not being able to stay still. There was a sense of urgency in the air, making him antsy. He couldn't put his finger on it, but he just knew his friends were danger. The real fear he wouldn't be in time to save them lingered in his mind.

****

"Rachael, stop," Chrissy said, her voice weak. "You're not yourself. I know you can hear me."

"Mine is the only voice she listens to, wizard."

Rachael stopped and Chrissy narrowed her eyes, trying to block out the pain. "Ezra Barghest, I command you, leave the body of Rachael McCafferty. Now."

She laughed with Ezra's voice. "Do not try your paltry magic on me, woman. You're weaker than Caine."

Rachael reached down and grabbed Chrissy around the throat, lifting her off the floor and holding her in mid-air. "I will enjoy snapping your neck."

Chrissy closed her eyes, murmuring a quiet spell. Rachael's grip tightened. If she didn't get Ezra out of Rachael's head now, Chrissy was sure she wouldn't survive the attack. Spots danced in her vision as she spoke the final word and slapped her hand against Rachael's forehead.

Ezra bellowed as Chrissy dropped to the floor, Rachael collapsing next to her. "That will teach you," she mumbled before passing out.

****

Joe paced in Damen's small kitchen. "I can't get ahold of Rachael or Chrissy. Something's wrong. I've got to get over there."

Damen grabbed his coat. "Right behind you."

They hurried out to Joe's car and tires squealed in protest as he sped from the parking lot. The two men were silent as they drove to Chrissy's apartment. Red and blue lights were flashing around the entrance as Joe pulled in. They jumped from the car and ran over.

A police officer stopped them. "Hold it. You can't cross the police line. Can I get your name?"

"Joseph Caine. I live in the apartment across from Christine Ford. She's a friend of mine. What happened?"

"Looks like a home invasion."

Joe and Damen glanced at each other. "Is she okay?"

"You'll have to go to the hospital to find out."

Joe stared over the cop's shoulder and saw Rachael sitting on the back of the ambulance, a blanket draped around her shoulders. "Rachael! What happened?"

She nodded to the officer and he let him over. She ran straight to his arms and clung tightly, crying into his shirt. "I don't know."

Joe's arms tightened around her. "It's all right." He looked at the medic. "Is she okay?"

"She's not hurt."

Joe turned to the officer. "My apartment is right there. Can I take her inside?"

The officer consulted his notes. "She's already given her statement. If we need anything else, we'll stop by before we leave."

Joe hurried her inside, with Damen following. As soon as the door was shut, she sagged against him. He picked her up and carried her to his room, laying her on the bed. It was when he went to cover her with a blanket he noticed her clothes were shredded. He lifted her hands and saw blood under her nails.

"What happened?" he whispered.

Damen laid his hand on his shoulder and led him to the living room, shutting the door behind them. "I think it's pretty obvious. The warlock's influence over Rachael is getting stronger."

Joe simply nodded.

"I'm going to the hospital to check on Chrissy. I'll call you when I find out how she is."

Joe nodded again, not really hearing what Damen had just said.

"Joe!" Damen said loudly, snapping him out of the stupor he'd put himself in. "Pull yourself together. We've defeated greater enemies before. We can do it again."

"But this is the first time the enemy has had the

upper hand. He hit us where we live. Chrissy wasn't that much of a threat to him. Why take her out?"

"He's sending us a message. He doesn't want any more interference."

Joe stood a little straighter and turned to his friend. "He's going to get interference on a major scale now. He doesn't know who he's messing with."

"Give me your car keys." Damen opened the door. "I'll call you."

After Damen left, the apartment was silent. Joe stared at the bedroom door, willing answers to come to him. When that didn't work, he took his shoes off and walked over to his plants. He took a pinch of dirt from each one and rolled it between his thumb and forefinger, letting the steady heartbeat of the earth calm him.

He walked to the middle of the living room floor, sat down, and closed his eyes. He needed to renew his connection to his magic, or he was going to be in big trouble going forward. He silently prayed for Chrissy to heal quickly. He didn't know what he'd do if he lost his friend.

****

Rachael tossed and turned in Joe's bed. It was a nightmare. It had to be. Chrissy had been so kind to her; she couldn't have hurt her. Could she? Was she a danger to everyone in her life? Or only to those who opposed the warlock trying to control her?

Apparently, he didn't have to try anymore. He had her in his power, and she didn't know if she could break out of it. A memory surged through her, making her relive how it felt to take Joe's power and feel life draining from Chrissy's body and she smiled. Did she want to break out of it? Power was a heady thing, letting you control your enemies and take what you wanted from people weaker than you.

She grabbed her head and curled into a tight ball. No. Those thoughts weren't hers. She couldn't, *wouldn't,* willingly hurt anyone. There wasn't enough temptation on the planet to make her do that. Ezra's voice laughed in her mind, making it look more and more like she didn't have a choice in the matter.

I won't be anyone's puppet, she silently swore. Leave me alone, warlock. I will no longer do your bidding.

"Your wishes make no difference to me. I own you, shifter, whether you like it or not."

Tears streamed down her cheeks, and she tried to push him out of her mind. Bile burned the back of her throat as nausea rolled through her. She could still feel Ezra's touch in her mind, and he made the stolen power streak through her veins, making her whimper and shake from the force of it.

"To relieve yourself, all you have to do is take Caine again. Steal more of his power, and you will feel better than before."

"Get out of her mind, warlock. I've told you before, she is under my protection," Joe said from the doorway. He wove his fingers in an intricate pattern in the air and Ezra howled in protest.

Rachael leapt off the bed, knocking Joe off his feet. "You will not harm the master," she growled.

"Yes. I will."

Joe placed his hands on either side of her head and finished the spell. Her back arched, and she fell forward as Joe felt the warlock's presence diminish. He lay on the floor with Rachael laying on top of him, breathing heavily.

"Are you all right?" he murmured, stroking her hair.

She nodded. "I tried to fight him, but I couldn't. His hold on me is so strong."

"You did good. You held him at bay long enough for me to complete the spell I needed. I tried to reduce his link with you so your mind can be your own."

She sat up and gazed at him. "Thank you. I think it would be best if I left. Go someplace where I can't hurt anyone. I don't think I could stand it if I hurt you again."

Joe let his hand slide down her arm. "Then I think you'd better put some clothes on first."

She looked down and her cheeks turned bright pink. "Probably a good idea."

He cupped her breast. "Or I could join you and we could discuss leaving options later."

"How can you want me after everything I've done?" she whispered.

"You're lying on top of me naked. How could I not want you?"

She stood and walked back to the bed. "Well, we have talked about it, and we did try the last time I was here."

He smiled and pulled his shirt off, absently scratching his left hand.

Chapter Thirteen

Joe gazed at her, drinking in the sight of her body. She was petite, yet strong. Thin, but with toned muscles. Those beautiful, violet eyes could be so serious, but the twinkle in them was never truly absent. Then there was her hair. Black and curly, that striking white patch making her completely unique. Combine all that with her light Irish brogue, and he couldn't ask for a more perfect woman.

He'd never met anyone like her before and doubted he would again. He ran a finger down her spine, smiling when she trembled. He drew circles on her butt cheeks, noticing goosebumps break out on her arms. He walked to the front of her, letting his hand slide around her hip to rest on her belly.

"What are you doing?" she asked.

"Damen said you tried to seduce me. I'm just returning the favor. I've strengthened the wards so it'll be just us. No unwanted evil people."

He let his hands move to cover her breasts, and he squeezed them gently, making her moan. He leaned down and took her mouth in a light kiss that soon became insistent, then demanding. The melding of their power and the resultant sparks again surged through them, but it felt stronger, deeper. He welcomed it and from the tight grip she held him in, knew she felt it too.

Fireworks exploded behind his eyes. In his soul, he

knew he felt it was right. The time was perfect and he sensed his joy match the wild abandon he sensed in her. He could tell she'd been as ready as he was for the moment they joined their bodies, minds, and souls. He could feel the earth beneath his feet even though they were inside. The connection deepened, becoming richer and stronger, filling him with energy the longer he kissed her. Her light touch on his skin was nothing like before. Now, it was healing him, mending the small fractures he begun to detect in his spirit.

They broke apart, and he saw the same joy in her eyes he knew she could see in his. Her impish grin broke out, making him almost fly apart just from seeing it. He knew that little smile would always be just for him. He stroked her cheek, her eyes closing from his touch.

She pressed closer to him, and his body jumped to attention, making him wish he'd taken time to remove his pants. He felt her fingers fumbling with the snap and then the tell-tale sound of the zipper being pulled down. He groaned into her mouth as she found him and held him lovingly.

She let her fingers trace his stomach and up his chest. She placed light kisses along his collarbone before pulling his face down to hers. His knees buckled when her tongue explored the depths of his mouth and his own answered the challenge. At the same time, she rubbed her nipples against his chest.

He lifted his head and smiled at her as his fingers found her, ready for him. She sighed when he dipped inside, and she pushed her hips closer to him. Her head fell back, and he kissed her throat, letting her build and explode against his hand. Her hands rested on his shoulders as he held her close.

Neither said anything. Words were unnecessary. The symphony of their breathing and cries of pleasure were enough. Instinct took over as they automatically knew what the other liked. He definitely liked it when her hands found him and held him. He'd reached the point where he didn't know where he ended and she began. They started as two. They were quickly becoming one.

He backed her up until she was right against the bed. He raised his head and smiled before laying her back. He stripped off his clothes and just stared at her until she squirmed beneath his scrutiny. Her nipples were peaked, looking like they were begging for his mouth. He laid next to her, taking one in his mouth.

He felt her fingers tangle in his hair as she held him there. He moved to the other one and let his hand trail down between her legs, where she willingly parted for him. He kissed his way down while his fingers delved within her, making her buck beneath his hand. She cried out, arching off the bed, her hands curling tightly in the sheets.

Her smile dared him to continue as he gazed at her. Her body was flushed pink, making her more beautiful now than she had been a moment before. He ran his finger down the outside of her sex, sensing she was ready for more. Just looking at her, ready and waiting for his next move, made his erection grow bigger.

He entered her slowly, savoring the feel of her around him. He didn't want to rush things, but he wasn't sure how much longer he could last. Her eyes showed love and laughter, joy and desire, as he filled her completely. Her legs wrapped around him, encouraging him to move with her.

She met him thrust for thrust, laying her arms above her head, making her breasts more prominent. She screamed out as she fell over the edge and that was enough to take him with her. He closed his eyes as he laid his head on her chest and took a deep breath. When he opened them, there was that perfect breast, right there for the taking. And who was he to deny what was being offered.

He nipped the underside, and she jumped just before he pulled her nipple into his mouth and pinched the other one gently. As she ground her hips against his, he knew they were both getting ready to go again. Would he ever have enough of her? He already knew the answer was never.

****

Ezra threw the crystal vase across the room, shattering it against the wall. How dare Caine lock him out of Rachael's mind! Things had been going well. He felt her will begin to weaken from his assault when that pathetic excuse for a wizard had come in and ruined everything.

"Ithick!"

Footsteps clattered across the tile floor in the hallway as the doppelganger skidded into his master's study. "Yes, master? What can I do?"

"I need to be rid of this meddlesome wizard. How much longer must I wait for the ceremony to open the gates to his world?"

"Not too much longer, master. The charts say within the next seven days, conditions should be right for you to take his life to keep the gates open forever."

Ezra scowled and turned to the window. The view

was of the void where his home was located. He could only open a few portals, and those had sapped most of his strength. Curse the Circle of Nine! And curse him for not killing all of them when he had the chance. The few members who escaped him had managed to reproduce, and their offspring were just as interfering as they had been.

"I need you to distract Caine. I must re-establish my connection with the shifter, or it will all be for naught. It could be my last chance for another hundred years, and my patience has run out. I will not wait that long when I can have everything I want now."

"I will do what must be done, master."

Ezra scowled. "Do not kill him. That will be done when I'm ready."

Ithick bowed before leaving, and Ezra turned around, stalking from the room. Time to see if he could still contact the shifter and make her do what he wanted. Caine would be sorry he ever tried to fight him. Glancing at his hand, he pictured it curled around Joe's neck, squeezing the life out of him.

Within seven short days, he would have everything he'd been dreaming of for the past century.

****

Joe pulled Rachael closer to him. Her steady breathing told him she'd finally fallen asleep. The few times she'd drifted off before, she would suddenly sit up, her eyes wide, her breathing rapid. He'd gotten her to calm down and talked to her the whole time. He'd known the instant she'd settled down.

He let himself drift off and sensed immediately when he'd been dragged to the dream plane. He looked around and, seeing a slight rise, climbed it. At the top stood Ezra Barghest. Joe hesitated, watching the warlock smile at him.

"Come closer, wizard. I'll not harm you yet."

Joe took a few more steps up the hill. "It's the 'yet' that worries me. What do you want, warlock?"

Ezra laughed. "I want the soul of the little shifter. I want you dead and bleeding at my feet." He leaned closer. "I want to watch your world burn."

"That's a pretty heavy 'to do' list. Why me? I didn't even know who you were until a few days ago."

Ezra's hand shot out, grabbing Joe by the throat and lifting him off the ground. "Your family banished me and stripped me of most of my powers. I'm just returning the favor. I will use you, Caine, to destroy everything you love. Then I will take the little shifter for my own and make sure you see it before I end your pitiful life."

Joe pulled at the fingers around his neck and shivered, feeling Ezra's hate roll over him, through him, and around him. He had no doubt if he couldn't stop him, Ezra would do everything he'd just outlined.

"I'll stop you by any means necessary," he croaked out. "I won't let you get back to the world."

"Even if that means destroying Rachael?" Ezra said pulling him close.

Joe hesitated for a fraction of a second. "Yes. If it keeps her out of your hands and leaves you stuck in the void, then yes."

Ezra tossed him aside and laughed. "You lie, wizard. You could no more harm her than you could your own mother. I will take what's mine, and there's nothing you can do to stop me."

Joe began shaking, and as it got harder, he realized

someone was shaking him. He forced his eyes open and saw Rachael leaning over him.

"Wake up! Please, wake up."

"I'm up. What's wrong?" he croaked.

She pointed at his neck. "How did you get those bruises? You were talking and then you got restless. I didn't know what to do."

He groaned and closed his eyes. His neck hurt. A lot. He swung his legs over the side of the bed, waiting as a momentary bout of dizziness hit him. He finally stood and went to the bathroom. His flicked on the light, cringing when he saw the damage Ezra had done to him on the dream plane. Those were going to be ugly in a few days.

He looked at Rachael. She was still on her knees on his bed. She hadn't covered up. He smiled a little. Apparently, she wasn't modest around him anymore. Of course, after the night they shared, why should she? As a matter of fact, why should he? He looked down at himself. Yep. Still naked as the day he was born.

He frowned. There were more marks on his body than just the bruises. Had they really been that energetic last night? He didn't think so, but he couldn't explain what he was seeing on his chest. Long scratches went down to his waist and were scabbing over. That meant they were deeper than they should've been.

"Do you know how I got these scratches?" he asked, sitting next to her.

She shook her head. "They weren't there a second ago. What's going on?"

"The warlock is hurting me from the dream plane." He reached for his discarded clothes. "I need to go see how Chrissy is and see if Damen's found out anything else."

"Are you sure you need to leave right now? It's five in the morning."

He shot a quick glance at her. "I would've thought you'd be tired. After all we were up kind of late."

"I will never be tired when you're near." Her hands went to his shoulders and she straddled his lap. "Of course, if you're too tired, I can just go back to sleep."

He held her on his lap and grinned as she slowly took him inside her. "You saying I can't keep up?"

"Not at all," she panted. "Now hush."

He guided her hips against him, and she laid her head on his shoulder. When she increased her pace, he reached down, rubbing the sweet spot, making her clench hard around him. He felt her teeth on his shoulder and, as she bit down, he pushed inside her hard one final time.

He stayed inside her as he pulled her tight against his chest, her tongue diving into the wound she'd just created. He shuddered as she kept her mouth on him.

"Touch me again, Joe. Just once more."

Doing what she wanted, his fingers rubbed the small nub and she moaned. She tightened around him and he felt her bite him again. He didn't seem to mind, though a small voice told him she should stop her. It was what led to his weakness before.

When her body finally stopped trembling, she lifted her head and gazed at him. He searched her face, but Rachael didn't look like herself. She smiled at him, his blood running from the corner of her mouth. Her eyes were solid black. Her tongue flicked out to lick the blood off.

"Rachael?" he whispered.

"I will deliver you to my master," she said. "And I will have your heart as a trophy. The master has promised."

Chapter Fourteen

Joe grabbed her shoulders, giving her a hard shake. "Rachael. Come back to me."

Closing her eyes, she shook her head, and when she opened them, they were back to the light violet he knew and loved. She was still on his lap and could feel him inside her. Blood ran down his shoulder from multiple bite marks. "I did that to you, didn't I?"

"Yeah, but I couldn't stop you." He paused. "I didn't want to stop you."

She pulled away and he let her go. She went to the bathroom. "I need a shower," she mumbled.

"Rachael," he said, his voice stopped her. "You're the most amazing woman. What we had here was special."

"Until I ruined it by treating you like a midnight snack." She finally turned. "You can't trust me. I don't even trust myself, especially where you and your friends are concerned. I keep thinking they need to be eliminated. I have dreams about cutting out your heart and eating it. That's sick. And it's not me."

"I know. He has plans for you." He walked over to her and took her hand. "I promise you, we'll all come out alive. We may get beat up a little, but we're going to defeat him."

"I wish I was as sure as you are, but I'm not."

She slipped into the bathroom, and Joe scratched

his palm.

****

Ezra sat back. He was very satisfied with how the night went. He'd distracted Caine long enough for Ithick to use whatever spell he had in his arsenal to wake up the mark in Rachael's hand. The doppelganger's magic was older than his and completely unpredictable but as long as it served him, he allowed Ithick to use what he wanted.

It had taken all of his self-control not to kill Caine on the dream plane. His own master had told him time and again he was too impatient. It was the one weakness he had that he just couldn't seem to conquer. If he had, he wouldn't have been banished to the void, locked out from the Earth.

Watching Rachael bite Caine and take his blood, made him sure his plan was going to succeed. These pitiful humans were fun to watch as they tumbled around on their sheets. It was laughable the importance they gave sex. He frowned, recalling a long dead memory.

He'd been human once. He'd been in love and did a fair amount of sheet tumbling himself. He'd been married at one point. She'd been a wild beauty with large breasts, a trim waist and had worn him out many a night. But when his master told him she had to be sacrificed so he could achieve greater power, he'd plunged the knife into her without a second thought.

He remembered smiling as she stared at him, accusing him of betrayal. Her blood had covered the altar, and he couldn't help tasting it. The rush it had given him, the feeling of invincibility as power flooded his body, every cell, every nerve. He knew why she'd had to die. She'd been a powerful mage in her own right. And then all that power had become his.

He'd then spent his time seducing witches and female wizards, taking their virginity or fidelity, finally murdering them and taking their powers. He allowed himself a small bit of satisfaction. He would let Rachael gut Caine and take his power. And when she turned to him, he would do the same to her, taking hers and Caine's magic. Then, the portals could be opened and his nether creatures could roam the earth.

And all he needed was the infernal patience he detested.

****

Joe made the quick trip to the church and back while Rachael was in the shower. He put her suitcase on the bed and went to the living room. Chrissy would've been here by now, making breakfast and talking. What had happened in her apartment the day before? Had Rachael knowingly hurt her? He sincerely hoped not.

His cell phone rang. "Hey, Damen. How's Chrissy?" He was quiet as Damen told him his friend's condition. He ended the call and turned as Rachael walked out of the bedroom. "We need to go to the hospital."

She wrapped her arms around her middle and looked away. "I didn't hurt her."

He grabbed Chrissy's spare car key off the hook by the door. "I know. Let's get down there, and we'll find out what happened."

They rode in silence, Joe feeling it every time Rachael glanced at him. He pulled into the parking lot and got out. Rachael stared at the building and shivered.

He put his arm around her and pulled her close.

"Whatever went on in her apartment, I know you wouldn't hurt her on purpose."

She stepped out of his embrace. "Are you sure? Even I don't know what happened, and I was there. I could've ripped her apart and wouldn't remember. You and your friends are in danger, and I know I'm the cause."

"Then you need to stop blocking our attempts to help you." He spun her around. "Stop running from me every time something bad happens. We've got to face all the problems, the fear, and him head on or the warlock wins. Let go of the fear we all see in you. Remember, you have an angel's heart. Knowing that will give you the strength you need to beat your fear."

She gave him a single nod. "Let's go inside. I need to see her."

Joe followed her through the automatic doors, scratching his left palm. Muted voices and beeping machines surrounded them as they waited for the elevator. On Chrissy's floor, even the music seemed quieter as they walked down the bright hallway, passing computers on rolling stands and carts with linen. They stopped at the desk before heading to her room.

Rachael gasped, and Joe's heart iced over at her condition. Both her eyes were black, and two IV's were in her left arm. Her right was in a cast. Bruises circled her neck, and bandages peeked out from the hospital gown. Damen dozed in the chair by the large window, sitting up when they came in.

Joe grabbed the cross around his neck as Rachael sank down on the only other chair in the room. "What happened to her?"

Damen shook his head. "No one knows. The scratches were too big and too deep. I'd never seen anything like them before. In addition to everything else, she's also got a pretty bad concussion."

"But she is going to make it, right?" Rachael asked.

"The doctors think so. They just gave her some pain meds about an hour ago. She's going to be hurting for a little while."

Joe walked over, leaned down, and kissed Chrissy on her forehead. Her eyes fluttered open and she groaned. "I guess that means you're not feeling so great?" he said.

"How'd you guess? What the heck happened?"

"The police are calling it a home invasion," Damen said. "What are you calling it?"

"I'm calling it an ass of a warlock busting my wards like they were children's scribbles." She groaned again. "If I didn't hurt so much, I'd be a lot angrier."

Rachael walked over to the bed. "Chrissy, I'm so sorry. Everything that happened was all my fault."

"No, it wasn't," she said. "You've got to stop blaming yourself. The more guilt and fear you allow yourself to feel, the stronger his hold gets on you."

"I almost killed you."

"Rachael, listen to me. I'm a little banged up. Lord knows, we've all been in a hospital bed more than once." The two men nodded in agreement. "We fight over and over, even knowing what could happen, because, like you, there are people who need us. We put our lives on the line, not because we have to, but because we want to. I know you understand. The Angels do the same thing all the time."

"Yes," Rachael said softly. "We do. I was so afraid

125

I'd killed you. I remember a lot of blood."

Chrissy took her hand. "Stay with Joe. Now that you two have made actual love, there is a bond between you. The warlock will try to break it, but it can't be done. When you're afraid, call on that bond, and it will help you through anything the warlock tries to make you do."

"I'll remember."

"We're going to go," Damen said. "You need to get some rest. I'll be back later to check on you."

"Okay," she said, her eyes slowly shutting as her breathing evened out.

They walked back down to the parking lot. Rachael glanced back at the building. "Should we really leave her alone?"

"I blessed the room, and I brought her cross to her. I also lined all the thresholds with salt, and raised my own wards around her. Nothing will happen to her."

"But can you protect her from me?"

Joe put his arm around her shoulders. "We're going to follow Damen back to the rectory. We're going to try and take the mark out of you."

She glared at her right hand. "It needs to go. Right now."

They got into their cars and headed for St. Michael's. Again, tense silence hung over them all the way to their destination. They pulled in, and Joe shut the car off. He turned to Rachael.

"You know we don't blame you for anything, right?"

She nodded. "I know, but the doubt, the fear, is still there. Can we beat the warlock? A small part of me doesn't want to."

"I know, but I will help you. For one thing, I promised Kristin I'd help you."

"Any more reasons?"

He took her hand and kissed her knuckles. "I want you with me for a long time."

"Is that a proposal? Because it's not what I was expecting."

He smiled. "I think you could consider it a proposal. I know we've only known each a short time, but it's time that matters. Things always move quickly in the magic world. You're a very special woman, Rachael. I don't want to lose you, and I damn sure won't let some evil spell-caster take you from me. We need to be together. I knew that after our first kiss."

"I felt it too. I thought I saw an explosion of light, and there was a feeling of...."

"Being complete," he finished. "You know, there are such things as soulmates. It's just possible that's what we have between us."

"Except I keep trying to kill you and your friends."

He leaned over the center console and kissed her. "Small problem. It's going to build character. You'll see."

She opened the car door. "You have a strange idea of a 'small problem', my friend."

"With some of the things I been through and done to survive, trust me. This is a small problem."

As they stepped into the warmth of Damen's home, that irritating itch was worse, making Joe scratch it all the harder.

Chapter Fifteen

Rachael looked up as Damen came downstairs and smiled. "I just finished a cleansing upstairs. I found a weak portal the warlock used to get in and sealed it for good. He won't be getting in that way any longer."

"Good. Was it only in the one room?" Joe asked.

"Yes. I've been over the whole place. Can you feel the difference?"

Joe closed his eyes and turned in a slow circle. "I can. It feels like it should again."

"Come to the study." They followed the priest down the hall, then watched as he took a small box from the top drawer of his desk and handed it to Rachael.

She took the lid off and frowned. "My mother's Celtic cross." She looked up. "Where did you get it?"

"I found it on the floor of your room here," Damen said. "I felt the years of love and protection in it. It's been blessed with holy water, and I've started laying protection spells on it. Joe can continue doing so now that you two have joined."

She fastened it around her neck, and a wave of dizziness came over her. "I don't feel so good."

"The warlock is trying to make you take it off. It limits his access to your mind."

Joe helped her to the couch and eased her down. "When can we try to remove the mark?"

"Now." Damen stared at Rachael. "It's not going to be pleasant. Once we begin, you can't stop. If you do, it will make the next attempt harder."

"I understand."

Joe squeezed her hand. "I'll be right here with you. Once the mark is removed, you'll have an easier time fighting him."

She nodded and turned to Damen. "You need to remove Joe's mark, too."

"I'm not marked."

She turned his left hand over and it was bright red. "You keep scratching it, just like I do with my right hand. I think Ithick marked you when you went to see him."

Joe looked at Damen. "What do you think?"

"She's right. I notice you keep digging at your hand when you think no one's looking. We'll take care of Rachael's first, then yours."

"I don't think it's a coincidence that it's her right hand and my left," Joe said. "It's always been after our hands were together that the weakness came over me. The warlock may have linked them to have easier access to my magic. And the fact Ithick could do that to me, and I couldn't detect it, tells me his abilities are getting stronger."

"It would seem so," Damen agreed. "We may have to deal with him at a future time. I've got to grab some holy water. Back in a minute."

Rachael rubbed the back of her neck. "I really don't feel well."

"Lay your head back. It will pass."

She did what he said, still rubbing the back of her neck. Joe looked for Damen and when turned back to her, she held the cross out and dropped it to the floor. Her eyes blacker than a starless night. "You're a fool, Caine. You can't stop me with these silly trinkets."

He felt the tell-tale warm wetness of blood on his lip. "Barghest," he muttered. "Leave her be. If I'm the one you want, why attack her?"

"She's stronger than you will ever hope to be." Her arm shot out, and she yanked his cross from his neck and threw it across the room. "Sorry. No more protection spells for you."

He wove his hands in the air, murmuring ancient words. She grabbed his left arm and held it, her grip getting tighter and harder the more he tried to pull it back. "Now, Caine, feel the power of the marks I've branded in you."

Her right hand grabbed his left and immediately, he felt his power drain from him and bleed into her. "Rachael, no."

She leaned close and grinned. "Oh, yes. Taking power feels so good. It gives me a better sexual thrill than you could ever hope to. I will take everything from you until not even your bones remain."

Damen darted in and scooped her necklace up from the floor, hooking it around her neck, and stopped the attack. He laid his hand on her head, bowing his in prayer. She sagged against the back of the couch as he handed Joe his cross.

"I can't leave you kids alone for two minutes, can I?" Damen said.

Rachael thrust her hand toward him. "Get this thing out of me. I can't bear having that voice in my head anymore."

"With pleasure," Damen said.

He sat next to her and took her hand in his. First he prayed for strength, then protection. He held his hand over hers and spoke words she'd never heard before. Pain lanced up her arm, making her squeeze her eyes shut. Her left hand closed around her mother's necklace, and she could feel it warm under her hand.

She could almost hear her mother's voice telling her to be strong. She grit her teeth, determined to see it through. The lives of her friends depended on it. Fire screamed along her nerves, and it was all she could do not to curl her fingers up and rip her hand from Damen's grasp. How much longer? How much more could she take before she broke?

As soon as she had that thought, the pain ceased. Cold water splashed over her palm, relieving the burning sensation from only moments before. She sighed and her shoulders drooped. "Is it out?"

Damen held a glowing blue sphere above his hand. Inside, a small ball of red light frantically zinged back and forth, looking like it was trying to escape. Damen lowered it into an iron box, sigils and runes inlaid in the sides and shut the lid.

He turned to Joe and grinned. "Your turn. When it's done, you'll need to make a sizable donation to the church for me saving you yet again."

Joe rolled his eyes and held out his left hand. "Just do it and keep the snide remarks to yourself."

Rachael watched as Damen went through the ritual again, and Joe looked like he was in terrible pain. Had she looked like that? Probably. She came up behind Joe and put her arms around him. He relaxed a tiny bit and then, the procedure was over. He sagged in her arms as Damen washed out the area with holy water.

He locked up the second sphere and turned back around. He frowned and took Joe's hand. "Houston, we have a problem."

"What's wrong?" Rachael asked.

The priest looked up. "He's bleeding, and it hasn't stopped. Your hand didn't bleed at all. If Ithick used a different mark, a different binding spell, I could've just made things worse."

"Hang on a second. There's only one type of mark," Joe said.

"That we know of," Damen said, pressing gauze on Joe's palm. "Doppelganger magic is still an unknown factor. It's ancient. It goes back hundreds, possibly thousands of years."

"If Chrissy was here, she'd know exactly what to do." He grimaced and looked up at his friend. "Try some of Gizel's salve. That stuff cures anything."

Rachael held up her right hand. There was a small red mark in the center of her palm, and it was already beginning to fade. Why was Joe bleeding so heavily? Ithick had marked both of them, so shouldn't they have had the same thing in their hands? Apparently, that was not the case.

Damen grabbed the nearby tube, smearing the salve on the wound, muttering the healing incantation to make it glow pale pink. They waited for a moment and blood began to seep through again. The two men looked at each other. "I'm thinking it's serious," Joe said, his voice shaking.

"Help me get him upstairs," Damen said.

With Rachael on the other side, they managed to get him up the stairs and on the bed. Damen hurried out to get some different healing items while Rachael knelt by the bed. Ezra's voice tickled her mind, but it was more distant, weaker, than it had been before. She held the cross around her neck.

The warlock bellowed in her mind, and she sat back, pushing the heels of her hands into her temples. She could hear what he wanted her to do. She glanced at Joe laying on the bed, his blood seeping through the bandages around his hand. Ezra planted the suggestion that all that magical blood was hers for the taking.

"I won't do it," she whispered. "I'm a hero. I keep people safe. You can't make me hurt him."

"You will do my bidding, shifter. Whether you bear my mark or not, I own you, body and soul."

"No, no, no," she murmured. "Your power over me is ended. Leave me alone."

His laughter faded away as Damen hurried back into the room. "Rachael, what's wrong?"

"Psychic assault. He's so strong. He doesn't need the mark anymore. He can still get to me, no matter what."

"We'll find a way to stop him. Don't worry."

"Before I kill both of you? Like I almost killed Chrissy?"

Damen gave her a small shake. "We will help you. Remember what Chrissy told you. You have to stop being afraid. Fear is powerful. Don't give that to him."

She straightened up. "I will give him absolutely nothing."

"That's my girl," Joe said, his voice weak.

Rachael watched as Damen took Joe's hand and did whatever healing things wizards did. All the words were foreign, but there was a cadence to them, and an eerie, musical quality. Her soul was touched by their beauty. She swayed in time to the words being spoken when Damen turned to her, reaching out to her.

She walked over and, not saying anything, took the priest's hand. She could feel on a primal level, precisely what she was supposed to do. As Damen held her hand, she activated her power and shifted to a fox just enough to distort her features. Damen then laid her hand on Joe's.

His hand was hot and the warmth of the wound bled into her. She pressed their hands together, before curling her fingers around his. Damen was still speaking, but his voice sounded like it was coming from the next county, it was so faint. She said the incantation along with him, not even wondering how she knew words she'd never heard before, let alone spoken.

She glanced at their hands and green light peeked out from the cracks. As their hands remained joined, the light became brighter, sparking outward in colorful rays. Joy filled her until she thought her body would fly apart. How could one person contain so much happiness? Glancing at Joe, she felt their bond and knew she'd love him forever. She let the fox features melt away as she changed back to herself while the light faded.

"Joe," she said, her voice low. "How are you feeling?"

He gazed at her, laying his hand on her cheek. "Well, I don't think I'm in any danger of bleeding to death anymore."

Her fingers trembled as she smoothed his hair off his forehead. "That's good."

Joe sat up, and Rachael perched next to him on the

edge of the bed. "Have you been studying without me?" he asked his friend.

"Not really," Damen said. "I called Gizel and explained the problem. He gave me a new incantation to try. It's a lot easier getting in touch with him since he got addicted to cell phones." He glanced at Rachael. "Gnomes have always liked machines. Gizel thought something so small would be useless until he was proven wrong."

"So, how did you learn it that fast?" Joe asked.

"It was a slight variation on the one we always use." The priest looked at the two of them. "Our favorite gnome doctor knows a lot about doppelgangers. He's been keeping a journal for the past couple of centuries."

"Figures."

Rachael put her hand on Joe's. "How long do gnomes live?"

"They've got a fairly long life span. No one knows for sure though. A lot of the fairy races keep everything completely private." He nodded to the priest. "We may be wizards, but we're still just human. We don't get the secret member access."

"Wow. There's a lot I still don't get."

He grinned. "There's a lot we still don't get."

She stood and paced as far as she could in the small room. "How is the warlock still able to talk to me? With the mark gone, I thought his influence would end."

"We've got to find and close all the portals he's created to enter our world. That's got to be how he's still able to communicate. There can't be that many," Damen said. "The one here was weak. I think, with him being barred from here, he's using a lot of power to keep open the ones he does have control over."

"There's one at Chrissy's," Rachael said. "The warlock appeared there in shadow form. And there's at least two at Angel Haven. Remember? He attacked you in my room, and I've seen him out by the large oak tree on at least two separate occasions."

Joe nodded. "I remember. There's probably one at my place, too. His shadow form has been there a couple of times, so the apartments should be the next place we cleanse. We'll need a stronger spell to close the portals at Angel Haven. We need to make sure he can't open them again."

"Agreed. I'll do some checking and see what I can find," Damen said. "You need to figure out how to close off Rachael's mind to him. If he can still access our world through her, closing the portals won't do too much."

Joe nodded. "I'll go start the ritual at Chrissy's. Since he was only there once, hers will be the next easiest to do." He took a deep breath and slowly released it. "Then, I need to do my place. That's going to be a little harder."

"Why?" Rachael asked.

"He's appeared there multiple times. The more he uses the portal, the stronger it gets."

Jumping up, she hurried down the steps. "Then what are we waiting for? Let's go stop the warlock."

Joe followed her. "I like the way you think."

Chapter Sixteen

Ezra paced. With the church portal destroyed, he would now have to use his shadow self to dispose of the priest. He was getting in the way more and more. He could potentially stop his plans for killing Caine and taking the shifter.

He was running out of resources. Ithick's desire for power and position was irritating, and he was getting sick of his constant fawning. Ezra had tossed a novice spell-caster at him and let the doppelganger do what he wanted. The girl's screams had irritated him almost as much as Ithick himself.

Soon, everything he'd set in motion would come to fruition. Then, he'd be rid of all the annoyances around him, including Ithick. He turned to the mirror he used for scrying, passing his hand in front of the smoky glass.

He watched Damen go about his evening ritual before donning his robes and heading to the church for the mid-week mass. Glancing at the clear orb next to him, he frowned. To get back into the rectory, he'd have to use it. Devices were beneath him. To be reduced to using one was embarrassing.

Still, a moment of dependency was worth it for the chance to rid himself of an enemy. The image in the mirror faded. Unfortunately, he still couldn't see inside the church. Sanctified ground. He was lucky the rules of the dark arts governing him didn't apply to the rectory. That was more a home than holy ground. Flexing his fingers, a cold smile curled his lips. Damen Richardson's life was his tonight. Snatching up the orb, he strode from the room.

****

Joe and Rachael stepped carefully into Chrissy's apartment. He looked around at the damage. Glass crunched under his feet, and he stepped farther into what had been her living room. Gouges had been cut into the wall, and it sure looked like it had been done by claws to him. Her kitchen was basically untouched, as was the tiny dining room.

He walked down to her bedroom, where most of the fight had taken place. The bed was torn apart, and blood spatter dotted the door. Her dresser had been shoved over a little, but the stains on the carpet made him stop and just stare.

He closed his eyes and held his arms out in a V from his body. Blue mist filled the room and the events of the past played out. He saw Ezra's presence in the corner and knew the exact moment he'd taken control of Rachael. She couldn't have fought him, even if she'd wanted to.

He frowned when he watched her change into a nether beast. She physically wasn't capable of transforming into those types of creatures. Ezra had warped her abilities and with it, her mind and body. Watching the woman he loved viciously attack his dearest friend made his heart ache.

He finally let the past go back to where it was supposed to be and turned to Rachael. "Let's close the portal."

"What did you see?"

He crushed her to him, burying his face in her hair. "He's destroying you, a little at a time. You can't feel it, you can't fight it."

Her arms squeezed him tightly. "What can I do?"

"You trust me and you stop being afraid of your abilities." He took her mouth in a hungry kiss before letting her go. "Stay behind me and repeat what I say."

"All right. Let's do it."

He took salt, sage, and holy water out of his bag. He burned the sage in every room, and using holy water, blessed every door and window. When that was done, he lined all the entrances with salt.

"That was the easy part," he said. "Now all we have left to do is close the portal."

Rachael pointed to the bedroom. "It's probably there. It's where I attacked Chrissy, and people are more vulnerable when they sleep. It would be the most likely spot."

"I think you might be right." He smiled at her. "See? You are getting the hang of magic."

He spoke the spell to reveal hidden doorways. There it sat, in the back corner. It was stronger than he thought, for as small as it appeared. He wove his hands in front of him as his fingers danced through the closing spell. Orange signs and sigils appeared in the air, and flowing down his arms to swirl around his hands, weaving an intricate, magical web.

Sweat broke out on his forehead as the orange sigils were replaced by bright, blue chains. The light shot to the corner and portal collapsed in on itself. He closed his eyes and a tiny light trail zoomed through the apartment before zinging back to him and disappearing as he sat on the bed.

"The warlock no longer has access to her home. It's been cleansed, blessed, and the portal is destroyed." He glanced at her. "I can't detect anything else here."

Rachael put her arms around him. "That's a good day's work."

"Now we need to do my place," he said, leaning against the dresser.

"That can wait until after you've eaten and had some rest. You look beat."

He sighed. "It takes a lot of energy to do what I just did here. There's usually a team and everyone does one piece of the ritual. Closing portals is harder than opening them. To do every piece is draining."

"Let me take you home so I can get you something to eat." She nudged him gently. "I may not be as good a cook as Chrissy, but I manage."

"I can microwave. That's about it."

He leaned on her as she helped him to his feet. They walked across the short sidewalk, and he dropped the wards. He kicked the door shut and raised the wards again. Not that it would do any good. The warlock had already blown by them a couple of times. Until the portal was closed, if he wanted in, he was getting in.

Rachael began putting pans on the stove. He poked his head around the doorway. "I'm going to get cleaned up."

"All right. Don't be long."

He headed down the hall to his bathroom. He stripped off his clothes and stepped in the shower, sighing when the hot water hit his face. Was there anything better than a hot shower to ease away the tension? The shower door opened, and Rachael stood there, gloriously naked, her body just begging to be touched. Apparently, a beautiful, naked, Irish woman beat hot water.

"I thought I'd join you. Do you mind?"

He stared at her. Delicious smells drifted to him from the kitchen and he frowned. "I thought you were making dinner. Won't it burn?"

She laughed, making him smile. It was such a musical sound, full of life and beauty. "No. I lowered the heat on the stove." She stepped in and closed the glass door. "I want to be with you."

He gazed at her mouth, slowly leaning down to kiss it gently. Her arms twined around his neck and she pushed her hips against his. He groaned when her tongue slid into his mouth, taking his in an erotic dance. However, the sparks, the explosions of joy and love he felt were absent.

Her hands glided down his back and he lifted his head to ask her if she noticed and stopped. Her eyes were jet black. No white, no color, just an inky nothingness lurching out to drag his soul down to hell. He stumbled back and slipped, jarring his shoulder against the wall.

A voice filled with hate screamed through his mind. *"You're so easy to control."*

Blood ran freely from his nose, making him grab the cross around his neck and utter a protection spell. His mind cleared, and he looked around. He was alone, and Rachael was nowhere to be seen. The thought of her standing with him under the spray of hot water made his body ring with desire. He snapped the water off and wrapped a towel around his waist. He pinched his nose for a few moments before walking out to the kitchen where Rachael was still cooking. And dry.

She glanced at him and smiled. "Dinner's almost ready. Go get dressed."

How could she do that to him? Couldn't she see how badly he wanted her? How did she dry all that hair so quickly? "Have you been out here the whole time?"

"Yes. Where else would I have been?"

He walked over to her. "With me. In the shower."

"No. You were in the shower. I was here, making you dinner." She stared at his face. "You've had another nose bleed. What happened?"

Joe shook his head. "I don't know. Things aren't clear."

Rachael turned the heat down on the stove and went over to him. "That sounds a lot like what I go through when the warlock controls me. Tell me everything."

"I turned on the hot water. You showed up, naked, and joined me, but there was an emotional void. I wanted to ask you if you felt it, but you were different. Your eyes were solid black. There was a voice that said I was easy to control and then I was alone. I came out here to find you."

"I wasn't with you. You must have had some kind of dream."

"Or illusion," he said quietly. "I've got shields in my mind. He shouldn't have been able to control me. How powerful is he?"

"If he can get past your shields, a lot more powerful than we originally thought. Go get dressed. Dinner's almost done."

He nodded and headed back to his room to finish drying off and throw some clothes on. He'd be glad when they finally confronted the warlock. He wasn't sure how much more he could take.

****

When Joe appeared at the kitchen door, wearing nothing but a towel, Rachael had wanted to jump him. He looked so sexy standing there. His reddish-brown hair turned a deep burnished bronze from the water and clung to his forehead, dripping water down his chest. Droplets settled in the short stubble on his jaw, and the temptation to kiss that water away had been almost more than she could bear. She'd stared at his broad, muscular chest, her fingers aching to caress it and those shoulders. She sighed.

Whoa, girl. Thinking about any other body parts is going to make you burn dinner. She smiled. Yeah, but those legs and that butt. And she knew what he had in front. She glanced at the wobbly dining room table. Would it support their weight? What she wouldn't give to find out. She could see them there, her on her back with Joe buried inside her, making her scream his name. And, yes. He was that tanned all over.

A loud clang snapped her out of the daydream. She picked up the spoon from where it fell and threw it in the sink. He made her feel warm and loved and, above all else, not afraid. She never realized how much she carried with her until Joe's touch banished it. She always tried to be someone she wasn't to make others happy, but Joe wanted her for who she was and no one else.

She slowly stirred the gravy. When he was aroused, his light green eyes darkened, giving him a strange, mysterious look that made her insides quiver just thinking about it. That reddish-brown hair was always is disarray, even when she'd seen him brush it. His worn leather jacket made her think of a motorcycle jockey, riding on the open highway, not a wizard in a contemporary, metropolitan area.

He was easy on the eyes, and like a warm blanket to her emotions. The warlock had turned her inside out and upside down. Joe had set her on the path to regaining herself, and she knew he was determined to be there every step of the way.

Chapter Seventeen

Damen shook hands with the last parishioner and locked the church doors. After storing his robes, he headed back to the rectory to get on the research for Joe. The answers were out there somewhere. He just needed to look in the right places.

The instant he walked in the front door, he knew something was wrong. The feeling of peace he'd restored earlier was gone. Darkness hung heavy in every corner, every shadow, behind every closed door. He blessed himself, walking swiftly and silently to his study. Opening the top desk drawer, he removed the gun he always kept loaded with blessed ammunition.

He headed back out to the hall and looked both ways. Hair stood up on the back of his neck, making him glance behind. Nothing. He headed for the stairs and slowly ascended the steps. He closed his eyes, letting his senses scan ahead. Yes. The warlock was here. Damen set his mouth in a grim line and finished climbing the stairs.

"Come out, warlock," he called. "I know you're here."

An inky shadow form pulled itself away from the wall. "Very good, priest. What harm do you think you will do with that gun? I am shadow. You can't hurt me."

Damen aimed the gun and cocked it. "I can try."

145

He pulled the trigger, the bullet hitting the shadow dead center. It folded a little and flowed backward. Damen fired again, trying to hurt it as much as he could.

"If that is your best, you are woefully outmatched."

Damen dropped the gun. "Not even close."

He closed his eyes and white light flowed to him. He raised his hands and the light shot toward the shadow, making it howl in pain and rage. Damen moved his hand in a slow circle, getting faster and faster, summoning a screaming wind. The blast hit the shadow man, blowing him apart.

Damen ran for the stairs, wanting to be in a better position to fight the warlock. Halfway down, he was shoved from behind. He hit the floor and lay there for precious seconds, trying to get his breath back. Pushing himself to his feet, he staggered to the living area.

Black mist oozed around his neck, lifting him off the ground. "Your miserable life ends tonight. I tire of your interference."

"And I'm not real fond of you either," he choked out. His hand inched into his pocket, his fingers curling around the gift his mother had given him when he graduated from the seminary. He flung the small string of blue beads at the warlock.

As the rosary passed through the shadow, Ezra screamed in pain, dropping Damen to the floor. The blackness started to recede, flowing backward up the stairs. Damen grabbed the rosary from the floor, holding it in front of him while marching forward.

He followed the shadow to the back bedroom and saw the glass orb on the floor. He picked it up, holding it high over his head.

"No!" Ezra dived for the orb, snatching it just before Damen had a chance to dash it to the floor. "You are not the only wizard I must deal with tonight." He disappeared inside, and it winked out of sight.

"Chrissy."

Damen stumbled and fell. When Ezra's shadow hand had grabbed him, he felt his magic being drained. He and Joe were playing with a warlock of incredible power. For the rosary to hurt him like it did, he was positive now, Ezra Barghest had made a deal with dark forces. He needed to pull himself together and do that research. Right now, information was their best friend.

Grasping the rosary tightly and holding it close to his chest, he pushed himself to his feet and headed for his study. He grabbed his laptop and jumped in his car, driving straight to the hospital.

****

Rachael watched Joe pace. His movements were smooth with a natural grace that made looking at him her new greatest pleasure. He sat on the couch for a few seconds, then got up and resumed pacing.

"What's wrong?"

He shook his head. "I don't know. I feel like I should, but it's just out of reach." He stopped. "Maybe something's wrong with Chrissy. If not, she might know something."

Rachael snatched up their coats and tossed his at him. "Let's go. Maybe she'll be awake enough to tell you what's going on."

Joe took back streets to the hospital and tapped his foot impatiently while they waited for the elevator. The ding made him jump, and he hurried in as soon as the doors opened, Rachael right behind him.

"Calm down. If you go to her as agitated as you are right now, you'll scare her."

"I know," he said. "I can't help it. There's something wrong."

They hurried down the hall to Chrissy's room. She was sitting up a little and drinking orange juice. Damen sat in the corner, spots that looked a lot like bloodstains on his shirt. He had the look of a man who had been put through the wringer. Twice.

"Hey, guys," he croaked out."

Rachael sat next to him. "What happened?"

"I was attacked by the warlock. He managed to get back into the rectory. He's stronger than we thought. I was doing some research on him when I got here, but had to stop. Looking at the screen is giving me a pounding headache."

Joe glanced at Damen as he stood by Chrissy's bed. "Are you hurt?"

Her head rolled back and forth on the pillow. "No. The warlock hasn't made an appearance here."

"Yet," Damen said. "He said I wasn't the only wizard he had to deal with tonight. I thought he might have meant coming here. So I was determined to beat him."

Rachael looked at him. "He attacked Joe at his home. We thought he might have been after Chrissy. Joe was restless all evening. That's when we decided to come here." She glanced at Joe. "You must have sensed the attack on Damen."

"That has to be it. Are you sure he didn't do some serious damage to you?" Joe asked. "I can hear you wheezing all the way over here."

"I'm fine. Just a little banged up."

"You closed the portal you found and blessed the rectory," Rachael said. "How did he get back in?"

Damen turned to her. "When doorways are closed, beings have to find another way. He had one." He looked up at Joe. "He has an orb."

Joe ran his hands through his hair and it was all Rachael could do not to run to him and wrap her arms around his waist. She hated seeing him so upset. "What's an orb?"

"It's a way to walk dimensions," Joe said. "The orb itself isn't evil, but when someone who isn't the best person comes along, the magic they use can taint it. If the warlock has had the orb for an extended time, that thing is going to be as evil as he is. It needs to be destroyed."

Damen flipped open the laptop. "Agreed. All we need to do is figure out how to get to the void where he's trapped."

"And therein lies the rub," Chrissy said. "I knew you were coming and that you were upset about something. At least we know what was setting you off."

Joe didn't say anything, just looked away and continued walking around the room.

Rachael knew she had to do something, or she'd just watched him the whole time. She finally took the laptop from Damen and sat it on her lap. "Where do you want me to start looking?"

"Are you sure you don't want me to do that?" Damen asked.

She nodded. "I feel like I haven't done enough to help. You have a headache, and we need to start looking for the warlock. So, I can at least help with the online search."

Rachael started tapping the keys and pulling up different websites. She couldn't stop sneaking peeks at Joe over the top of the screen. He still paced, and his hair was starting to stick up more as he kept running his hands through it. She shot her gaze back to the screen and then, just as quickly, flicked them back up to the object of her true interest.

When she stared at the screen again, she swore she could feel his gaze on her. Her cheeks felt warm, and she tried to pay more attention to what Damen was instructing her to do. Knowing Joe was looking at her made her lady parts tingle.

"I'm going out for a minute," Joe said. "Everyone, please stay here."

Chrissy laughed which turned into a cough. "I don't have a choice."

Rachael watched him stride from the room and wondered where he was going.

****

Joe took the elevator to the ground floor and stepped out. He checked the directory and turned right, walking down a bright hallway. He found the room he was looking for and stepped inside.

The sounds of the hospital stopped at the doorway. Silence enveloped him, its peacefulness barring any noise from entering. Low, amber lights lent an atmosphere of calm, giving visitors the solace they craved. The hospital chapel had a stained glass window that wasn't really a window. It was back lit to make it appear that it was on an outside wall.

Joe was the only one there, and he sat in a front pew, staring at the simple altar. It lacked the adornments of the bigger churches, and he was grateful for that. It seemed to him church was more about image these days, than faith.

He gave thanks for Damen. His friend kept him firmly planted on the ground, like Chrissy. His friends were the anchor that gave him strength to go on. He was getting tired of all the battles, fighting every evil thing that could open a doorway. There were times, more often than not recently, when he wished he'd never left Nebraska.

Rachael's face formed in his mind. She was amazing. As he watched her make dinner earlier, her movements were quick and sure, almost like a bird. She never stayed still for very long, always turning to something else that needed her attention. Right now, he could use her attention. She made him feel like he was the only man on the planet. The sparkle in her eyes brightened every time she looked at him, making his manly bits twitch with pride.

She'd been the only woman so far to make him react that way. When they made love, her touch had been firm, yet gentle. He loved the way her hands explored him. He gazed at the altar again, his thoughts not very pious at the moment, but thinking about the woman who now held his heart. He smiled a little, pretty sure the Man Upstairs wouldn't mind.

A feeling that worse things were coming invaded his heart and soul. The warlock asked him if he would sacrifice Rachael if it meant keeping the world safe. He'd hesitated but said yes. At the time, he'd been lying. Now? He wasn't sure. It would destroy her to be kept as a slave, if the warlock didn't sacrifice her first. He rolled his eyes. There was a happy thought.

He stared at the plain, wooden cross hanging just

above the altar. It hit him that, yes, he'd do whatever was needed to make sure she wouldn't be used by the warlock. Could he be that strong? He'd have to be, for her sake and his.

As he came to terms with that, he felt strangely at peace. He'd been jumpy for so long, he'd forgotten what true peace felt like. He bowed his head, praying for the strength he'd need in the coming days to defeat the warlock and protect his friends. Both Damen and Chrissy had been hurt. That was going to stop as of today.

He smiled at the angel on the stained glass. The Archangel Michael was the most well-known of all the angels. He could use Michael's strength right about now. He was going into battle, and he'd like to have some of the archangel's skill in a fight.

"Protect us, Michael. We're going to need you more than ever before. Just watch our backs when the fight goes down." Joe stopped and closed his eyes. "Give me the knowledge and the strength to do what must be done to save Rachael's soul. I don't want her to be some puppet." He gazed back up at the picture, and it appeared Michael was looking right back at him. "Thanks for listening. I've got to get back upstairs."

Joe exited the chapel feeling a little better than he had when he'd first entered.

Chapter Eighteen

Rachael looked up and smiled when Joe came back into the room. Her heart beat a little faster, and she wanted to go to him and hold him. There was a peacefulness about him that hadn't been there when he left. "Everything all right?"

"Better than it was before. You guys find anything?"

"We think so," she said, turning the bedside table around so he could see the computer. He bent over a little and read the screen. She resisted her impulse to reach out and caress him. She cleared her throat. "We think he's trying to open a permanent portal between here and the nether dimensions. He wants the dark creatures to overrun the earth."

"Where did you guys find this?"

"A small website, and it was really obscure. I'm not even sure how we found them." Damen pointed out the web address. "Do you know them?"

"Magic Central," he murmured. "Never heard of them. How do they know so much?"

Damen shrugged, then groaned and rubbed his neck. "I'm not sure. It could be run by a smaller magic circle."

"But if it's run by someone with a bigger agenda, we could be putting ourselves in danger just having the page open."

Rachael's finger hovered over the keyboard. "Do you want me to close it out?"

"No," Joe said. "Send an email. Ask them how they know."

Rachael's fingers flew over the keyboard as she typed in the 'contact us' box. She glanced at Joe and he barely nodded, a signal to hit the send button. "There it goes. Hopefully they'll get back to us soon."

"Hopefully," Joe said. "Does it say how he plans to keep the portal open?"

Rachael glanced at Damen and Chrissy. "Yes. You're not going to like it."

He stared at the three of them. "What has to happen?" When everyone was still hesitant to say anything, he stared at each of them in turn. "Come on, guys, I'm a big boy. I can handle it."

"He needs the blood of a wizard. There's a specific day it needs to be done." She stopped talking, clamping her lips together.

"Go on," he said slowly.

She swallowed hard. "The blood needs to be taken by force to draw the creatures to where the portal will open."

"And?" he prompted.

"And a shapeshifter needs to be the catalyst for the drawing of the blood."

Joe ran his hands through his hair again. "Figures. Ithick had told me the same thing when I went to see him. I hate when he's right."

"It explains why he started with Rachael, then turned his attention to you," Damen said. "It also explains why you were both marked. I think Rachael's mark was the one to draw your power out so you'd be too weak to fight him."

"Makes sense. We've fought and beaten a lot of evil creatures, gang. So how do we beat him?"

They all shook their heads. Rachael couldn't believe no one had any idea how to fight Ezra Barghest. "We'll find some way," she said. "We're the good guys. The good guys are supposed to win."

"Not all the time," Joe said quietly.

****

They visited with Chrissy until the nurse told them visiting hours were over. The car clock showed it was after eleven, so they swung through a twenty-four-hour fast food place on the way to Joe's. While she started emptying the bags, he grabbed extra napkins from the kitchen. They ate in silence, and after he threw the trash away, he sat at the table, staring at her.

"I don't want to be disemboweled by you," he finally said.

"And I don't want to disembowel you. What can we do to make sure that doesn't happen?"

He sat back. "Not a clue. I've been underestimating the warlock since we began. We'll wait and see what the email says when they get back to us." He took her hand. "I promise I won't let him use you."

She felt the power in his gentle grip and squeezed his fingers. "I want you to promise that if he gets control of me and there's nothing you can do, you'll kill me. I don't want to live like that, and no matter how far he gets into my mind, there'll be a part of me that won't want to be his servant."

"I promise," he said quietly. "I won't let him use you. By the same token, if you get a chance to run, take it. Don't worry about me. He'll need both of us for the

155

ceremony, and if one of us is gone, he can't complete the spell."

He needed to hear it, but there would be no way she could leave him behind. She nodded. "I promise." I am such a liar. She walked over to his computer. "Do you want me to see if they responded yet?"

"You can, but you only sent it a little while ago. I don't think they'll get back to you quickly."

She pressed the power button and waited. "I know but I need to do something. I feel so helpless."

He finally grinned. "I understand. You do your thing and I'll do mine."

She watched as he kicked his shoes off and sat cross-legged in the middle of the floor. The computer beeped, calling her attention. She logged into her email and there was a reply. Taking a shaky breath, she opened it.

The reply was longer than she thought. Resting her chin on her hand, she scanned the email, slowly scrolling through the lines of type. What she read wasn't making their situation any better. As a matter of fact, it now felt like they were in way over their heads. She glanced over her shoulder at Joe, who hadn't moved. He needed to see the reply.

Her vision blurred and she sat back, rubbing her eyes. The back of her neck ached, and she massaged right below her scalp as her eyes drifted closed. There was something important she had to do, something she needed to tell him.

"Was there any reply yet?"

She glanced at him, then to the computer screen. "No, not yet. I hope they send something soon. We need to know what we're dealing with."

"I hear you. Maybe we'll try contacting them again if we don't hear something by tomorrow."

She stood and stretched. "Sounds good."

****

Joe listened to Rachael tapping the computer keys as he tried to connect with the earth. Just knowing she sat not six feet behind him made his concentration falter. He could smell her delightful scent wafting on the air current from the apartment's heater. She was all sweet and spice and woodsy.

He snuck a peek over his shoulder, and she looked so intent on what she was doing. She had leaned close to the screen. Whatever she was reading was certainly holding her attention. Her back was stiff, and he watched as she slipped a hand beneath that wild black mane of hair.

He tried to slow his heartbeat when she stood and stretched. The material of her blouse pulled tight against her chest as she raised her arms over her head. That small waist just begged for hands to be around it, the flare of her hips asking to be snuggled against his. His body sat up and noticed as he watched her. Yeah, meditation with Rachael in the same room was not a good idea.

All he wanted right then, was to strip her bare and have her beneath him screaming his name. They had fit together so well when they'd made love before, he was anxious to try it again. He knew it'd be just as special, just as amazing as the first time. Loving Rachael would be new and exciting every time. He felt it in his heart. He could still feel the silkiness of her skin in his fingers, making them itch to touch her again.

He watched her walk over and sit in front of him.

She took his hands, and he glanced at them. Her hands were so small, so delicate, compared to his. The smoothness of her skin soothed him, and he tightened his grip. She smiled and he wanted so much to smile back at her, but couldn't.

He gazed intently at her eyes, waiting for any sign the warlock was trying to assert control again, but nothing happened. The uncommon light violet color never wavered, never changed as she watched him. Sitting so close, and not doing unmentionable, but fun things to her, he saw the true color of them. Light near the pupil, fanning out to an almost bluish purple around the edges.

She was definitely one of a kind, a woman to be loved and cherished, worshipped and spoiled. He could see that tiny, mischievous sparkle gleam in her eyes. He loved that about her. Even with everything bad they faced and was still to come, she still had that twinkle. Would it still be there when they completed the mission? That, he didn't know.

"What are you thinking about?" she asked, her Irish brogue making him smile.

"You. Always you." He squeezed her hands. "I'm not going to leave, you know. I'll help you through everything to come. You don't have to be afraid. We're all going to make it."

"I know. You're too stubborn to accept any other outcome."

He grinned. "You really are getting to know me well." He stood and offered her a hand up. "It's getting late. We both need some rest."

Standing up, she kept his hand in hers. "Are you sleeping with me?"

"No. I've got to finish my meditations. I got a little distracted." He smiled. "You're the best distraction I've had in a long time. I'll stay out here when I'm done. You need your rest."

She stood on her toes and gave him a light kiss good night. "I'll see you in the morning then."

He watched her walk to his bedroom and turn before closing the door. She gave him a small wave, and then he was closed off from her. Strange he should feel like they were on two different worlds when he couldn't see her. He squared his shoulders and resumed his seat on the floor. Time to finish what he started.

He cleared his mind, letting the power of the planet flow into him. As long as he could concentrate on his power, maybe he'd stop thinking about the black-haired Irish beauty just a few steps away, sleeping in his bed.

****

Rachael lay awake for a long time, staring at the door, silently willing him to come in. She sighed and turned over, knowing he wouldn't because he was a man of his word. Pulling the covers up to her chin, her eyes drifted shut and she tumbled into sleep.

Instantly, she slipped into a nightmare. She was running, her breath coming in ragged gasps. The shadow figure was right behind her. She tripped, falling headlong down a hill as something coiled around her legs. She kicked hard and tried to scream, then bolted upright, her chest heaving, sweat beading on her brow. She looked down, her shoulders slumping in relief. The covers. Somehow, she'd gotten them tangled around her legs. She straightened them, jumping when a quiet knock sounded.

"Rachael, are you all right?"

"Yes," she called. "You can come in, it's okay." The door opened, and the low light from the living room cast Joe in shadow, but unlike the man in her dream, there was no menace from him. She took a deep breath. "Did I wake you?"

"No. I was still awake trying to find anything on the warlock." He walked over and sat on the foot of the bed. "Bad dreams?"

She wrapped her arms around her waist and huddled in the middle of the bed. "It was so much worse than the others I've had recently. I can't remember what happens, only that I'm scared and I need to run away. I wish I knew what to do about them."

"When did they start?"

"Right around the time the old man shook my hand." She looked up at him. "We both know what that was about."

He shook his head. "I don't understand how he can still be affecting you so badly. Maybe we missed something."

"Maybe," she said.

He stood. "Try and get some rest."

"Don't go," she said, grabbing his hand. "I'm terrified to close my eyes. I'd feel better if you were here."

He propped up the pillows and sat back, stretching his legs out. He gently pulled her down next to him and put his arm around her shoulders. She laid her head on his chest, letting the beat of his heart soothe her, his steady breathing a balm to her tormented spirit. As he stroked her hair, he hummed a quiet tune.

"What song is that?"

"It's an old Irish lullaby written at the beginning of the twentieth century. My mother used to sing it to me when I had a nightmare or was upset about something. She'd hold me and sing until I fell asleep."

"What's it about?"

"A mother and her love for her child. She tells him all the fairies and the Green Man are there to watch over him and keep him safe as he sleeps."

"Will you sing it to me?"

His voice was deep and soft, wrapping around her, weaving its own kind of magic. It was almost a promise he would keep her as safe as the baby in the song. She felt the vibrations of his voice rumble through her, soothing away her fear and doubt. His arms cradled her to his chest and she snuggled closer. The song ended and his shirt was wet. She wiped tears from her eyes.

Glancing up, she noticed his eyes shone with the same tears. He was just as affected by the melody and the simple words of love. "It's beautiful. Sing it again. Please."

"Sure," he murmured, pulling her closer to him. The tune haunted her as much as the words calmed her. He never stopped stroking her hair as he just repeated the song until her eyes closed and she couldn't stay awake and longer.

Her mouth curved in a small smile when she felt his lips lightly brush her forehead. Tonight, no fear, no doubt, and no evil could touch her.

Chapter Nineteen

Joe was right where he wanted to be. Rachael was curled into his side while he held her, trying to soothe away the terrors of the dream plane. The warlock was getting his hooks in deeper, and she was slowly losing what control she had left. He kept humming the lullaby, hoping it would get her through the night.

Their first intimate moment had been explosive but tender, sensual, yet sweet. The second had been just as special as the first. Would they be able to have more? If there was a chance, any chance, he'd find it. He'd given her a promise to protect her and he meant to keep it. There was no way his wonderful woman would now or ever be taken from him. He held her a little tighter and she sighed, making him smile.

He hadn't sung the Gartan Mother's Lullaby in years. It was one of his mom's favorite songs. She'd taught it to him when he was only five or six. It felt like he'd known it all his life. She'd told him her mother had sung it to her and told her to pass it on to her children.

Joe had no brothers or sisters. His mom couldn't have any other kids after him. So she taught him everything she knew, from how to take care of a home to the origin of his magic. Now that he'd sung the song to Rachael, he felt stronger, renewed, more focused on the job at hand. The lullaby always had the ability to get him through whatever tough time he was having, but sharing it had strengthened his spirit, increasing his determination to win.

He laid his head back and closed his eyes. Laying here with Rachael's head on his chest felt sexier and more intimate than anything they'd done before. He could still feel where her tears had dampened his T-shirt. He'd cried the first time he'd heard it, too. His mother had held him tighter and she'd continued to sing until he'd calmed down. He did the same now with Rachael. He sang the words quietly and let them ease his soul. Morning would be here soon. He needed at least a little rest. He let himself drift away.

****

Sunlight pushed its way into his room, and Joe opened his eyes. Rachael hadn't moved the entire night. He shifted a little and she woke, smiling up at him. He planted a light kiss on her forehead. "Good morning. How'd you sleep?"

She sat up and stretched. "Best sleep I've had in ages. You?"

"Same here. I think we need some breakfast. What would you like?"

She watched as he stood up. "Anything will be fine." She glanced back at the bed. "I wish we didn't have to get up."

"I know, but the sooner we deal with the warlock, the sooner we can go back to what we had last night."

"All you did was hold me," she said.

He leaned down and kissed her. "Sometimes that's the best way to spend a night together. Any couple can hop in bed, and that's fine, I'm not judging. But to just be together, to just hold each other, that's what's important." He stood back and grinned. "Get ready for the day. I'll start making food."

****

Rachael watched him leave the room, his gait sure and easy. He was content just holding her the previous night. He'd made no move, didn't try anything. It was like he knew exactly what she needed at the time. And that lullaby he sang. She couldn't get it out of her head. She quickly dressed and walked out to sit at the dining room table.

"You know, I still have that song in my head," she told him.

Pushing bread down in the toaster, he turned. "It does get into you. I'm convinced it's got some magical properties to it."

"I'm sure it does. I felt so much calmer after you sang it to me. I didn't have any nightmares or see the shadow that haunts me."

He brought out two plates with scrambled eggs, bacon, and toast. "I'm having tea. I've also got orange juice."

"Tea, thank you." Eyeing the plate, she said, "I thought you said you could only microwave."

"I can make eggs as long as you want them scrambled. That's about as far as it goes. My mom taught me a lot, but I never mastered cooking."

"Your mother sounds amazing," Rachael said, taking a bite of her eggs.

He nodded. "She is. When everything is over, maybe we'll go visit my parents. I know they'd love you. After breakfast, let's check your email again and see if there's any word from those people."

She frowned and rubbed her head. "Okay."

"Are you all right?"

She hummed the song and looked up, smiling. "I'm fine. I'm sure there'll be some word. We'll check as soon as we clean up."

"Sounds like a plan."

They finished and put the dishes in the dishwasher. Joe walked over to his computer and turned it on. He looked over his email, then let Rachael sit down. She punched up her email and stared at it. The lullaby echoed through her mind, and she moved the cursor over to the trash icon and clicked it.

There was the reply from the website. "I deleted it last night," she said, her voice sounding far away.

"Why?"

She curled her hands into tight fists on the keyboard. "The warlock wanted me to. We are going to stop him. I don't care what it takes. I won't be under some lunatic's control any longer."

Joe's arms circled around her. "We'll get him. Don't worry."

She leaned against his chest. "It's so much easier beating up bad guys. Super powered villains are always more straight forward in their goals. They want the world; they take out the good guys. In public. In broad daylight. There's no skulking in the shadows stuff."

"I know. Unfortunately, magical bad guys are sneaky. They have to be. I think it's in their union contract."

She smiled, grateful for his quick sense of humor. He pulled up a dining room chair, sitting next to her as she opened the email. The answer came, not from the site, but from a personal account. Rachael could almost feel the other person watching her as she scrolled down.

Rachael and Joe were greeted by name, and they glanced at each other. The writer went on to say they had been waiting to be contacted by them so they could tell them the warlock's history. Knowledge, after all, was power. Ezra had been a warlock of little ability in the mid eighteenth century. When he discovered he was going to be arrested for witchcraft, he snuck out of his village before the law could grab him.

He wandered for several years before marrying and settling down on a small farm in France. A master warlock had found him and began training him in the dark arts. His wife was a powerful wizard in her own right. When Ezra's master ordered her death so he could achieve more power, he did so without a second thought.

As his abilities gained strength, he made a pact with dark forces. In the middle of the night, he killed his master and took his power. It was then he came to the notice of the Circle of Nine. They hunted him all over Europe, always one step behind, arriving too late to stop his murderous rampage.

Finally, in the late 1800s, they cornered him, exiling him to the void, and binding him there. Recently, the doppelganger, Ithick, had found the way in to Ezra's dimension and had been trying to free him. The warlock swore vengeance on all members of the Circle of Nine and their descendants. Ithick had already dispatched two of them, and all that were left were Father Damen Richardson, Christine Ford, and Joseph Caine.

Having found the spell to help his master permanently open the door between dimensions, Ithick marked the two people that would be the strongest for

Ezra to achieve his goals. The time was getting near for the warlock to use them to open the doorways. Rachael's power as a shapeshifter was unprecedented and only she could complete the ceremony to destroy the lock on the portals. The fact that Caine was a descendant of the Circle of Nine made it all the sweeter to the warlock.

The writer of the email explained there was a new Circle of Nine forming in secret after they'd found the history of the original Circle. They wanted to help, but for now, they weren't at full strength and had to stay in the background. They knew Joe and Rachael had everything they needed to defeat Ezra and seal the portal forever.

Joe glanced at Rachael. "If I'm a descendant, what about my family? Are they in danger? Are Chrissy and Damen's families at risk?"

A line of type appeared. We are watching your families closely. They will not be harmed.

"Great. I'm talking to a computer without sounds." Joe sat back. "They say we have everything. It would be nice if they'd tell us."

You know magic doesn't work like that, Wizard Caine. You have everything. It will all become clear in time.

The email disappeared and left them with a blank screen. "That's inconvenient," Rachael muttered.

"I can see their reasoning, but it's still really frustrating." Joe began to pace. "There's a new Circle of Nine being put together. Interesting." He grabbed his cell phone. "I've got to let Damen know."

She listened to him talk to his friend. She rubbed her eyes and leaned back in the chair. She hadn't been sitting here that long, so why did she feel so wrung out? She glanced at Joe and felt the stirrings of irritation. Why was he always talking to his friends and not her? Didn't she deserve his attention too?

She got up and walked over to him. "I need you," she whispered. "Now."

He hung up and turned. Rachael pressed herself to him, forcing his head down to kiss him. He pushed her back slightly and pressed the back of his hand to his nose. Blood. He wove a quick pattern in the air and touched her forehead with his index finger. She stumbled backward and fell to the floor.

"What happened?"

"Guess," he said, his voice muted as he pinched his nose shut. "We've got to conclude the situation before we all go insane."

She grabbed his hand, pulling herself up. "You'll get no argument from me."

Chapter Twenty

"I can't believe there's a new Circle," Damen said as they sat in his study.

Joe nodded. "Yep, and you, Chrissy, and I are the last descendants of the originals."

"It makes sense. What now?"

Rachael glanced at the two of them. "We still have to cleanse Joe's home and do Angel Haven. I have a feeling it's going to be bad, and things aren't going to go our way."

"Why?" Joe asked, watching her closely. "Did you have some kind of vision?"

She shook her head, frowning. "I don't know. I just feel like when we get to Angel Haven, everything is going to go wrong."

Joe pulled her close. "I know better than to discount intuition. We'd better make sure we have everything in place, take every precaution we can to make sure things work out in our favor and we all come out still breathing."

"Agreed." Damen walked to his desk and pulled out a large, leather bound book. Sitting down, he laid the book across his knees and opened it. "There are some passages in here that tell how to permanently destroy portals between worlds. We need to memorize these spells to make sure we get them right."

"The reply from Magic Central said the time was

getting close. We should expect Ithick or the warlock to make their move any day now."

"We'll start learning the spell later today," Damen said.

Joe ran his hands through his hair. "I should've closed the portals in my apartment as soon as I finished Chrissy's place. I don't know why I waited."

"You waited because you were wiped out by doing the cleansing and closing the one at Chrissy's," Rachael said. "You didn't have enough energy to repeat the process at your place. And then, there were so many other things that needed to be done, there wasn't time."

Damen grinned. "I guess she's the smart one in your relationship? Come back after dinner. I should have it memorized by then."

"See you then," Joe said.

They drove back to his apartment, and he made no move to get out of the car. She glanced at him, and he knew she had to be wondering why he was hesitant to open the door and get out. He just stared at the window to his living room, thinking about what might be waiting for them inside. Some type of nether beast? Ithick? The warlock himself?

The building looked so innocent, but he could feel the taint rolling off it like heat on a summer day. Dread filled him, and he forced himself to not turn the car back on, speed away, and never look back. One thing he learned a long time ago, you can't run from evil. You've got to stand and face it, fight it, defeat it. Whether it was here or somewhere else, he was going to have to do his best to make sure the warlock was gone for good.

"Are we going in?" she asked.

He nodded. "Yeah. We don't have a choice." He shoved the car door open. "Let's go before I'm tempted to hightail it out of here."

She stood beside him and wrapped her arms around his waist. "I know we can do it. Together, we're stronger. I'll help you as much as I can. I'm sorry you have to do most of the work, but I'll be by your side the whole time."

He smiled at her and pulled her close. "When we finish this, I mean when it's really over, you and I are going to Barbados and lay on the beach."

"I'll buy the tickets," she said. "Now let's go take care of business."

They marched toward Joe's front door, and he dropped the wards. He opened it slowly and nothing jumped out to tear his face off. That could change in a New York minute, he thought.

He chucked his jacket on the couch and went over to his plants. Yellow leaves dotted the floor under the stands and in the track of the sliding patio door. Kneeling on the floor, he picked them up, murmuring to them. The vines tacked to the wall were turning a sickly brown, the leaves drooping. They hadn't been gone that long. How could the warlock's influence fill his home so completely and it such a short amount of time?

"I'm so sorry, guys," he murmured. He passed his hand over them, but there was no movement, no response. He went to the kitchen and filled a glass with water. Pouring a little on top of the dirt, it pooled for a few seconds before draining all the way to the tray under the pot.

"My plants are sick. The warlock has done something to infect them."

Rachael rubbed her arms. "Maybe they feel the taint in the air. It's so oppressive in here."

"You're right. They won't even take water in. I tried a quick healing spell, but they don't feel it." He got up and grab the items he needed for the cleansing. "Let's do it. Tomorrow, we'll tackle Angel Haven. I'm going to need Damen for that one. It's where everything originated."

"I'll be there, doing what I can to help you."

Joe started the ritual in the kitchen, then moved to the dining room. When he got to the living room, he faltered. Grabbing the cross around his neck, he continued, not breaking the cadence of the blessing. Finally, he turned to the bedroom and headed back that way, Rachael at his back.

She pointed to the corner near his bathroom. "There's the portal. I can sense it."

Joe cleansed the room then called forth the orange signs and sigils once again. They flowed around his arms and formed the familiar bright, blue chains. His arms shook from the strain, and the chains faded a little. He poured more energy into them, making them flare before sending them into the portal, sealing it off for good. He sat on the edge of the bed and took a deep breath.

"Are you okay?"

"Yeah. I just need a minute to catch my breath. See if you can sense any other portals here."

She nodded and left the room. The warlock's magic was incredibly strong, and he didn't want to tell her he almost couldn't get the doorway closed. Ezra had only appeared in his home a few times. If it was hard here, what kind of a battle were they in for when they got to Angel Haven? He prayed he would be strong enough to handle it.

Rachael poked her head back in. "I can't sense anything else. Your plants look a little better, though."

Joe pushed himself up and staggered out to the living room. He sat on the floor near the plant stands and checked them over. Yes, they looked a little brighter. Summoning the healing spell again, he felt it take hold and the color on the vines returned to deep green.

"Way to go, guys. I got your backs."

They waved a little, making him smile. He got to his feet and went to the kitchen, grabbing the carton of orange juice from the refrigerator. He drank half of it and put it back. He glanced at Rachael, who had a small smile on her lips.

"What?"

"If you'd drunk out of the carton at my mom's house, she would have gotten a switch and your bottom would be raw."

"Oh?"

She laughed. "Just ask my brothers." She winked at him as the small, special smile was back. "I was smart enough not to get caught."

He pulled her into his arms and held her tight. "You may look all sweet and innocent and you may be one of the heroes, but I think you've got a trouble maker in there somewhere."

"Don't tell my parents that. They'd never believe you."

"I could make them. All it takes is one little incantation."

She stepped as close to him as she could. "It's a

good thing they aren't here then, isn't it? I wouldn't want to ruin their perception of their baby girl."

He kissed her lightly. "I wouldn't do that to you anyway. You're my trouble maker, and I don't think I want to share."

When he tugged on her hand, she willingly followed him down the hall to his bedroom.

****

Rachael gazed at Joe, watching his chest rise and fall as he slept. She knew the cleansing he'd performed here had taken more out of him than he wanted to admit. Sweat had shown on his forehead, and his muscles trembled until he'd sat down for a few minutes. When they went to Angel Haven, what would happen to him there? Hopefully, Damen would be able to shoulder some of the burden. Fear settled on her shoulders as she thought about him expending so much magical energy, he would have nothing left for himself.

She reached over and grabbed the first shirt off the floor. His T-shirt hung to the middle of her thighs and she got up to go get something to drink. Tiptoeing down the hallway, she walked into the kitchen and put some ice in a glass before running water in it. She went to the couch and sat down, looking around his apartment.

There was definitely a feeling of peace here now. The plants looked better as sunlight shone off their leaves. On an end table was a small wooden box she hadn't noticed before. She picked it up and stared at it, turning it over in her hands. Flowers and a single hummingbird were carved into the lid and a leafy vine circled the sides.

On the bottom was a small, silver knob. She turned

it just a few times, then opened the lid. A haunting melody played, distorted by the tinny, metal sound of the music box. She'd never heard it before, yet it was familiar in a way that defied explanation. It had the rhythm of a waltz but it was like no waltz she'd ever heard.

The music stopped and she rewound it so it would play longer. She held the box and let the tune fill her, the feeling that she knew it, tickling her memories and making her heart ache. The tune repeated several times before needing to be wound again, which she did.

"What are you doing?"

He stood in the doorway, wearing only jeans. His hair was in more disarray than usual. The early afternoon sun shone in, making him almost glow in the light. Magic flowed from him, filling her heart with joy at his presence. She could see bright light dance across his skin. Could that be his aura, and if so, how did she learn to see it? She'd carry the memory of how he looked right now for the rest of her life.

She held up the music box. "I was listening to it. I hope you don't mind."

"Not at all." He laid his left arm across the middle of his back and held out his right hand. "Shall we?"

Winding the music box and letting it play, she stood and took his hand. His steps were easy to follow, even though she'd never waltzed in her life. They twirled around the living room, the music seeming to get larger and fuller the longer he held her. As the music box wound down, they slowed and eventually stopped.

"That's such a beautiful melody. First the lullaby, then the music box. Your family knows the prettiest, and yet somehow incredibly haunting, tunes."

"It's part of our charm." He wound the music box again, holding it with a kind of reverence. "It was my great grandmother's. My great grandfather had it made for her. She'd heard the song somewhere, and he had it turned into the music box. The craftsmanship is beyond anything that's around today."

She covered his hands with hers. "It's incredible. Just like you."

"Thanks. I take after the woman I'm beginning to love more than anything, even more than the music box."

"I'm glad I'm not alone, though I'm pretty sure I loved you first."

He tucked her hair behind her ear. "If you say so. And it's got more to do with your angel's heart than how great you look in my T-shirt."

They stood there for several heartbeats while the box wound down again. He put it back where it belonged before holding her gently. "There's so much that needs to be said."

"We'll have time. As soon as this situation is settled, we'll have plenty of time."

Chapter Twenty-One

"No, you can't," Damen said as Joe sat down.

He'd dropped Rachael off at the hospital to visit Chrissy so he and his friend could study the spell. "I don't understand. What do you mean, I can't?"

Damen pointed to the page. "You can't perform the binding on the portal."

"Why not? What's the problem?"

"The spell was used so rarely because it's dangerous. It takes a long time to cast. It could, potentially, cause harm to the caster. If the portal is used while the spell is being spoken, it could splinter. We'd have portals everywhere."

"Okay, so how do we circumnavigate the problem?"

Damen hung his head. "I'll do the spell while you make sure nothing comes through. Your offense is stronger than mine. My magic is basically blessing items to cause more harm to evil creatures."

"So, if I'm hearing you right, if I let one creature through, you could potentially get killed, Rachael is doomed, and the warlock comes back to wreak havoc."

"Yep. That's about the gist of it."

Joe ran his hand through his hair. "Figures." He walked over to the book. "Let's get studying. Maybe if we cast it together, we can get it to close faster. Then Rachael won't have to worry anymore."

Damen laid his hand on Joe's shoulder. "I know." He grinned. "What about the rest of us?"

"Oh, yeah. You guys will be safe, too."

They sat down and began to study how to block Ezra from ever coming back to their world.

****

Rachael sat next to Chrissy's bed. Her new friend was eating dinner and made a face every time she chewed. "It can't be that bad," Rachael said.

"Want to bet? I'll be glad when I get back home and can make my own food again."

"I'm sure. Joe and I got a response yesterday from those people we emailed."

Chrissy raised her eyebrows. "That was fast. What did they say?"

"You, Damen, and Joe are descendants from the original Circle of Nine. That's why you've been targeted."

"I knew someone had been a powerful spell-caster in my lineage, but I didn't realize they were part of the original Circle. Anything else?"

Rachael stood and looked out the window. "There's a new Circle forming in secret. They gave us all kinds of background on Ezra."

"You're still afraid he's controlling you," Chrissy said.

Rachael nodded. "I know he is. I haven't told the others, but there's still a part of me that welcomes him every time he speaks to me. I'm not sure they can save me."

"But they won't stop trying." Chrissy pushed herself up a little higher in the bed. "It will all be coming to an end soon. You mustn't give in to the fear I see in you. You're going to have to be stronger than you ever thought possible."

"I know."

"If it comes down to a choice, will you do what's necessary to stop the warlock from entering our realm?"

Rachael turned, staring at her. "What are you trying to say? Am I going to have to hurt someone, like you or Damen or…."

She couldn't finish the thought. Hurting Joe, or possibly killing him was out of the question. Wasn't it? She had to put the needs of the world above her own, but could she? Could she find the strength to not only kill the man she loved, but her new friends as well? Would Ezra make her do it?

"No, but he's going to try," Chrissy said. "Everything is starting to come together."

"Damen found a spell for closing the portal in an old book. Will it work to keep the warlock from coming here?"

Chrissy's eyes took on the familiar faraway look Rachael was coming to recognize as her trance. "Yes, it will work. The portal will be sealed forever. I sense you guys will destroy him, not just bind him as a prisoner in the nether dimension."

Rachael sagged into the chair she'd just vacated. They were going to succeed. Joe would be happy to hear that. "When we win, you're welcome to join us in Barbados."

"I think I will."

As they continued to talk, Rachael thought she heard a bit of sadness every time Chrissy mentioned Joe. What had she seen in her vision? From the look in her eyes, it wasn't anything good.

****

Joe wiped his hand across his forehead. The spell was harder than anything he'd learned before. It wasn't like summoning an element from the earth. It was messing with the fabric of time and space. He could see in his mind it was like folding a piece of paper before ripping it to pieces. Except, instead of paper, it was a natural opening between worlds they were trying to bend on itself.

He looked up as Damen handed him a glass of water. "Thanks. How much longer do you think we have to try and perfect the casting of the spell?"

Damen shrugged. "Who can say? I think the faster we get it down, the better. The warlock is going to be making his move soon. Did the reply say when the optimal day is supposed to be?"

"I think it's supposed to be in a few days at most. Why does bad stuff always happen sooner than expected?"

"Because evil knows how to cover its tracks," Damen said. "A better question is, why do the good guys always find out too late?"

Joe stood and stretched, trying to work the kinks out of his back and shoulders. "I think we should save the portal by the oak tree at Angel Haven for last."

"Agreed. From what you've told me, it seems that's his main point of entry. We take care of any we find in the house, then move outside. Once that portal is destroyed, he shouldn't be able to come back into here."

"Unless he uses the orb," Joe said. "We've got to make sure that thing is destroyed."

Damen leaned against his desk, folding his arms.

"Well, unless you picked up a dark summoning spell, we're not going to get our hands on it."

"What if I go to his dimension and steal it? I could go in the portal in Rachael's room, snatch the orb, and come out at the one by the tree, meet you, and collapse the portal."

"You're nuts."

Joe grinned. "Like you've never said that before. It might work."

"And it might not, which is what I'm thinking. We'll see what Chrissy says before you get your heart set on committing suicide."

"For a priest, you sure seem to see the downside to everything." He walked back to the book. "Ready to start again?"

"Whenever you are."

They stood at the book memorizing the words and hand gestures they would need to close Ezra's gateway once and for all.

****

Joe and Damen arrived at the hospital just as the sun was beginning to set. Chrissy and Rachael were talking and laughing quietly. They looked up as the two men walked in the room.

"You look worse than I do," Chrissy said. "What were the two of you doing?"

"Learning how to bend n-space," Joe said, as Damen nodded.

Rachael walked over to him, laying her hand on his shoulder. "I guess it's harder than you thought?"

Joe shook his head. "No. It's precisely the pain in the rear end we knew it was going to be. Closing portals is always hard, but we're not just trying to close the portal. We're trying to destroy it. We figure his main point of entry is by the tree at Angel Haven. That's where we're planning to use the binding spell."

"I have seen him outside more than I did inside. Come to think of it, I never really saw him inside. He just appeared to me in dreams. I think the only time his shadow form appeared was the night I met you."

"You're probably right," he said. "That's why we're going to start inside. We want to do a cleansing on the whole house to make sure he or his monsters can't get back in."

"And you can stop thinking about your plan, Joseph Caine," Chrissy said. "It won't work. You'll be able to get the orb, just not in the way you want to try."

"Seriously?"

She nodded. "Oh, yeah. You'll doom yourself. The answer will come to you when you need it to."

"Right."

"So, when are we planning to start the big showdown?" Rachael asked.

"Day after tomorrow," Damen said. "We need to gather the items for the spell and the cleansing. If you could call your teammates and tell them to have everyone out of the house, it will make our job a lot easier."

"Why?"

"Too much risk to innocent lives. If a nether beast comes through, we'll barely be able to protect ourselves, much less anyone who doesn't know how to handle those types of animals."

"Maybe I could call the hunters to assist us. We know I can talk to them now, so maybe they could help."

"We don't know enough about how you communicate with them," Joe said quietly. "They might be able to help, yes, but they also may turn on us just as easily."

Rachael's shoulders slumped. "I feel like I've brought all these problems to you guys, and there's nothing I can do to help."

"There may be something she can do," Damen said. "It would be dangerous."

Joe glanced at him. "What?"

"She could distract the warlock until we're almost finished casting the spell."

"No."

"But…"

"Damen, I'm trying to keep her safe, not throw her under the bus to keep myself safe."

"I'll do it," Rachael said.

"No."

She laid her hand on Joe's cheek. "I don't think you can tell me what to do. I've been in plenty of dangerous situations before and came out okay. I can do the same thing here. I know you won't let him hurt me. If I can keep his attention away from what you guys are doing, you have a better chance of stopping him." She smiled. "And taking me to Barbados."

Joe wrapped his arms around her and pulled her tight against his chest. "I don't want you to put yourself in harm's way. Not for me."

"You don't have a choice."

"She's right," Chrissy said. "Rachael will be instrumental in helping you stop the warlock. You need to begin in the time frame you've set. The cleansing of Angel Haven will take longer than you think. Then you can work on destroying the portal outside."

They looked at each other and nodded. "I'm going to take Rachael and get some food."

"And that's why I insisted on bringing both cars. I'll see you tomorrow at the rectory."

Joe nodded and he and Rachael left, fingers entwined.

Chapter Twenty-Two

Joe left Rachael sleeping as he stepped quietly into the living room. He walked over to the plants and noticed they were still healthy, telling him the warlock hadn't tried to come back in. He got a glass of water and poured it into a couple of the pots, smiling when he sensed their contentment.

He went over to the end table and picked up the music box Rachael had played the day before. He ran his finger lightly over the lid, seeing her doing the same thing. He could almost feel the warmth from her touch still lingering in the wood. She'd felt the power of the song, heard the beauty in the tinny melody. He'd felt those same things the first time he'd heard it as a boy.

There were some things in life that absolutely defied description, like a perfect day, a sunset, or a song with a subtle sadness to it. His music box was one of those things, as was the lullaby he'd taught her. Those two songs always made him remember growing up and the fun he'd had as a child.

His parents hadn't been very strict with him, as he was their only child. When he began displaying his talent for earth magic, they'd nurtured it and taught him how to control it. They'd also introduced him to the fairy court in their region. As he grew older, the fairies had taken over his training until he'd left home.

It was in the Middle East where he'd met Damen.

The two had become fast friends and Joe moved to New York to help the priest protect the city against supernatural threats. The city's defenders had little to no experience with magical creatures. He'd met plenty of heroes and heroines, but none had ever affected him like Rachael.

He'd told her she had an angel's heart, and he'd meant it. The warlock was trying to corrupt her soul and taint her abilities so she would be under his complete control. He couldn't, *wouldn't*, let that happen. Rachael was a beautiful woman, inside and out. She'd get out with her heart, her mind, and her soul intact.

He closed his eyes and gripped the music box tighter. The back of his neck ached, the tell-tale sign a vision was coming to him. Instead of fighting it, like he wanted to, he let it come. He saw himself as a prisoner of the warlock and Rachael was changed. She had become a thing of evil, of hate, and right then, what she hated most, was him.

He felt her claws rake him and his blood running down his body. A light appeared, and he saw himself free and running with Rachael toward the open portal. As they jumped for it, the vision ended. He opened his eyes and forced himself to loosen the white-knuckled grip he had on the box. He set down and looked at the bedroom door.

This was the second time he'd "seen" her attack him. The difference being, he knew they would both live through it. Questions nagged at him. How was the wizard going to get Rachael in the first place? And how would he find her in time to save her? He walked back to where she waited for him. It didn't matter. He would be there to save her, come hell or high water.

****

Rachael listened to Joe move around in the other room. He was trying to hide the fact he was worried about the warlock and the power he possessed. She knew he'd do anything to stop the evil trying to control her, and she was grateful for that, but not at the expense of his life. She sighed. And according to Magic Central, she was going to sacrifice him so the warlock could take over the world.

"Say my name, little shifter. You know it. All you have to do is speak it."

She shook her head. Chrissy told her to stop saying his name. Speaking it aloud gave him power over her. She clamped her lips together and refused.

"I said, speak it!" he shouted in her mind.

Sweat lined her brow and her fingers dug into the sheets. She wouldn't give him control over her, not now. Not ever! She sensed he backed off a little and relaxed. He slammed into her mind with the force of a thrown sledgehammer.

"Say it!"

"Ezra Barghest," she whispered.

His joy filled her mind, and her back arched as his presence entered her soul, filling her with the desire for power, for blood.

"Sleep now. I will come for you when the time is right."

Her eyes drifted shut and, as she fell asleep, she wondered what woke her in the first place. It felt like a bad dream, but it was done now. She sighed and snuggled deeper under the covers.

****

Rachael woke to the smell of eggs and bacon. Joe had apparently been up for a while. Warm, moist air drifted from the bathroom, and the smell of soap and shampoo filled the bedroom. She must have really been wiped out to sleep through the sound of water running. Usually, any sound woke her up. Smiling as she lay back on the pillows, she thought about the previous night. They were a bit energetic before falling asleep.

A memory tried to push its way to the front of her mind. Did she have another encounter with Ezra on the dream plane? She frowned. She didn't think so but feared that wasn't the case. He'd done something to her, talked to her. What was it? Why couldn't she remember?

She threw the covers back and headed to the bathroom. A shower did sound good right about now. She stepped in and turned on the water. Hot spray hit her in the face and she let it work its own magic. Was there anything better than hot water to ease tension away?

"Can I join you?"

Rachael wiped the water from her eyes and saw Joe standing there, gloriously naked and waiting for her to say something. Apparently, an incredibly hot, naked guy worked as good as hot water. "By all means."

He stepped in and took her in his arms, kissing her hard. He pressed her against the wall, lifting her up and wrapping her legs around his waist. When he raised his head and stared at her, a gasp slipped from her lips.

His eyes were black, their inky depths trying to suck her in. She pushed hard at his chest and he dropped her, laughing while he did so. "Give yourself to Ezra," he said.

Goosebumps broke out on her arms despite the hot water. "Never. The warlock doesn't control me."

"No? Say his name."

Control over her body fled. She stood still and calmly said, "Ezra Barghest."

Joe leaned close to her ear. "And who is Ezra Barghest?" he whispered.

"My master. I will do what he says. Always."

His figure began to turn transparent. "Very good. The master will let you know what you are supposed to do very soon."

She blinked several times and looked around. She was alone, and the water was turning cold. She shut it off and wrapped a towel around herself. She hurried out to the kitchen, her body shaking.

Joe stood over the stove, stirring something in a pan. How did he get dried off and dressed so fast? His hair, for now, was neatly combed and he looked up as she stood there. "Go get dressed. Breakfast is almost ready."

"Have you been out here the whole time?"

He stopped what he was doing and stared at her. "What happened?"

"You were just with me in the shower," she said. "We were getting ready to have a repeat performance of last night, but when I looked at you, your eyes were black. You made me say the warlock's name. Everything is fuzzy after that."

"This seems real familiar."

"I know," she said. "It just happened, except in reverse."

Joe walked over to his plants, and they were still healthy and happy. He stroked the leaves between his thumb and forefinger. They had sensed nothing out of the ordinary. He glanced over his shoulder at her. "I don't know how, but he's able to connect with your conscious mind now. Before, he was only communicating on the dream plane. What's changed?"

She shook her head. "I don't know. I'm so tired."

He gathered her into his arms, holding her until her trembling stopped. When she finally looked up at him, he smiled. "Maybe you'd better get dressed before we really do have a repeat performance from last night."

She placed her hand on his chest and stepped back, reluctant to leave his arms. "Right. I'll be out in a minute."

She hurried to the bedroom and slammed the door.

****

When Rachael had appeared at the kitchen doorway wrapped only in a too short towel, Joe's mouth instantly turned into the Mojave Desert. She was gorgeous and sexy, and he'd had a hard time not running over to her immediately and taking her back to his room. He stopped the minute he'd seen fear cloud her eyes.

When she said almost the exact same thing he did, he knew there was a problem. He glanced over at his plants and knew they hadn't felt anything. How had the warlock gotten to her? They had to have missed something. Maybe there was an after effect they didn't know about from the mark that had been implanted in her.

Joe stood still as a thought occurred to him. Another mark. They hadn't even considered Ithick could've marked her twice. If it were true, the warlock still had access to her mind. Time was of the essence to find out if it were true. Her body was shaking and he decided a few more minutes wouldn't hurt.

He gathered her in his arms, holding her until she stopped trembling. "Go get dressed. Breakfast is almost ready. We'll figure out what's going on. I promise you, he won't get a chance to hurt you."

She eased out of his hold, her hands sliding down his arms to rest in his hands for a moment. She slowly pulled them from his grasp, then hurried down the hallway. He flinched when he heard the door slam.

Chapter Twenty-Three

Joe sat across from Rachael at the dining room table. He took her hands, gazing at her the whole time. "There's a possibility you're carrying another mark. That's the only thing I can think of as to why the warlock could still control you."

"Well, that's something I didn't expect to hear. Can you take it out like Damen did?"

"I don't know," he said. "I've got to see if it's true first."

She nodded and gripped his hands tighter. "Do what you need to. I can't deal with the way he makes me feel. It's not me."

"Hold on to that thought. Let me see what I can find."

He opened his mage sight and stared at her. Her aura was dull, the colors turning an ugly gray. That confirmed his suspicions. Now to find the thing and remove it. He started at her head, moving down a little at a time. He got to her chest. There! The other mark. He frowned and sat back. Not good.

"What did you see? Is there another mark?"

"Yeah," he said, rubbing his eyes. "There's another mark. I can't remove it. No one can."

"Why not?"

"It's right over your heart. If we try, it could kill you. I'm not willing to risk doing it, and I'm pretty sure

Damen won't either."

She sat back, folding her arms. "Terrific. So now what? Do I live out the rest of my life as some evil warlock's personal servant?"

"No. All we have to do is kill the warlock. With him gone, any spell he's cast will be negated, and that includes marks."

"But you said Ithick marked me. Does the same hold true for doppelganger magic? You said you didn't know that much about that race."

"It's true for any spell-caster, so I'm pretty sure it will be true for doppelganger magic, too."

She finally smiled. "You're quite the optimist, aren't you?"

"I guess I am." He walked over and pulled her to his feet. "I'm going to save you, Rachael. I've given you my word. I'll make sure he can't control you anymore. Just keep the faith."

"In what?"

Wrapping his arms around her, he held her tight. "In me. I will keep you safe."

She laid her head on his chest. "I like the sound of that."

****

"Are you sure it's wise to bring her?" Damen asked.

They sat in the hospital cafeteria while Rachael visited with Chrissy. Different aromas drifted to them, but instead of making him hungry, nausea made Joe want to run from the building. He turned the soda can around in a circle on the table, dragging his finger through the water it left behind to make sigils of protection.

He ran his hands through his hair. "No, but we can't leave her alone. She's more vulnerable when she's by herself. We need to keep her with us at all times."

"The mark you found. It's over her heart?"

"Yeah. It was put there deliberately, so if we try to remove, it will more than likely kill her. You saw the pain she was in with the one in her hand. She wouldn't survive that kind of stress so close to a vital organ."

Damen poured himself some more hot water, picking up a tea bag and three sugar packs. "I know she wouldn't, but I think it's a risk to take her when we close the portals. The warlock could exert control over her at any time."

Joe stopped tracing on the table and glanced up. "You think he wants us to bring her, don't you?"

The priest looked down at the table. "I didn't say that."

"You didn't have to. I've been thinking the same thing myself. I made her a promise, Damen. I mean to keep it."

"And that's what makes you who you are. You're a good man."

"Let's hope I'm good enough to beat the warlock before he kills all of us."

The clinked their drinks together and stared at each other.

****

"It's almost time for us to go close the portals at Angel Haven," Rachael said.

Chrissy stared at her for a moment before taking her hand. "You know he'll protect you. You don't have to worry. Joe's a big boy. He's faced a lot of threats and come out on top every time." She smiled. "Sometimes a little more banged up than he would like."

"His luck has to run out one of these days."

Chrissy laughed. "It would, if he believed in luck. He's got faith that he can get the job done. I think it rubs off from Damen."

Rachael smiled. "I guess that's what happens when your friends with a priest." As quickly as it came, her smile faded. "I've had my own vision. I know he's not going to make it out, and I'm going to be the cause. I saw myself actually enjoy killing him."

"That could be the warlock's influence, trying to get you to turn more to his side. Just remember everything he shows you is a lie. It's all illusions and trickery. Now, tell me more about the second mark."

"Joe says it's right over my heart, and it can't be removed because doing so might kill me."

Chrissy nodded. "He's right. It was put there just for that reason. It must be smaller to go unnoticed for so long."

"If Ithick placed it, I don't even think it can be removed. Joe says they know so little about doppelganger magic."

"Let me take a look."

"Are you sure you're strong enough?" Rachael asked. Her friend still looked bad but she was awake more than she slept and she was restless to go home.

"Yes. I've been casting my own healing spells before I go to sleep every night. I still have a long way to go, but I feel so much better than I did a few days ago. Sit still and let me see what's going on."

Racheal sat perfectly still while Chrissy looked her over. She watched the wizard, noticing the intent look and the blue light glowing around her eyes. After a few minutes, Chrissy blinked and lay back.

"Well? What did you see?"

"It can't be removed, but I don't think it's from Ithick. I think the warlock gave it to him and he did plant it, but it doesn't have the oily vibe of doppelganger magic."

"That seems to be a bad news, worse news type of thing."

Chrissy shrugged. "If you guys can destroy the warlock, the mark will vanish on its own. It's tied to him so if he goes, it goes."

Rachael began to pace. "Joe said the same thing." She stopped and glanced at Chrissy. "I'm afraid to go to Angel Haven. I'm afraid not to go. I have the feeling something bad is going to happen there, and I don't know what it is."

"There are some things we have to do with no information."

Rachael laughed a little. "My team leader says that's what gets heroes killed. I have a tendency to agree."

"I would too, except I've been a spell-caster all of my life. There's always unknown variables in magic. We just go with feelings and pray we get to come home to battle another day."

"I guess that's the difference between magic and science."

Chrissy laughed. "Sometimes, and sometimes they're the same thing."

They turned when the door opened, and Joe and Damen walked in. Rachael stared at them, wishing she could see some sign of hope, something to tell her they knew everything was going to be all right. Neither man's face held that kind of promise. In the short time she'd known them, she'd never seen them look so grim.

"It's time to go," Joe said.

Rachael squeezed Chrissy's hand. "We'll see you soon. Get better."

"I'll be out of here in no time," she said, then looked at her friends. "You guys take care. It's going to be hard, but you'll come through."

Joe nodded and leaned down to kiss Chrissy's forehead. "I'll see you when you get home."

The three of them walked out and down to the elevator. Rachael slipped her hand in Joe's and glanced up at him. He pulled her close and walked to the car with his arm around her shoulders. Damen started the car, and they headed out of the city.

As they drove, Rachael remembered the night she met Joe. The van was silent, just like now, tension thick, choking words in her throat before she could get them out. She sat in the back seat, staring at the back of Joe's head, wondering what he was thinking about.

She knew what she was thinking. She was worried the warlock might actually be able to make her hurt him and then keep her prisoner forever. She'd die before she'd let that happen. Somewhere along the line, Joe had become her whole world. He wouldn't die at the warlock's hands. Or hers, she silently vowed.

They pulled up to the gate, and Rachael gave them the key code to get in. The house was dark and the grounds, eerily silent. They got out and stood by the car, looking up at the second story. None of them moved for several moments.

Rachael finally pulled out her key and took a deep

breath before heading up the steps. The door swung open on silent hinges and the house had the sense of no other living things around. Well, they had requested for everyone to be gone, so they had clear access. As soon as they stepped inside, Joe began sniffing. They all knew what that meant.

She glanced at the two men with her. "Where do you want to start?"

"Ground floor," Damen said. He and Joe went from room to room, performing the cleansing ritual and blessing every lintel.

Rachael took them to the lower levels where the Angels trained and watched them repeat their actions. They headed to the third floor next. When they finished, the second floor, Rachael's floor, was all that remained. They did the cleansing in all the other rooms first, then stood outside her door.

They looked at each other, and Joe pushed the door open. Blood ran from his nose freely, and he stuffed a tissue in his nostril, needing both hands for the task at hand. The warlock's presence filled every corner, every shadow, every inch of her room. Damen blessed the outside of her door, then stepped inside.

"I think it's going to be harder than we thought," Damen said in a hushed voice.

Joe glanced at him. "This is nothing. Wait until we get out to the tree."

As they began the ritual, shadows pulled themselves from all parts of her room. They flowed into each other, coalescing into a large man. "You cannot stop me, wizards. I will have my revenge on you."

Joe summoned a red flame and flung it at the warlock. It hit him dead center in his chest, and the shadow just brushed it off. A wind blew through her room with the force of a tornado, and Rachael figured Joe was trying to dissipate the shadow before it could get any more solid.

She shifted to a condor, trying to help strengthen the wind already screaming through her room. The warlock reached out, knocking her to the ground. Well, for a shadow that felt pretty solid. She shifted again to a large tiger and clawed at the arm that had hit her. The shadow staggered backward, and she leapt at him again.

Turning his attention to Rachael, he batted her away like she nothing more than a small nuisance. He swung his arm and Damen and Joe were swatted across the room to land against the far wall. Shadows swirled around their bodies, trying to choke them. Damen summoned the light that he'd used before, and the shadows recoiled back around the man. Joe shot bright green light from his fingers at the same time.

"Your pitiful holy light won't work again, priest. And you are so desperate, wizard, you use your own personal energy?" He laughed, a dark sound freezing their souls. "I've not come to fight you, yet." A black, smoky tendril shot out from the shadow to curl around Rachael's waist and lifted her in the air. "I've come for my little shifter."

A portal opened behind him. Joe jumped to his feet and grabbed Rachael's arms. "You can't have her."

"Help me," she screamed, clawing frantically at his hands.

Tendons strained in his arms, and veins stood out in his neck. Damen grabbed her around the waist as she was pulled closer to the warlock's shadow form inch by excruciating inch. Their feet slid across the carpet as they tried to free her from his grip. A final yank and the warlock disappeared into the nothingness behind him, Rachael held tight in his grip as the portal winked out.

"NO!"

Just like that, she was gone and in the hands of the warlock. Joe collapsed on the carpet, his hand brushed something. He looked down. Rachael's Celtic cross. If it was here, she was in more trouble than he realized. Ezra would have an almost impeded path to her mind, and there was nothing he could do to help her.

Chapter Twenty-Four

"Pull yourself together," Damen said, shaking him. "We've got to close the portal."

Joe pushed his friend's hands off him. "I can't! I've got to get her back."

"Listen to me. We're both wiped out. Chrissy told us it was going to take longer than we thought. You can't go after Rachael while you're so upset. He'll kill you before you know what's happened. You've got to rest and get some food. We need to close the portal so we can finish the cleansing of the house."

"But Rachael…"

"He needs you to be there before he does anything to her. She'll be all right for now. Come on. Help me finish what we started."

Joe nodded once and stood up. "Right. Doesn't mean I like it, though."

"I know. We'll get her back, and everything will work out, just like Chrissy said."

They began the closing ritual, the orange signs and sigils glowing brighter than ever before. Joe hesitated a fraction of a second before sending the blue energy chains into the portal, sealing it forever. He dropped to his knees, his heart breaking as the portal collapsed on itself and winked out of existence. As soon as it shut, his nosebleed quit.

They headed back to the rectory, Damen glancing

at Joe. "I've never seen you so emotional, my friend."

"I promised I'd keep her safe, and I failed. She was screaming for me to help her, and I didn't. Now she's with the warlock, and I couldn't stop him."

"We'll get her back and take care of him once and for all. We've got to get a few more items, and we both need something to eat. I can't believe you used your personal energy to try and fight him."

"It was a long shot, but I thought it might blow his shadow form apart. I've used it like that before."

Damen pulled up to the rectory and helped Joe inside. "I remember and it wiped you out then, too. You need food and rest."

Joe simply nodded and let Damen take care of him.

****

The room wasn't the dungeon she expected. There was a deep green, plush area rug on the floor. A canopy bed stood in the middle of the wall behind her with a large wardrobe nearby. A small table with a candle was to the right of the bed. A fire danced merrily, casting flickering shadows on the *fleur de lis* wallpaper.

"Let me out of here," Rachael shouted, even though she was pretty sure no one was going to hear her and, if they did, listen to her. The walls were solid stone, and the door was bolted shut. She shifted to a grizzly bear and clawed at the wooden door, but it held steady.

She shifted back to herself and watched the scratches she'd made fade away. She sighed. "I should've known. Magic bad guy, magic door."

She shivered. Once again, she'd shredded what she'd been wearing. What would it cost to have her entire wardrobe made out of the same material as her

Angel's uniform? She stopped. She wasn't getting out of here. Joe had tried to save her, but he couldn't get her out of the warlock's shadowy grasp. Before she knew it, she'd been dumped here in the torn remains of her clothes.

She pressed her ear to the door, thinking she'd heard something. She half shifted to a wolf and with the more acute hearing, definitely picked up movement on the other side of the door. She backed up and fully shifted to the wolf as a key turned in the lock.

A servant walked in and laid a gown on the bed. "The master asks would you please dress and meet him in his study. I'm to wait for you outside and show you the way." He went out and closed the door until it was almost shut.

She turned back human and looked at the gown. It was light violet, almost the same color as her eyes. It was a Victorian-era gown one pictured at parties and ceremonies of the time. She held it up to her body, and it appeared to be her size. Anything was better than standing around in clothes so destroyed they weren't even close to comfortable. She threw what she'd been wearing in the corner and pulled the gown over her head.

Following the servant down the long hall, then up the stairs, Rachael grew more nervous by the second. What was the warlock going to do to her? How was he going to exert his final control? Was she strong enough to stop him? She tried to dampen down the fear threatening to consume her.

The servant pushed open the study doors, and a familiar, large man turned to her. She'd seen him many times in her dreams. His outfit matched the era of her gown, and she felt a ridiculous urge to curtsy. He had deep brown, almost black eyes. His black-brown hair hung to just below the collar of his coat. He was bigger than she thought he'd be, with wide shoulders and thick legs.

He held a hand out to her. "Rachael, welcome to my home."

"Um, thank you?"

He laughed at her uncertainty. "I know the two men you were with have filled your head with lies about me."

"You marked me and tried to use me to hurt one of my friends."

He poured wine from a decanter and handed her a glass. She stared and took it, but never tasted it. He escorted her farther into the room and sat her down on the small loveseat. "The mark was so I could find you. I've been looking so many years for you."

"I read the information on you. You're trying to open a permanent portal between worlds so you can have access to go wherever you want in the world. Are you going to kill off all the wizards and take their abilities?"

"You have been reading." He sat in the chair across from her. "I just want to end my exile. I told you that before when we met on the dream plane."

Rachael looked at the glass in her hands. The light sparkled in the red liquid, making it look like it was winking at her. He had told her that before, and she'd believed him then. Why couldn't she do that now? What had changed?

"I've never hurt you, have I?"

She glanced up. "No, but you've terrified me a

lot."

"It was necessary for them to believe you were not my servant."

"Am I your servant?"

He hurried to her side and took her hand. "You would never be anyone's servant. You are my partner, nothing more. I wish for us to become great friends."

She drank a little of her wine, and nodded slowly. The warmth of the drink spread through her, and she wondered what she'd been so worried about. Ezra ordered their dinner to be brought in and they ate in companionable silence.

****

Ezra watched as Rachael's dress disappeared down the hallway and shut the study doors. What a fool. As if he needed a partner to do what he needed done. All he wanted her for was to gut Caine so he could take his power. Then, the lovely Rachael would follow. The doors between worlds would then open and be his to command.

He'd been worried at first, when she resisted his attempts to calm her down. Soon, though, she'd succumbed to the subtle spell he'd been weaving since dragging her to his realm. He scowled out the window. His realm was nothingness, a black void waiting just beyond to devour him.

If Ithick hadn't found the way in, he might have spent eternity here, slowly going mad. He'd recently been reconsidering doing away with Ithick. Yes, the doppelganger was ambitious, but he made a good servant and was always eager to do Ezra's bidding. He walked back to chair in front of the fire that constantly burned.

All he had to do now was wait for Caine to arrive. The wizard would try to save the shifter, and Ezra would kill them both. He sat down, smiling. It no longer mattered he didn't have access to the Angel Haven house. There was still the main portal at the tree. Caine would use that to come to him and then die. Today had been a good day.

****

"Not a good idea," Joe murmured as he stretched out on the bed at the rectory. He took a deep breath and closed his eyes. As he relaxed more, he sent himself to the dream plane.

He looked around as he stood on a small hill that rose out of dense woods. He could hear the howls of wolves in the distance and took a deep breath. He started down the hill and headed into the woods. Darkness closed around him and he held up a pale yellow light.

Someone was leaning against a tree. He squinted his eyes. "Hello?"

Whoever it was pushed away and walked toward him. In the ring of light, he saw Rachael. She was dressed in a lavender, Victorian gown. Her shoulders were bare, and the swell of her breasts made his breath catch.

"What are you doing here?" she demanded.

He stroked her cheek. "I was trying to find you. Are you all right? He hasn't hurt you, has he?"

"No. I'm fine." She twirled around. "He gave me this dress, though. Don't you love it?"

He caught her hands. "Only because it's on you. I'm coming for you, Rachael. I won't let him make you a slave."

She laughed. "I'm not his slave. We're partners."

Joe backed up as her features changed into something otherworldly. Scales formed over her arms and face, and she hissed as she closed in on him. Her eyes had turned solid black.

"The master and I will destroy you, Caine. We will dance in your blood."

Claws flexed out from the ends of her fingers, and she slashed the air in front of him. He ducked out of the way, but not before she caught his shoulder. He fell to the ground, and she stood over him. "You can't stop us, wizard. All you can do is pray we kill you quickly."

Joe shot straight up in bed, his chest heaving. His shoulder was on fire, and he looked over, already knowing he'd see the scratches she'd left. The second mark must have let the warlock into her mind with no problems if she had been turned so quickly.

He got up and pulled his pants on. Quietly grabbing Damen's keys, he hurried across the parking lot to the church, the remaining snow numbing his bare feet. He opened the side door and slipped inside. He padded over to where votive candles still burned. He put one in an empty cup and lit it, bowing his head.

He rose and walked to the altar and looked up. He reached in his pocket and pulled out a necklace, gripping in his right hand. The chain on Rachael's cross bit into his skin as he clenched it in his fist, the cross itself dangling from between his fingers.

"I'm losing her," he said, his voice echoing off the high ceiling. "I don't know how to get her back. She's being turned against her will and I need to stop it. Please, God. Tell me what to do."

Kneeling at the railing and folding his hands, he

laid his head on his arms and felt tears burn his cheeks.

****

Damen frowned at the empty bed. Joe wasn't here, the bathroom, or downstairs. The car was still in the parking lot. He couldn't have gone for a walk because his shoes were still by the bed. He went downstairs again and grabbed his coat. He reached for his keys, and they were gone. It was then he smiled, knowing exactly where to find his friend.

He walked in the church, and Joe was sleeping on the floor in front of the altar, no shirt, no shoes. A sense of peace filled him, even more than usual as he slid into a pew. He bowed his head, praying until he heard Joe start to stir.

"Good morning," Damen said.

Joe rubbed his eyes and pushed himself up to sit on the kneeler. "It's morning?"

"Yep. I couldn't find you in the house, then I noticed my keys were missing. Did you get a good night's rest?"

"I did. I tried to contact Rachael on the dream plane. She's become his. She's been enthralled, and it's almost complete."

Damen pulled Joe to his feet, and they walked back to the rectory. "I'm not surprised. We felt how strong his control was getting."

Joe sat at the kitchen table and watched Damen put the kettle on and drop bread in the toaster. "I know what I have to do now."

"Oh?"

He nodded. "I prayed for guidance, and I was given the knowledge on what to do. We need to get back to Angel Haven soon. I'm going to go into the portal and find her. Once I bring her out, we can close it."

"What about the mark? If we just close it, he'll still be able to contact her. She'll never be her own person."

Joe sat straighter and looked at the priest making breakfast. With the nature of what they were dealing with, doing something so ordinary was almost surreal. "He's not going to be able to control her. When I go in, I'm going to destroy him."

Damen put the plates on the table and sat down. A feeling crawled through him that he wasn't going to see his friend again after he crossed the doorway. "I guess you'd better put your shoes on."

Chapter Twenty-Five

Joe shrugged into his jacket and joined Damen in the car. Today was the day. He would either save Rachael, or he was doomed. If they were in a movie, he'd confront the warlock and summon a magic blade from somewhere and smite the villain. But they were in the real world, and he'd never swung a sword in his life.

He held his cross in his right hand and really hoped he knew what he was doing. It had all been so clear last night. The morning had brought all the doubts and fears back in force. He knew he could beat the bad guy. The warlock would finally be out of their lives, and Rachael would be her own person again.

Damen turned up the drive to the large house and the car crunched to a halt as he stopped and put it in park. He cut the engine, and they sat there, knowing what lay ahead of them. Rachael's absence was a knife to Joe's soul. He'd known when she was staring at him when they drove up yesterday. He ached to curl his hand around hers again, and his side was cold where she usually held him.

He looked out over the grounds and spied the oak tree. "That's where we need to go. The last and strongest portal is there. We need to open it so I can get to him and grab Rachael. Have the spell prepared and as soon as we're through, close it. It needs to be destroyed."

They walked up the slight hill as Joe glanced at the priest, making sure he knew what had to be done. When Damen nodded, he turned and opened the portal. He took one last look at his friend before allowing himself to be swallowed up by the blackness on the other side. He stood there for a moment, trying to get his balance and listened to Damen begin the binding spell. A deep breath, a forced first step, and he was on his way.

The farther he got from the portal, the more he missed the sound of his friend's voice. "Come on, Caine, man up. Rachael needs you."

A lighted pathway, wide enough so four people could walk side by side, stretched before him, cutting through the inky darkness. He knew from his studies, he was in the void. The path had been created by the warlock to show where the portal waited. Joe stepped carefully down the winding path, expecting something large to jump out and eat him at any second.

Lights appeared in the distance, and he hurried toward them. The absolute black was already getting to him. Glow from windows in a large house greeted him. There was nothing underneath supporting the structure, and Joe knew that, again, it had to be the warlock's doing. He took a deep breath, trying to still the unsettling feeling growing stronger in his soul. His nose began to run with blood again.

He pounded on the door, and it opened slowly. Ithick gave him a toothy grin and stepped to the side, allowing him entrance. "The master has been wondering what has kept you."

Joe wiped at his nose and sniffed. "The master can go back to whatever hell he came from."

Ithick practically giggled as he took Joe to Ezra's study. Joe stepped inside, and Ezra turned, a smile playing around his lips. "I was beginning to think you'd never show up."

"I'm here for Rachael. Where is she?"

Ezra move to a chair and sat, crossing his legs. "She will be arriving any time now. I let her go on a hunt, so she would know precisely how to end your miserable life."

"What did you do to her?"

Ezra picked up a brandy snifter and swirled the liquid around in it. "I've unleashed her true power. She is greater than I ever thought possible. The fact that you two have done whatever it is humans do when they need relief, just makes it better."

Ezra was going to try to use their love making as a control over her. Joe stepped forward. "You'll never implement your plan, warlock. I'm taking her from here, and we're going to close and bind the portal so you can't get out again."

Quicker than Joe could react, Ezra was out of his chair and had him around his neck. "Don't think to threaten me, wizard. You are in my world now. You'll play by my rules." He threw Joe across the room and sat back down.

The door opened, and Rachael breezed in. "Oh, Ezra, I had the most wonderful time. We hunted a man dressed as a deer. He thought he'd lost us at one point, but we found him. Your friend got the kill, and we had the most wonderful party afterwards."

"Rachael," Joe croaked out.

She turned, and he cringed from the look in her eyes. "What's he doing here?"

Ezra took her hand and walked her over to him. "He's my present to you. Tonight, we'll do the ceremony I promised and you will feast on his heart."

"I can't wait."

Ithick appeared and grabbed Joe by his shirt collar and dragged him to the dungeon. He flung him in the cell and shut the door with a clang. "You will wait here until the master wants you," Ithick shouted through the door. "I can't wait to hear your screams as the shifter guts you."

The doppelganger's laughter faded away, and Joe sat back against the wall. "Well, this is a fine how do you do."

He scanned the cell, already knowing there was no way out. He wasn't leaving without Rachael any way. He readied a few spells, keeping them in his mind. Better to be prepared when they came for him. He held his cross and the warmth of the wood comforted him while he sang the lullaby he'd shared with the woman upstairs.

****

Rachael sat at her dressing table, brushing out her hair. She'd had a fun day and tonight was going to be grand. Tonight, the wizard would be sacrificed so her master could walk between worlds, gathering more followers and power. She hoped he wouldn't push her aside for someone new.

She removed her dress, standing in the middle of the room. Wearing only her underwear, she caught sight of herself in the mirror and turned, admiring her body. Ezra would like it, too. As a hero on Earth, she kept herself in great shape.

She frowned. A hero. On Earth. She touched her

213

finger to the glass and leaned closer. Her eyes were black. That wasn't her normal color. They were usually a light violet. "What's happening to me?" she whispered.

She squeezed her eyes shut. Someone, a friend, told her it was all illusion and trickery. She had to find herself. Closing her eyes tightly, she murmured over and over, "This isn't real. This isn't me."

"It is you," Ezra said behind her.

She jumped and turned around, grabbing her robe from the vanity chair. "I wasn't expecting you."

"I can tell." He closed the robe and tightened the belt. "As soon as we take care of business tonight, I will be happy to satisfy your every whim."

He took her hand and raised it to his lips. She stood there, her legs trembling as his hand found its way beneath the thin robe. He laid his hand over her heart, and she stiffened. She watched his lips move but couldn't hear the words he spoke.

He stepped back and smiled. "Are you better now?"

She slowly nodded. She couldn't remember why she'd been so frightened a moment ago. The wizard in the dungeon. It had to be him playing with her mind. "I'm sorry. I don't know what came over me."

"It will all be over soon. Another couple of hours and the wizard won't be able to harm you anymore."

"You're very kind to protect me and teach me how to use the power you've given me."

"I saw you in my future and knew you would be important to me. I have to prepare for the ceremony. I have waited generations, and I will trust no other to make sure things are ready. I'm sure you can keep yourself amused until it's time."

She smiled as he bowed and left the room. Yes. She could keep herself amused. A faint tune reached her and she stopped. It was familiar and made her think of another time, another place, with Joe. His home. It was the lullaby he sang her. She rubbed the area over her heart and straightened her back.

The wizard waited in the dungeon for his fate. She took a dark green gown from the wardrobe and quickly dressed. She had to go see him and find out what he was doing to her mind. She yanked open the door, the silky material flowing around her ankles as she walked purposefully to the lower levels.

****

Joe's butt was freezing, and he was getting on his own nerves, constantly sniffing, trying to stop the blood flow. There wasn't any hay, threadbare blankets, or anything else to get him off the stone floor. Of course, being locked in a dungeon was going to be the least of his problems if he couldn't find a way to save Rachael and himself.

When she'd glanced at him, she had looked so...evil. Ezra's control was almost absolute. If only he could talk to her. He knew he could bring her back to herself, and they'd have a better chance of escaping. The lock turned, and he jumped to his feet.

Rachael stood there, a hunter green gown clinging to her body. The dark color made her fair skin look even paler. The half sleeves couldn't hide the toned muscles in her arms. Her black hair had been pinned back on the sides with white combs, the curls skimming her shoulders. The white patch hung over her eyes, which were as black as her hair, as she stared at him.

They stood in silence before she finally spoke.

"So, you came to save me."

"Yes."

She sidled up close to him. "That's most heroic of you. Did you ever think, though, maybe I didn't want to be saved? Just since I've been here, Ezra has opened up more and more of my powers that I didn't even know I had."

His heart sank with her words, colored with hate from the warlock's influence. "He's using you. He's going to sacrifice you as soon as he's done with me."

"I don't think so," she purred in his ear. "We have a special relationship."

Joe cupped her chin and gazed at her, trying to call her back to herself. "Oh, Rachael. You need to remember who you are. He's making you lose yourself."

She stepped back, her eyes narrowing as she glared at him. "That's what you keep saying, but I see things more clearly now that I'm here. I think it's you who's been messing with my mind. Tell me, wizard, what spell have you put on me to try to make me turn on my master?"

"Your master? Listen to yourself. You told me you wouldn't be anyone's puppet, and that's exactly what he's made you."

She backed up until she was against the wall. Joe could see the fear and confusion in the darkness of her eyes. He stepped closer, never breaking eye contact. He could sense she was terrified of him and had a feeling the warlock had placed it there.

He reached out, and she flinched. He laid his hand over her heart, his fingers laying against her skin above

216

the dress. "You know who you are in here. You have an angel's heart. I told you before. Try to remember."

"I can't," she whispered. "It hurts to think about the past. Why are you doing this to me?"

"Because I love you. I won't let him take you from me. The world needs your strength, your courage. All I need is for you to love me in return."

As he watched, the black faded, and her eyes were the violet he dreamed of at night. She threw herself in his arms. He held her close, humming the lullaby. Soon, she picked it up and they sang together.

"How do we get out of here?" she asked.

"I'm still working on that part. I didn't think his control over you would be so complete, so fast." He smiled at her. "I will get you out of here. You just have to keep the faith."

"You say that all the time."

"It's because I believe it," he said. "There's always a way out. We just have to wait for it to appear."

She nodded. "I'm going to stay here with you."

He chuckled. "I'm pretty sure the warlock wouldn't care for that one little bit."

"I don't care what he likes."

The door to the cell opened. Ithick stood there scowling at the two of them. "It's a good thing I do care what the master likes. He would like you in his study, right now." He grabbed Rachael's arm and pulled her through the door.

"Remember who you are," Joe shouted. "He can't take that from you, no matter what he does."

He listened to their retreating footsteps and sat back down. It was all happening too soon. He wasn't as prepared as he'd wanted to be, but the spells he'd had in reserve still swirled in his mind, waiting to be unleashed at a moment's notice. His nose continued to drip blood down his face.

Chapter Twenty-Six

Ezra frowned when Rachael walked into his study. He knew she'd been to see Caine, had counted on it. What he didn't foresee was the wizard being able to reach her true self. He needed her to be completely under his control. It was almost time for the ceremony. If she didn't play her part, it was all for nothing.

"And how did you find the prisoner?" he asked.

"Ezra, you need to let us go. I won't help you open the doorway."

He strode over to her and grabbed her arm. "You have no choice. You will do as you are commanded to do."

She pulled her arm from his grasp and backed away. "No. You can't make me kill Joe. I'm not your slave anymore."

"Yes. You are."

Ezra followed her as she backed up, smiling when confusion filled her face. "What's the matter? Can't use your power?" He stood over her. "Your power is mine to control. You've given yourself to me freely."

"Freely? Ha! You used illusions and lies to get what you wanted from me."

"And I won't hesitate to do so again." He snapped his fingers, and Ithick held her from behind. "Caine is right. As soon as you take his life, I will take yours. Between the two of you, I will have more power than

I've been able to take in a very long time. I will enjoy killing you. I think I will do it slowly so I can enjoy every scream from your beautiful throat."

He laid his hand over her heart and uttered a spell. He knew the instant her will became his again. Caine couldn't save her, and Ezra would finally have the revenge he so craved.

"I await your orders, master," she said.

"Very good. Go sit down. It's almost time to begin."

****

I was going to do something important, Rachael thought. Why can't I remember? She glanced at Ezra, who'd become her whole world. He was going to let her take the wizard's life. She was proud to be chosen for such an honor. She watched him get everything ready. They would be performing the ceremony soon.

Did he say he was going to kill her, too? He couldn't have. She must have misheard him. He wouldn't do that, would he? She rubbed the back of her neck. Too many questions, too much confusion. He said he would take care of her, that they were partners.

"The time draws near, master," Ithick said from the doorway.

"Very good. Get the wizard ready. We'll be down shortly."

He walked over to her and extended his hand. "It's time, my dear. Shall we go? The sooner Caine is dealt with, the sooner you will be free of his influence."

She nodded and stood up, taking Ezra's hand. "I have been anxiously waiting to do just that. I will serve you well, master."

She frowned. That wasn't right. She and Joe were

here to destroy the warlock and she was nobody's slave. Her chest began to ache and she rubbed it. What was she thinking about? The fog she was constantly in worried her.

"Ezra, I think I may be ill," she said.

He came up next to her, putting his arm around her waist. "Why do you say that, my dear?"

"My mind is so foggy. I can't remember anything. I don't want to ruin the ceremony."

He laughed. "It's just nerves. As soon as the ceremony is done, you'll be fine. Trust me."

She smiled but was unconvinced. Just keep the faith. She stopped suddenly. Joe said that all the time. What was she planning on doing?

Ezra spun her around to face him. "You are planning on doing whatever I tell you to do. Understand?"

She nodded but silently said, keep the faith. They continued to where Ithick had prepared Joe for the ceremony.

****

The doppelganger had come into Joe's cell. "It's time to get rid of you. The shifter will rip you open and eat your heart."

"That's really sick, Ithick."

The doppelganger laughed. "It will be fun to watch."

Joe frowned and stood straight. "You evil people need some better hobbies. How about taking up knitting? That's not gross nor does it involve killing people. Or how scrapbooking? On second thought, maybe not. I'd hate to see what the pages would have on them and what sort of nasty sayings you'd write."

He paused. "I know. Comic books. Some of the stories are really good, and they go up in value."

Ithick frowned. "I tire of you, wizard, as does my master. He is preparing the shifter for the ceremony right now. She thought she could defy him and not do his bidding. She is learning she is wrong."

Rachael was fighting the warlock? He must have helped her find herself when she came to see him earlier. He didn't know how he was going to get them both out, but all he had to do was keep the faith. The way would come to him at the right time.

He allowed Ithick to bind his hands and take him to where Ezra would be performing the ceremony. Getting out of the bonds would be child's play. All he needed was for every player to be in position and to stop Rachael before she gutted him.

They walked deep into the bowels of the house. A large Y frame stood in the middle of a magic circle, the writing on the edge so ancient, Joe had no idea of the meaning of the symbols. Bluish purple flames danced in shallow pits at the four corners of the room, raising the temperature considerably. A marble table stood in front of the frame with a trio of knives on them.

"The master will be here soon," Ithick said.

Joe snorted. "The suspense is unbearable. How do you stand it?"

"Your pathetic jokes will not bother me any longer, wizard."

He nodded to an open hallway and two trolls came forward, grabbing Joe and slamming him into the Y frame, securing his wrists above his head. "What are the knives for, Ithick? I thought the warlock's grand plan involved Rachael."

"It does. The knives are to trigger the shifter into killing you." Ithick was just about dancing with glee. "I can't wait for things to get started."

Oh boy, Joe thought. The whole situation is worse than I thought. Ithick stood in front of him and ripped his T-shirt down the front. "Hey! I just bought this shirt."

"You won't miss it."

Ithick scowled at the cross around Joe's neck and backed away. It glowed in the low light, and Joe felt its warmth fill him. They both turned when they heard footsteps approaching. Ithick bowed low when Ezra walked in, his hand resting on the small of Rachael's back.

"Well, wizard. Are you ready to meet your destiny?" Ezra said as he picked up a knife.

Joe smiled. "Are you?"

Ezra laughed at him. "A good answer. I would've expected no less from a descendant of the Circle of Nine. I recall your ancestor. He was just as arrogant as you. That must be where you get it from. He fought all the way until the end. It made his death sweet to the pallet. I have yearned for more ever since."

"But you didn't get it, did you? The Circle locked you in here and now you need help to get out."

Ezra walked over, leaning close to Joe's face. "And you will be the one to help me. After Rachael kills you, her life will be mine. There will be no stopping me after that."

Ezra pricked the skin over Joe's heart until a small drop of blood welled. As if the blood running constantly from his nose wasn't incentive enough. Joe saw Rachael's eyes gleam with anticipation as the drop rolled down his chest. He barely heard Ezra and Ithick begin to open portals to the nether realms, summoning the creatures that lived there. He glanced up at the shackles holding him in place and let his fingers begin to weave in the air.

Ezra kissed the back of Rachael's hand. "Now, my love, it is time to claim his heart."

Rachael began to shift, but it was into a beast Joe had never seen before. Her face elongated into some type of reptilian creature. Her dress ripped as her back bulged with muscles that filled out her arms and legs. She grew, towering over everyone present.

Black claws stretched from her fingers, matching the lengthening of her teeth into sharp fangs. Lifting her head, she roared a challenge just as Joe broke the metal holding his right wrist in place. She stomped over to him, the large nostrils at the end of the long muzzle flared. Her forked tongue darted out, tasting the blood on his chest.

Joe could swear she almost smiled as she growled. He was getting a tad frantic as he knew what was coming next. After all, he'd had a vision of it. She was going to gut him where he was held. She pulled her right arm back and with one swipe, left three deep, diagonal cuts down his torso.

Joe cried out and freed his other hand just as she swiped him again. His blood dripped on the floor, making the symbols in the circle glow. "Rachael," he gasped. "Stop! You're doing what he wants. You're not yourself. Stop before he makes you kill me."

"No," she hissed. "I shall feast on your living heart this night."

She raised her arm up again and he began to sing.

She stopped and stared at him, her arm slowly lowering. She narrowed her eyes as he finished. Her body shrank a little and she stepped back.

"I know that song," she said, the hiss still evident in her words.

Joe dropped to his knees and held his stomach while he gazed at her. "I taught it to you. You'd had a nightmare and I held you, singing my lullaby to you."

Her face started to change as she stared at him. Ezra came up behind her, laying his hand on her head. "You are mine, shifter. Do as you are commanded."

She lurched forward, closing her jaws on Joe's arm. He cried out and, before his instincts kicked in to strike back, spoke a word. Light flared from his hand, making her scream and let go. He began the song again, trying to ignore the pain raging through his body and the fact she was covered with his blood.

When he finished, she stared at him. "Why do you not defend yourself, wizard? In another moment, I will rip you open and you will die at my hands."

Ezra stood next to her, lightly caressing her scaly head. "He can't defend himself. He's no hero. He's not one of his God's army. He is just a man, weak and expendable."

Joe smiled up at Ezra. "It's true. I'm neither a hero nor an angel. I'm an ordinary human." He turned to Rachael. "I'm a man who loves you." He laid his hand on her chest. "You're the angel. You have an angel's heart."

Before anyone could stop him, he grabbed Rachael's face and kissed her. Her fangs cut his lips, and he tasted his blood in her mouth, but he didn't care. The moment had arrived. The time his faith had been telling him was coming was here. He needed to prove he loved her, no matter her appearance. He'd seen her true self. He knew her heart. This scaly abomination wasn't her. The real Rachael was deep inside, shining bright and beautiful, blazing hotter than any magic, where Ezra couldn't find her or touch her.

"I love you, Rachael. All I need is for you to love me, too."

She stumbled backward, clutching her head. Her body shifted rapidly into different creatures while she screamed at the top of her lungs. She spun around, knocking over the marble table, sending the knives skittering across the stone floor.

"Master, we are running out of time," Ithick yelled. "The wizard must die now."

Ezra picked a knife off the floor. "The shifter has drawn his blood. Now, I can finish it."

He marched to where Joe still knelt on the floor. He raised the blade high in the air but couldn't bring it down. An ear-piercing roar filled the room as a huge black bear with a white spot on its head held his arms. Rachael flung him away and picked up Joe, running from the chamber.

She burst through the study doors, slamming them shut. She sat Joe on the loveseat before finally shifting back to human and turning the lock. He pulled a tube from his sock and smeared the salve on the claw marks on his chest and the bite on his arm.

"The good thing about visions, is that you can always be more prepared than usual," he said.

Rachael sat beside him. "I was ready to kill you. I knew I didn't want to, but I couldn't stop myself."

"I know," he said. "Why do you think I sang the

lullaby to you over and over? It gave you an anchor to your true self." He said the incantation and the salve glowed pink as the healing spell took effect.

She smiled while she watched the wounds close. "So, you're actually my anchor."

"In a matter of speaking."

They sat for a few more minutes, giving the healing salve as much time as possible to work. Joe finally pushed himself to his feet, and Rachael stood with him. He laid his ear to the door and didn't hear anything from the other side.

Over by the window, stood a square pedestal. Sitting innocently on top, was the orb. Joe approached it and lifted his hand. He could tell the orb had been completely corrupted from Ezra's possession. He felt bad for the device, but it had to be destroyed so the warlock couldn't use it to come back to their world.

"What's that?" Rachael asked.

"An orb. I'm not sure if it's the last one, but they are getting increasingly rare with every passing year. They can be used for different things, but mainly to open doors between worlds. I've got to destroy it."

Rachael stared into it. "It feels like it's alive."

"In a sense it is. To take a life is never a good thing, but it's been turned by the warlock's influence over it. There's no choice. It can't be reclaimed."

He took the torn remains of his T-shirt and draped it over the orb. Going to the fireplace, he grabbed the poker. He held his hand over it and cast forgiveness. He raised it high above his head, then brought it down hard. Glass cracked, and he did it again and again until shards fell to the floor, the light in them fading.

He dropped the poker on the floor and went to the

door, his fingers resting on the lock. "The warlock knows we need to head to the portal. That's probably why he hasn't chased us up here. He'll be marshalling his forces to stop us from leaving."

Rachael tore off a piece of the gown that had tangled around her legs. "Well, we shouldn't keep him waiting. And we need to be where we belong."

"Agreed. Remember, you have an angel's heart." He kissed her soundly. "And I love you."

"I love you, too. You're not anywhere close to ordinary." She laid her hand on his cheek. "You are a hero and you are my angel."

He opened the door and glanced back at her. "Let the games begin."

Chapter Twenty-Seven

They hurried down the long hall to the front door and the path home. They flung the door open to be greeted by a cacophony of unearthly animal sounds. Growls, snarls, ear-piercing shrieks, and other noises bellowed at them from the darkness beyond. Rachael trembled as she took his hand. He squeezed it, and they took their first steps onto the lighted trail. A tentacle shot out from the blackness, just missing them.

"Run!" Joe said, giving her a little push.

She heard Joe behind her, rapidly firing off spells. A huge feline appeared in front of her. She skidded to a stop, recognizing it as a witch-cat. Shifting to a large tiger, her haunches bunched, giving her more power as she leapt at the creature before her. The witch-cat howled as she raked her claws across its face.

The cat tried to clamp its jaws around her throat, but she ducked, ramming her shoulder into its wide chest. The witch-cat slashed downward, catching her right flank, making her howl as she sprawled on the path. She looked up and saw it getting ready to pounce. She scrambled to her feet, backing up when a dark blur slammed into the witch-cat, knocking it into the void.

Her features flowed back to human as she looked at the great beast loomed over her. She stood, realizing what the creature was that looked at her.

"Rachael, get back!"

She glanced over her shoulder at him at he tossed another creature off the path. "It's okay. This is the hunter I spoke to at the church. He's here to help us."

Joe walked up to it and she smiled as he offered his hand to the beast. "I'm sorry for hurting you."

The hunter looked at Rachael and rumbled deep in its chest. "He forgives you. He understands what you were feeling."

"Let's get to that portal and have an end, once and for all."

The three of them ran toward the doorway, the hunter shoving aside any creature not smart enough to get out of the way, Joe firing off magic bolts, and Rachael shifting to any animal that would benefit moving whatever stood before them. Soon, a light appeared at the end.

He pointed. "There it is. Once we're through, Damen will seal it forever."

As they drew closer, Ezra stepped out from the darkness. "You must get by me first, wizard. I assure you, that won't happen."

Joe eased Rachael behind him. "Yeah, blah, blah, blah. Stop talking and start fighting."

He fired a bolt of pure energy, which Ezra blocked easily. The warlock returned with a fire strike that bounced off a hastily erected shield. Joe was blown backward and landed near the hunter as it stood growling at Ezra. Using the beast's broad shoulder, Joe pulled himself upright, whispering in his ear.

The hunter lifted his muzzle and made a strange high-pitched keening as Joe whipped around, daggers made of pure light aiming straight for Ezra's heart. The warlock flicked his wrist, and the blades flew off into the darkness. A shambling creature shuffled forth, leaving a trail of murky slime behind it. The odor wafting from it smelled of damp, mildew, and decay. It raised its moss green arm to take a swipe at him. Joe ducked under the lumbering blow, backing up as the hunter leapt over him to knock the swampy creature off the path into the void.

Joe circled around, keeping Rachael behind him as they backed toward the portal. The hunter stayed with them, attacking and pushing away any of the horde trying to approach them. He took a quick glance over his shoulder. They were almost in position.

"I know what you're trying to do, Caine. You won't make it through the portal before I kill you."

Joe smiled. "You have no idea what my plan is, warlock. If you did, you'd have stopped me by now."

Ezra summoned a ghost wind. The lost spirits howled around him, their skeletal fingers trying to pluck him off the path to his doom. Joe held his ancestor's cross, calling a counter-clockwise cyclone to disperse the ghostly tornado. Air crackled around his hand and he opened it, firing snow and ice at Ezra as though shot from a cannon.

The warlock staggered back, howling with rage as he wiped the snow from his eyes. He stomped his foot hard on the path, the tremor pulsing at them in a wave, making them fight to keep upright. Joe countered with increasing the gravity around Ezra so he could barely move.

He threw a shield up in front of them as Ezra flung medium sized fire balls at them while still trying to dispel the gravity spell holding him in place. Rachael watched as sweat broke out on Joe's forehead, and his chest heaved as he drew in labored breath after labored breath.

"You're running out of strength, and he's stuck in one spot." She grabbed his hand and pulled hard. "Now's our chance. Let's go."

He kissed her. "I can't leave. Not until he's dead. The hunter will take care of you. I will be back. I will find you. Keep the faith."

"I don't understand. We've got to get out of here. Now!"

"Listen to me," he said. "I can't leave him alive. If he lives, that mark will plague you forever. I have to stay until the job's done."

Tears streamed down her face. "The job *is* done. You can't leave me." She glanced at the portal, seeing Damen on the other side, strain of holding it open showing on his face. "Please. Let's go."

He pressed her mother's cross into her hand. "I can't. Forgive me. Always remember, I love you."

Rachael was shoved through the portal, the hunter by her side. As she watched, it immediately closed in on itself and exploded out of existence. She fell onto the grass beneath the oak tree at Angel Haven. She stared up at Damen, but he looked as surprised as she did.

"Open the portal!" she begged. "Joe's still in there. He needs us."

"I can't. It's not just closed. He's destroyed it from the other side. I can't undo it."

She grabbed his jacket and yanked him forward. "Open it!" she demanded. "You're a wizard and a priest. There's got to be something you can do."

"I'm sorry. The portal is gone." He bowed his

head. "And so is he."

Rachael stared at where the portal had been just seconds before. "It can't be," she whispered.

The hunter whimpered, nudging her as she cried into his tough hide.

****

"No!" Ezra backhanded Joe, knocking him off his feet. Standing over him, his chest heaved and his eyes darkened to an unearthly black. "You fool. What have you done?"

Joe stood, rubbing his cheek. "I trapped us here. I told you I had a plan. You weren't leaving here. I've had the binding spell for the portal ready since before I got here. You were beaten as soon as you started your insane plan. You just didn't know it."

"You won't leave here, Caine. Ever."

"If that is what it takes to make sure you don't either, I'm good with it. Better that I stay here to keep fighting you for eternity than to let you have the chance of hurting Racheal."

A spectral hand grabbed Joe around the throat. "You don't have eternity. You will be dead very soon. You are alone here. Friendless. Helpless. And I will escape your damned prison. I have the orb."

"The orb is destroyed. You're not getting out." A high-pitched keening sounded in the darkness, and Joe smiled, dispelling the hand that held him. "And I'm not as alone as you think."

A huge burst of force knocked Joe off his feet. "That orb was priceless. Neither one of us is leaving without it." Out of the darkness, a pack of hunters barreled down the path. Ezra's mouth hung open in shock. "Those creatures are *my* servants."

Joe heard something clatter to the path but couldn't see the object around Ezra's broad shoulders. Whatever the warlock dropped, it was bound to be something that would make Joe's life incredibly unpleasant. He was tiring quicker than he would've believed. The energy it took to use his magic here was unbearable. He struggled to draw a decent breath, sweat trickling down his face. If he didn't stop Ezra soon, the warlock just might win.

"Those *hunters* are no one's servants." Joe's magic coalesced around his hands. "This ends, warlock. Now. One of us isn't walking away."

"And that will be you," he snarled.

As the hunters gathered behind Joe, he looked around. "We'll see."

****

Rachel sat on the loveseat in the family room. The Angels and the household staff weren't expected back until the next day. She held the cup of hot tea, shivering so hard it sloshed over the rim several times. The hunter had squeezed his huge body in to lay near her.

Damen sat across from her, waiting for her to say something. He held his rosary in his hand, murmuring the prayer for each bead.

"He can't be gone," she finally said.

"He isn't. He'll find a way back. The warlock had the orb…."

She looked up. "Joe destroyed it. He's left himself no way to get back. Did you know what he was going to do?"

Damen shook his head. "No, but I should have. He was too confident. I should've suspected he'd have something up his sleeve. I can't believe he kept his plan a secret. The pain had to have been intense to keep such a powerful spell at bay for as long as he did."

She suddenly sat up. "Joe can open portals. I've seen him do it. When he sent Arlen back, then when he went into the house to confront the doppelganger. Why can't he just open a portal and come back?"

"Portals are a lot harder to create than you think," Damen said. "Yes, he can open them, and he's good at it. But that's here. He's in the void now. We don't know a lot about the void, but we do know that magic there is unpredictable. The warlock only got out because Ithick created the portal to let him out."

"Why can't you or Chrissy open one to get him?"

"We don't have Joe's skill to open one and sustain it. Closing them is a different story. Yes, it takes a lot of energy, but not as much to open it."

She sat back, rubbing Arlen's head. "Joe really is powerful, isn't he?"

Damen nodded. "Unless he can find some way of opening and maintaining a portal long enough to get through it, I'm afraid he's gone."

She glanced at him, started to speak, and hesitated, before finally saying, "Do you think Chrissy knew?"

"I'm not sure. She told you she knew you were going to succeed."

Rachael stood. "The last time we were there, she seemed sad. If she knew, why wouldn't she say something?"

He sat back. "She may have seen something in her vision that let her know she had to keep silent. Clairvoyance is tricky. Reveal too much, and you can upset the natural order. Revealing too little can have the same result. It may have needed to happen."

She slowly sank down on the loveseat, scratching the hunter behind his ears when he nuzzled her hand. "But why?"

He shook his head, and she knew he had no answer.

****

Rachael was sitting under the oak when her teammates returned. The hunter rested at her side, her hand absently stroking him. He raised his head as Kristin walked up the hill, a low growl coming from deep in his throat.

"It's all right," Rachael murmured. "She's a friend."

Kristin looked at the hunter. "Who's your companion?"

"Arlen. He's a hunter from another dimension."

"Okay," Kristin said slowly. "And how did he come to be here?"

Tears pooled in Rachael's eyes. "Joe told him to protect me."

"What happened?"

Rachael stood, the hunter right behind her. "He's gone. He purposefully trapped himself in another dimension to save me from the warlock who was trying to control me." She turned away. "There's no way out. Joe is stuck in the void forever."

Kristin glanced at the tree. "I don't know what he did, but the oak looks better. Why are you out here?"

"It's where he disappeared. He may come back here. I'm going to stay put until...until..."

Kristin pulled Rachael into her arms and let her cry on her shoulder. "I'm so sorry. Let's go to the house, and I'll get you something to eat."

They headed for the house, Arlen right behind them. Rachael kept glancing at the tree, hoping the portal would open and Joe would step through, safe and sound. Arlen looked back every time she did. She hoped he'd be able to sense if the way opened again and Joe could come home.

****

A wispy figure appeared, trying to call out. Arlen lifted his head and stared at the tree, but saw nothing. He turned, taking a couple of hesitant steps toward it, then stopped. Rachael waited for him by the door.

"I'm trying…way….back," a quiet voice said before being lost on the breeze.

Chapter Twenty-Eight

Chrissy dropped the wards on her apartment as Rachael and Damen helped her inside. She sat on the couch, taking a deep breath and slowly released it. "It's amazing how much a car ride tires you out when you've been in bed for over a week. It's good to be home."

Rachael nodded and turned away. She and Damen had cleaned her apartment so she wouldn't have to do it when she got home. She went outside and stared at Joe's door. So many things had happened. She laid her hand on it and could almost hear his voice. A movement in the window caught her eye, and she walked closer. She pressed close to the glass and saw something inside. The figure turned, reaching out to her.

She gasped, jumping back. Arlen appeared at her side, and she smiled at him. Invisibility for a large friend was a huge asset. He rumbled and she turned around. Chrissy and Damen stood in the doorway, watching her.

"I think I saw something inside," she said.

Chrissy shook her head. "I haven't picked up anything. It's possible you want to see him so much, your mind is trying to play tricks."

"Oh." She reached down to pet Arlen. "You're probably right."

"It's been two weeks since he got trapped," Damen

said. "Did you want to check his apartment and see if his plants need water?"

She nodded and stepped aside to let Damen open the door. "Thanks. Arlen and I have got it from here."

She closed the door behind them and looked around. The air was stale, the room dark because of the closed blinds. She shoved them aside, sunlight immediately flooding the room. She walked over to his plants. They were still green, but they looked faded and a little droopy. She went to the kitchen and filled a glass with water.

The dirt in all the pots was dry. "I'm sorry Joe's not here to take care of you. It's all my fault. He was trying so hard to protect me; he did something incredibly brave and self-sacrificing. We could've made it back together, but he chose to save me so he could stay behind and defeat the warlock."

The leaves rustled, and she stared at them. Glancing at Arlen, she thought he looked like he was smiling. She turned her attention to the plants again. "Are you guys trying to talk to me?"

Leaves moved again. "Who knew?" she said.

After tending to the plants, she sat on the couch, rubbing Arlen's massive head. "We could stay here. It was his home. If, I mean when, he returns, it's very likely he'll come here, not to Angel Haven."

Looking around, she decided it was a good idea. She could look after his home and take care of his plants until he came back. "Arlen, I'm going to leave you here to guard the place. I'll be back soon. I've got to go home and get some things. Will you be all right for a bit?"

He nodded his great head, and she went back over

to Chrissy's. "Arlen and I are going to stay at Joe's place. I can keep an eye on things. I'm sure he'd want his plants cared for."

"You don't know how to raise and lower the wards," Damen said.

She smiled a little. "There's going to be a hunter on guard. I think we'll be okay. I've got to go home and pack some items. Back soon."

From the look Damen and Chrissy exchanged, Rachael knew they were worried about her. She knew in her heart, they feared she hadn't gotten over Joe's loss.

****

Rachael put more clothes on the bed next to the open suitcase. Kristin had tried to talk her out of leaving, but she couldn't stay here. She wanted to be near him and that meant keeping his apartment clean and intact until he found his way back to her. She paused, squeezing her eyes shut. Memories of him affected her at the worst times. Tears blurred her vision and ran down her cheeks. He had to come back to her. Soon.

Getting herself under control, she finished packing and set the case by the door. She went to her desk and unplugged her laptop. She coiled the power cord in her hand and caught a movement out of the corner of her eye. She turned her head, and the cord slid out of her hands, hitting the carpet with a muffled thump. Joe's image appeared faintly and faded away.

"I'm losing my mind," she murmured. "I want to see him so badly, I'm starting to."

She stuffed the cord in the bag and walked back to the bathroom to make sure she grabbed everything she would need. She pushed the shower curtain aside, and yes, she got everything from there. She turned to the medicine cabinet and stopped cold. A faint outline of Joe's face lingered there for a few seconds before disappearing.

As she watched, words began to form on the glass. *Remember me.* She stumbled out of the bathroom, worrying she really was going crazy. She hurried out, slinging her laptop case over her shoulder. She picked up the other bags and practically ran out the door to her car. It was all tricks of the light and wishful thinking. He was gone. He wasn't coming back. End of story. She headed for his home. She would keep it for him and Arlen would protect it.

She entered and Arlen looked up, growling a greeting. "Hello to you, too. Anything happen while I was out?"

Arlen swung his head toward the bedroom. "What happened?" He woofed quietly. "The mirror?"

She walked down the hallway to the bedroom and stared into the mirror over the dresser. Arlen padded behind her, squeezing in to sit and watch. "It's not doing anything now," she said.

She laid her hand on the glass. It was warm. She frowned and leaned closer. "What is going on?"

Joe's face appeared, and she screamed stumbling backward until the end of the bed stopped her. He lifted a fist, and she heard it thump against the glass. His face twisted as though he was in a lot of pain. Pale red light began to build and it hit the mirror, shattering the glass on the inside. Cracks radiated out from the center, shards falling slowly to the dresser.

She took great gulps of air, trying to calm her

racing heart. Tears streaked down her face as she leaned as close as she dared. He was alive! Alive and trying to contact her. "Joe, can you hear me? I'm here. Tell me what to do."

"Coming…soon."

His voice faded, and she lifted her hand. Trembling started at her legs, working its way up her body, until her teeth started chattering. Arlen pressed his large body against her. "You heard him, didn't you?" The hunter nodded. "Can we help him?" Arlen shook his head. She wrapped her arms around his thick neck. "We still have to wait, don't we?" She took the small whine as a yes.

"We have to tell Chrissy. She may have an idea on what to do." She glanced at Arlen. "Maybe it better just be me. Wait for me and don't let anyone in."

She raised her hand to knock and Chrissy opened the door. "I knew you were coming. Come on in. Where's Arlen?"

"Defending the homestead. I have to tell you something."

Chrissy sat on the couch. "Okay. What's up?"

"I just saw Joe in his bedroom mirror." She leaned down, taking Chrissy's good hand. "He's alive. He'll be coming home soon."

"Are you sure it's him and not an illusion?"

She nodded. "I saw him multiple times in my room when I was packing. He was almost transparent, then faded away like a ghost. I think he wants us to know he's all right."

"Did he say anything to you?"

"Not that time, but Arlen alerted me to the bedroom mirror when I got here, and I saw him again.

All he said was 'coming soon.'"

Chrissy rubbed her chin. "Mirrors have been used for communicating in the past. It makes sense he would try that to get in touch with you. Was there anything else you remember?"

She shook her head. "Could it mean he's still alive? Could the warlock really be dead?"

"Let me check for the second mark. If I can't see it, then the warlock is no more."

Rachael nodded and sat up straight. Chrissy laid her hand just above her heart and closed her eyes. "I find no trace of the mark. It's gone."

"Then it *is* him. How can we help him?"

"I'm afraid we can't. When he collapsed the portal and destroyed the orb, he also destroyed any chance we had of helping him on from here."

Rachael stood and smiled. "Then we just keep the faith. That's what he'd want us to do."

"It's exactly what he would say. Let me know if you hear or see anything else from him."

"Will do." She walked back over to his place and closed the door. "Good news, Arlen. It really is him, and the second mark is gone from me. Isn't that exciting? I wish you knew how to get him home."

She swore the hunter shrugged. "How about some dinner?"

He plodded to the door and turned invisible. She opened it and let him do whatever it was he did. She walked to the kitchen and began fixing something to eat. Joe must have recently gone shopping because nothing was expired. As she stirred gravy in the little saucepan, she remembered the last time she'd cooked here.

Joe had come out of the bathroom wearing a towel slung low on his hips. She'd stared at him, not believing a man could look that good. The broad shoulders, the defined chest, the abs that had been partially hidden by the terry material. Oh, and what that material hid. She knew how his legs felt, how easily he'd slipped into her when they made love.

His reddish-brown hair plastered to his head and those green eyes that had been wary at first, then confused. She'd denied being with him in the shower, but how she wished she'd been. He was a tender lover, putting her needs before his, making her feel like the only woman in the world. She smiled as she remembered wanting to tear the towel off and admire him before having her wicked way with him.

She still felt the warmth of his skin in her hands. She loved the way he responded when she touched him. Everywhere. His weight on her had been comforting and she knew at that moment, she loved him. A man of faith and magic, he was unique, and she had claimed him as her own.

Gravy popped out and splashed her hand. She jumped and snapped the heat off. She fixed her plate and sat at the table, still seeing him sitting across from her. It wasn't fair. The bad guy was beaten. Why couldn't her ending have been like her teammates? Why did the man she love trap himself?

Her shoulders slumped. Because he loved her. Because he would've done anything to protect her, even if it meant they wouldn't be together. A soft scratching told her Arlen was back. She got up to open the door and he sauntered in, picking his way carefully to lay over by the patio doors. "You really need to be smaller," she said scratching behind his ear.

She went back to the table and picked at her food. She was hungry until she'd made it. There was no doubt she needed to eat, in case she had to do something to help get Joe back from the void. Sliding the fork under the potatoes, she nibbled at the meal until it was gone.

After washing the few dishes, she sat on the couch. She never realized how much the television was on at Angel Haven until she moved in here. Picking up the stereo remote, she started the CDs Joe had left in there, not having the heart to change them. As she put the remote on the table, the music box caught her eye.

She held it in her hands, caressing the carvings. The darkening wood was smooth and shiny, a testament to its age. Joe had said it was from his great grandparents. She closed her eyes, holding the box to her chest. She missed him so much. Was he actually trying to come back or was she just wishing too hard?

As she thought of him, she smiled. "Just keep the faith."

Chapter Twenty-Nine

Spring had finally arrived. The last of the snow melted, and Rachael opened the windows to let some fresh air blow away the cobwebs of winter. Arlen had learned to control his size, and she wondered if he was learning from her own shapeshifting abilities. He was now more the size of a large dog, rather than, say, a Buick.

She paid the rent on his apartment and kept everything straight. She'd taken to going to hear Damen at his church every Sunday with Chrissy. She always half heard the sermon, instead praying the whole time for Joe to come back to her. It had been three months since he'd saved her and collapsed the portal. He hadn't appeared to her since the few times right after he'd been trapped.

She got back home, kneeling down and hugging Arlen tightly as she did every time she had to leave. If it wasn't for the hunter, she was sure she'd have gone crazy. She was understanding him more and more every day. At first, it was through a little bit of telepathy, but that got too hard for both of them.

Soon, she learned how to read his facial expressions, and there were plenty. He was getting good at reading her, too. She began taking him with her on the Angels' missions, his invisibility a valuable asset. Her team wasn't too sure about him at first, but quicker than she would've believed, they accepted him.

Rachael stood in front of the window, the warm breeze clicking the long blinds together. Three months. Joe had been gone for three very long, incredibly lonely months. She glanced at Arlen. "I don't think he's coming back."

The hunter blew air out of his nostrils.

"Easy for you to say 'have patience.' You're not in love with him."

Arlen rolled his eyes, making her chuckle. "I know. Keep the faith."

****

The spring night was quiet as police officers completed the shift change at the Red Lion station in southern New Jersey. Traffic at the Rt. 70 circle wouldn't pick up now until rush hour the next morning. A low crime rate, thanks to the local heroes, and it being close to ten at night, the officers had no reason to expect anything different from any other night.

Until the explosion.

Officers in the back came running to the front counter and they all looked at each other before hurrying outside. Across Rt. 206 was a large open field with trees bordering it from houses and farms just beyond. Smoke rose from the middle of the field and a figure collapsed. Several officers ran across the street, while someone called for medical help.

The first officer to arrive was Nate Kendall. The rest of his company would be here in a second. As he quickly looked the man over, his skin tingled and he knew whoever this guy was, he'd been in a big time magic battle. The signs were all there. Thankfully, the hospital would be able to take care of him. He couldn't detect any supernatural infection. As the newest member of the Circle of Nine, he'd been told to be on the lookout for anything odd that may happen.

Well, it qualified. The man on the ground was smoking. All he wore was a pair of badly damaged jeans. His skin was pale, and he had a long growth of beard on his face. His hair was shaggy and greasy, matted with blood and dirt. Around his neck was a leather braid with a wooden cross that looked, surprisingly, undamaged. His palms had been scorched, almost to the bone. Blood still seeped out from multiple cuts on his body. Ugly, purple bruises covered his arms, chest, and back.

All the police looked at each other. "He's been in one hell of a fight. He's lucky he's alive."

The man on the ground moaned softly. "Rachael."

Nate looked at his fellow officers. He leaned close. "Sir, can you tell me your name?"

"J…Joseph Caine."

"Do you remember what happened?" he said, trying to keep the excitement from his voice. The Wizard Caine was back, and Nate had found him.

Joe's head rolled back and forth. "Dark. Too…much…pain."

"You called for someone named Rachael," Nate said. "Who's Rachael? Can you tell us how to get in touch with her?"

"Love," Joe gasped. "Keep…the faith."

His eyes closed, and they knew he wasn't saying anything else. The officers just looked at each other as another glanced over his shoulder when they heard sirens blaring in the distance. "Do you think that explosion we heard caused those burns?"

Everyone shook their heads and stood back as the paramedics took over.

"I'll follow them to the hospital, see if we can get more information," Nate said. He'd also be in a better position to defend him if necessary.

Joe was loaded into the ambulance, and Nate and his partner jumped in their cruiser to follow them to the hospital in Marlton. He was hoping he could get some information from Joe so he could report to the rest of the Circle. His own group had also been trying to retrieve Joe from the void. With the portals destroyed, though, it had made a hard task impossible.

Standing at the nurses' counter, Nate punched up Joe's name on the small tablet he carried. His picture came up, and the officer showed it to his partner. "That's him. He's originally from Oakley Lake, Nebraska. He lives in New York. He's a freelance journalist for a small paper. Says he disappeared at the end of January. Could he have been kidnapped and just got free?"

The other office shrugged. "Anything is possible. It say anything about a 'Rachael'?"

"Not a thing. It does say one of his contacts is a Father Damen Richardson, a priest at a small church called St. Michaels. We're going to have to wait and see if he can answer any other questions when he wakes up."

"Let's try to get in touch with the priest. Maybe he can help."

Nate pulled out his cell phone and dialed St. Michael's church.

****

Damen pushed himself to his feet and grabbed his

keys. It was late, his favorite time to sit in the church. The silence soothed him, and he could pray for a way to retrieve his friend. It was already close to the end of April, and he hadn't come up with a way yet to save Joe. They had even gone so far to try to contact the Magic Central website people again, with no luck.

He gazed at the cross over the altar. "Help me find the way to bring him home. Everything I've done, everything I've tried, has failed. I didn't keep him safe when he was here, and I let him down when he needed me most. What else can I do?"

A quiet voice whispered, *"Keep the faith, buddy. I'm coming."*

He smiled. It was only his mind telling him that in Joe's voice. "I'm trying to keep the faith, but sometimes, God, even a priest has doubts. If I could just bring him home."

Damen sat there a little longer, his legs starting to bounce with impatience. He kept glancing at the door, until he could stand no longer. He got up and hurried home, just in time to hear the phone in his office start to ring. The caller ID showed it was a New Jersey area code.

"Hello?"

"May I speak to Father Damen Richardson?"

He frowned. "Speaking. How may I help you?"

"My name is Officer Nathan Kendall. I'm with the police in Red Lion, New Jersey. Do you know a Joseph Caine?"

Damen's spine stiffened as he straightened up. "Yes. He's a good friend of mine. Did something happen?"

"We have him at the hospital in Marlton. Do you

think you could come down here and answer some questions? He's been beaten pretty badly."

"Give me a couple of hours. I'm heading out now."

Damen grabbed his cell phone and keys, running out to his car. He'd call Rachael and Chrissy once he had more information. He backed out, heading for the Garden State. Time to pick up the turnpike and head south to get his friend.

****

Damen burst into the emergency room and headed for the desk. "I'm Father Damen Richardson. I received a call a friend of mine was here?"

A police officer approached him. "Father Damen, I'm Nate Kendall."

"You're the one who called," he said, shaking the officer's hand. He let Nate escort him to a private room where they could talk. "How is he?"

"The doc thinks he's going to be okay, but his hands were burned pretty badly. What do you think happened to him?"

Damen wasn't sure how to answer him, so he simply shrugged. He watched Nate walk to the door and look up and down the hall before pushing is closed and coming back over. Light began forming over Nate's hand.

"You can trust me with the truth. I'm part of the new Circle of Nine. We've been trying to retrieve Wizard Caine ever since he trapped himself in the void. Now the only time I've ever seen burns like the ones on his hands was the time I fought a fire djinn."

"They're nasty pieces of work. How are you in law enforcement and a wizard?"

Nate grinned. "Why are you a priest and a wizard?

We all do what we must. Now, what happened?"

Damen shook his head. "I don't know. We went to close the portal at Angel Haven. Rachael, one of the Angels, had been taken by the warlock. Joe went in after her. I saw them coming. Next thing I knew, Rachael stumbled out of the portal with a hunter, and it exploded. I knew then, that had been his plan all along. He was going to destroy the portal and kill the warlock. That was the last I saw him."

"Who is Rachael?"

"The love of his life," Damen said quietly. "They're crazy about each other. His power has grown in strength ever since he started trying to free her from the warlock's influence."

Nate nodded. "But the burns. You didn't see a djinn or any fire type after him?"

"I'm sorry, but no. How are you going to write up the report?"

"Kidnapping and assault by a cult. It's the best way right now. The rest of my company doesn't know I'm one of the heroes they admire, and I'd like to keep it that way."

Damen smiled. "Who keeps secrets better than a priest? Can you imagine what my congregation would say if they knew I carried a gun with blessed ammunition?"

"It'd be interesting." Nate stood. "Let's go see how he's doing."

The two men left the room, heading straight for the nurses' station.

****

Chrissy knocked on Rachael's door and was greeted with a short huff and a scratch. She opened it, leaning down to rub the hunter's head. "Thank you, Arlen. How you been?"

He rolled his eyes and glanced over at Rachael. Chrissy nodded, understanding what he meant. She watched Rachael, come out of the kitchen and water the plants, talking to them the whole time. "Hi, Chrissy. Arlen said you'd be stopping by. I think he's picking up a little of your clairvoyance. I didn't know hunters adapted like that, did you?"

"There's a lot about hunters we don't know, but I think Arlen here, is amazing."

Rachael gestured to the couch, and they sat. "What would happen if he started hanging around Damen?" The women giggled a moment.

Chrissy cleared her throat. "Speaking of Damen, he just called me. He wants us to come to south Jersey as soon as we can."

"Has something happened?"

"Joe has come back."

Rachael sat back, stunned. He was here on earth? After so much time had gone by? "Why didn't he get in touch with me? And how did he end up in New Jersey?"

"I really can't answer that question. Damen says he's been hurt. He's in a hospital in Marlton. He won't wake up." She took Rachael's hands. "He's hoping the three of us can come up with something. You up for a road trip?"

"To see him again? What are we waiting for?"

Arlen nudged her legs. "I need you to stay here and protect the place."

"I can raise the wards if Arlen wants to come," Chrissy said.

The hunter turned to Rachael and raised an eyebrow. She sighed. "Fine, you can come. But stop saying 'I told you so.'"

They piled into Chrissy's car and headed south.

Chapter Thirty

Rachael eased the door open to Joe's hospital room and smiled when Damen stood to greet them. He hugged her, then Chrissy, stumbling when he was bumped into by nothing. When he looked down, she grinned as Arlen appeared.

"I told him to wait in the car, but he didn't want to."

Damen rubbed his head. "As long as you stay invisible and out of the way when the nurse comes in, you should be fine."

Rachael stepped closer to the bed. His short beard had grown longer, his reddish-brown hair now streaked with white. She smoothed it back, kissing his forehead. Thick bandages covered his hands, and he had small, assorted dressings over all the cuts. She traced the bruises on his arms.

Tears slipped down her cheeks and she gazed at him. "What happened to him?"

"That's what I'd like to know," Nate said from the doorway.

"Officer Nate Kendall, I'd like you to meet Christine Ford." Damen walked over, laying his hand on Rachael's shoulder. "And here is the Rachael you've been asking about."

"Now I have a face to go with the name."

"I don't understand. How do you know me?"

Nate smiled. "You were the first person he called for when he came back." He glanced in the corner. "How did you get a hunter?"

"Arlen is a friend. He protects me." She stopped and stared at him. "How can you see him?"

"It's one of my talents. I can 'see' the invisible. I'm a member of the new Circle of Nine."

"Oh." She glanced again at Joe. "Why won't he wake up?"

Nate shook his head. "We don't know. I've tried every spell I can think of, but no luck. Damen has also tried."

"I even called Gizel to see if he had any thoughts," Damen said. "But he'd never heard of an injury that robs the mind."

Rachael touched Joe's forehead, trying to hold herself together. "So I have him back, but not all of him. He's gone somewhere inside himself."

Damen took her hands. "If anyone can bring him back, I know it will be you."

Silence filled the room as they waited for some sign Joe would wake up just from Rachael's touch. Nothing.

"Can I be alone with him, please?" she said, not looking at the group behind her.

They left quietly, and Rachael pulled a chair up next to the bed. She held his hand carefully, trying not to hurt him. Her eyes burned, and her throat tightened as she watched him. She stroked his forehead as her tears fall, dotting the hospital sheet.

"What happened to you after you shoved me through the portal?" she whispered. "I know you weren't hurt this badly when I left, so what happened to you?"

His chest rose and fell, but his hand remained still in hers, and his eyes remained shut.

"If only you knew how much I've missed you. I knew you would come back, and I had a feeling your body would be hurt, but I didn't think your mind would be, too." She wiped her eyes. "You've got to come all the way back. You won't get better unless you do."

She sang the lullaby to him, her voice breaking every few words. When she finished, she started over, her voice stronger as the words and melody filled her. As the last note faded, his hand twitched in hers so she started again. Her back straightened, and the melody rang true through the room.

His head moved back and forth, and his face scrunched up, like he was suffering great pain. He groaned and she stood, singing as she laid her hand over his heart. His eyelids began to flutter before slowly opening to gaze at her.

"Rachael," he said, his voice cracking. "Sing it again."

And she did, softly, next to his ear so only he heard her. When she finished he smiled, and she lightly kissed him.

"I missed the sound of your voice," he said.

"I missed everything about you. I'm glad you've come back to me."

The door opened, and their friends walked in, surprised to see him awake. "Why are the nurses crying in the hall?" Chrissy asked.

"Because a special song has brought my love back to me," Rachael said.

The four of them gathered around his bed. "Joe,

what happened to you in the void?" Damen said.

"Well, for one thing, I got my ass kicked." He closed his eyes. "The warlock came after me. It was a long fight. The hunters helped keep the other creatures back, so I could concentrate on the battle. Trolls are still not my favorite people."

"But how did you get back?" Rachael said. "We've tried everything to bring you home. What exactly happened?"

"What indeed," Joe murmured. "It all started when I destroyed the portal…"

****

Joe spoke the final words of the binding spell, and the portal exploded behind him, burning his back. The warlock bellowed his rage and charged at him, slinging points of magic light at him. Joe shielded himself from most of them, but a few hit, cutting him open. He ducked under Ezra's grasp and ran for the house, the hunters following him.

With the building at his back, he turned and summoned lightning. The bolt struck Ezra, shearing away his hastily erected shield as the electricity burned his clothes. He created an energy axe, throwing it at Joe's head. Joe shunted it off to the darkness, smiling when something yelped. Behind him, the hunters seemed to chuckle. He wasn't sure how he could talk to the hunters now, and he knew it wasn't the best time to solve that particular mystery.

Ezra charged toward him, summoning anything he could think of to throw at Joe, to stop him. "I will destroy you, wizard!"

He raised his arms, calling more dark creatures and gesturing them to attack Joe. He listened to the nails, claws, and just very large, heavy feet creep closer to him. The nether beasts stood behind Ezra, looking at the warlock as if waiting for a signal.

Joe glanced back at the hunters. He heard them in his mind say the other beasts were waiting for the outcome of the magic battle to see who they would follow. Turning back to Ezra, he determined it wouldn't be him they fed on.

"You can try, warlock, but you couldn't even get the job done when I was tied up and bleeding. What makes you think you can do it now?"

Blood red energy zoomed at him from the warlock, knocking him off his feet. He slid on his back a few feet before hitting the step. One of the hunters swung its massive head at him and raised an eyebrow.

As Joe pushed himself to his feet, he glanced at it. "All right. So maybe taunting him wasn't the brightest idea. I'm doing the best I can."

Joe swept his arm upward, and Ezra was encased in a block of ice. At least momentarily. The ice exploded, and Joe threw up another shield, protecting him and the hunters from the flying shards. He flung dozens of tiny fire darts at Ezra, silently giving thanks when some hit, doing damage. The rest Ezra shunted off into the void.

He glanced at the hunters. "I'm not sure I can beat him. You guys got any ideas at all?"

One of the hunters looked in the other direction, nonchalantly dropping something on the path at his feet. Joe looked down and saw the knife Ezra had used to open his skin. He picked it up, concealing the blade behind his back. As the warlock approached, finally standing over him, Joe murmured a spell over the knife. He'd never used a knife at close range before, and the accuracy incantation was the insurance he needed to make sure the blade hit home.

"I will end your miserable life now, wizard. You're beaten. As you die, I will take your power. Then, the little shifter will be mine. I will toy with her until she begs me for death."

"Yeah. About that…" Joe surged to his feet, driving the blade deep into Ezra's chest. Ezra's eyes opened wide in shock, and he stared down at the knife protruding from his chest. He crumpled to the ground, Joe following him down, making sure the knife stayed in.

"That plan just doesn't work for me. I'm sorry things worked out this way. You are forgiven, Ezra Barghest. Be at peace in the afterlife you have chosen."

The shock on Ezra's face faded as his eyes drifted shut. Shadows blacker than the darkest night seeped out of him, flowing on invisible winds back to the void. Joe scurried back and watched as Ezra's body turned to dust to be blown away. The hunters sat around Joe, eyeing the other creatures.

A heavy silence fell over them as the beasts looked around. They finally gazed at Joe, as if waiting for him to do something. He looked at the hunter. "What do they want me to do?"

The hunter rolled his eyes and snorted.

"Are you serious? I can't send them home. Portals can't be opened in the void."

The hunter head-butted him lightly on the shoulder and got up, walking into the house. Joe got up and followed him. He walked back into the study and sat down. Joe looked at the bookshelves.

"Don't you think if there was a spell in here, Ezra

would have found it?"

The hunter huffed and nodded toward the curtains. Joe looked over and saw feet sticking out beneath. He walked over and, reaching behind the heavy fabric, yanked out Ithick and threw him to the floor. "How do I get the nether beasts home?"

The doppelganger cringed. "There are portals along the path. All they have to do is walk along and the right one will open as the creature gets near. It was a spell I used to help my master."

"Yeah, well, you don't have a master anymore." Joe looked at the hunter, who nodded. "Thanks for all your help. You'll make sure everyone gets home?"

The hunter huffed again and walked out.

Joe turned again to Ithick. "How do I get home?"

The doppelganger laughed. "You and I are stuck here for all eternity. When you destroyed the main portal, you destroyed all my links to your world. The creatures can go home because the links to the nether realms are easier to manage."

"Why can't I just use one of those portals to their world and then gate myself home?"

"You humans are so stupid. As soon as you step one foot into their world, they will destroy you."

Joe grabbed him, jerking him to his feet. "Not the hunters. They'd protect me."

"You would not live five seconds there. Hunters are adaptable. Their atmosphere is poison to humans. They can breathe your air, but you cannot breathe theirs. You are stuck here, wizard, whether you like it or not."

Joe pushed Ithick away from him. There had to be a way out. He'd had a vision of him and Rachael together in the future. There was a way out. All he had to do was find it and keep the faith.

"Do not forget about my trolls and goblins. We'll make sure you've got plenty of company."

"Figures," he muttered.

Joe threw Ithick into the hallway and slammed the study doors shut behind him. He turned to the books lining the walls. He started at the top, thumbing through them to find something, anything that would get him out of here. There was a scratching at the door. He opened it carefully, and the hunter stood there, staring at him. He opened it wider, allowing it to come in.

The hunter walked in and sat in front of a small alcove at the far end of the room. Joe watched as the hunter nodded to it. He walked over and pulled the velvet curtain back. A magic mirror. Joe grinned at the hunter, who just rolled his eyes and lay on the floor.

Magic mirrors were easy to activate. It was one of the first things a novice wizard learned to do. He could at least get a message to Rachael and let her know he was alive. He looked at the cuts and bruises covering his body. He didn't look too great, but he was alive.

He opened the pathway and saw her in her room. She was packing a suitcase. He frowned. He tried to call out to her. She turned and gasped. He tried again when she went into her bathroom. He sagged into the chair behind him. It had never taken so much effort before to communicate through a mirror. It had to be the void.

After the fight to free himself and Rachael, then using the spell to destroy the portal, his body was beginning to fight to remain upright, let alone work anymore magic. His muscles trembled as if he'd run a bunch of marathons non-stop. His power dimmed from not being able to connect with the earth to renew himself.

His eyes drifted shut and as much as he didn't want to, he let sleep claim him. He'd try again after resting.

Chapter Thirty-One

He woke a couple of hours later, heading straight for the mirror. He opened it again and saw his bedroom. The hunter he sent with Rachael gazed back at him. He let the image fade. Rachael. He needed to concentrate on her. He took a deep breath and stepped closer to the mirror.

When he looked again, he saw Rachael staring intently into the mirror. He could barely hear what she was saying. "Remember me." he shouted. "I'm working on a few ideas. I'll be coming home soon."

The look on her face told him she could barely understand his words. Frustration bubbled up and he smashed his fist against the mirror, the damage traveling to his own and shattering it. Just brilliant. He turned around and stumbled back to the loveseat. He laid his arm across his eyes and took a deep breath. He was beginning to think he was as trapped here as Ezra had been.

The study doors burst open and trolls charged in, with Ithick in the lead. Joe threw up a shield as they hurled anything they could get their hands on at him. He sent a blast of icy wind at them, blowing them out the door. Joe shook his head at the latest attack. He was going to have to put a stop to the constant battles and soon. Ithick was always irritating but leading goblins and trolls against him every day was getting out of hand.

He felt blood run down his face, and he sat on the loveseat and wiped it off. He laid his head back and closed his eyes. How was he ever going to get home? Something cold and slimy nudged him. He opened his eyes, and the hunter sat there, a disapproving look on his face. "Don't judge me. I'm doing the best I can. I've barely scratched the surface of these books. If you got a better idea, let's hear it. I can't even figure out how I'm talking to you."

The hunter rolled his eyes, making Joe frown. "Saying 'it's magic' doesn't help. You got a name?"

The hunter stared at him, before making a rumbling sound.

Joe held out his hand. "Nice to meet you, Elek. Wizard Joseph Caine, at your service."

Elek walked over to the shelves, dragging a specific book down. He plopped it on Joe's lap. Joe looked at the title and almost threw the book across the room. "I am not summoning a fire djinn. They're too unpredictable."

Elek growled and sat directly in front of him, narrowing his eyes.

"Yes, I want to get out of here. I'm just not sure summoning an elemental is the best way to do it."

Elek whined and stared at him.

"It can't be April already back home. I haven't been here that long."

Another yowl ending with a yip and eye roll.

Joe sighed. "I know it's the void. I didn't know time moved differently here. Get off my case. I've never been here before."

He flipped open the book and began to read. It

seemed simple enough, but apparently he was going to have to pay a price. And that price could be anything. He looked up at the hunter, watching him expectantly. "It's the only way, isn't it?"

Elek's eyes held a hint of sadness and he nodded.

Joe took a deep breath. "Then let's do it."

Finding the spell, he read it over. It didn't appear too terribly difficult, but he needed to concentrate or the spell could backfire and that would not be pleasant. Elek looked like he had a grin on his face as Joe cast a circle and began to summon who was, hopefully, going to be his ticket home.

He traced patterns in the air, all the while speaking the words that would bring the fire djinn to him. The temperature began to climb in the room and the floor glowed with an eerie, orange light. A spire of flame appeared, reaching up to the ceiling. The fire parted and a figure stepped out. Joe swallowed. A very large figure, with bright red skin and white hair scowling fiercely at him.

"Who has summoned me?" the djinn bellowed.

"I did. I am the Wizard Caine, descendant of the leader of the original Circle of Nine. I know your race walks between worlds, and I need your help. I'm trapped here, and I need your excellent assistance to return home."

The djinn leaned close to his face. "There is a price, wizard, for my help. Are you prepared to pay?"

Joe thought of Rachael and how he longed to hold her again. "I am willing to pay the price you set."

"You will owe me three favors, wizard. Do you agree?"

Owing any magical creature a favor was bad, but

he needed to be home. "I agree. I will owe you three favors."

The door burst open, and Ithick charged in on his daily attack, his trolls behind him. They pulled up short when they saw the djinn. Joe watched the djinn's eyes narrow and instantly felt sorry for Ithick.

"I will not be interrupted," the djinn thundered. Flame shot from his hand and all that was left of Ithick and his trolls were scorch marks on the carpet. "Traveling with me will cause you pain. You will need to shield yourself in your mind to be able to withstand my touch. Now wizard, are you ready?"

Joe nodded. "I am."

The djinn grabbed his hands, making him scream as fire burned his palms. A bright gateway opened above them, and they shot through it faster than Joe thought possible. He sensed Elek next to him as they traveled through a tunnel vaguely resembling the wormholes he'd read about in school. There was an explosion, and he stood in the middle of a field.

He looked up and the sky was familiar. Nothing else was, but he knew he was back on earth. Elek had disappeared, and he collapsed to the ground. As he lay there, he heard voices talking to him.

****

"And that's what happened," Joe said. "Ezra couldn't use the fire djinns to get home because of the binding spell. I didn't have that limitation, so I tried it and it worked. I couldn't wake up when I was first brought here because I had to, basically, hit my reset button."

"But you're all right now?" Rachael said, laying her hand on his cheek.

He nodded. "I heard your voice. The lullaby reached me, and I knew it was time to return. I missed you so much."

"Same here," she whispered.

"We're glad to have you back," Damen said. "After all, what would I do without my sidekick?"

"Sidekick?" Joe repeated.

Damen just grinned. Chrissy stepped up. "Joe, I'd like to introduce you to Nate Kendall. He was first on the scene when you re-appeared. He's part of the new Circle of Nine."

"Nice to meet you, Nate." Joe held up his hands. "I'd shake your hand but…"

"Not a problem. I can't believe you promised three favors to a fire djinn."

Joe shrugged. "I did what I had to do. Fire djinns have their own code of honor. It may be a little iffy, but I felt comfortable with it. Did you see Elek anywhere nearby? He came with me, but I can't find him now."

Nate grinned. "I gave him your address. He'll probably be at your apartment when you get home." He squeezed Joe's shoulder. "If you need help with anything, give me a yell."

"Will do."

Damen walked over to the door and opened it. "We'll be back tomorrow to see you. Rachael, you coming?"

She shook her head. "No. I'm staying here tonight."

The door shut and she leaned over and kissed him lightly. "I was so afraid you'd never come back."

"I told you I would. All you had to do was keep the faith."

She smiled. "I did and here you are. It worked."

"It will always work, especially for you."

"And why is that?" she asked, smoothing his hair back.

"Because you have an angel's heart." He lifted a bandaged hand and caressed her cheek. "And because love is the greatest magic there is and you have my love for all time."

"Same here." She leaned down to kiss him while Arlen re-appeared and rolled his eyes.

A word from the author...

I graduated from Mercy High in Baltimore, Maryland, in 1981 and got married to an Air Force man in 1982. We have two amazing boys who have grown into amazing young men. We spent sixteen years in southern New Jersey, four of them at McGuire Air Force Base and the rest in Hammonton. We currently live in Memphis, Tennessee, where science fiction, wrestling, and hockey take up what time the cat doesn't.

Thank you for purchasing
this publication of The Wild Rose Press, Inc.

If you enjoyed the story, we would appreciate your
letting others know by leaving a review.

For other wonderful stories,
please visit our on-line bookstore at
www.thewildrosepress.com.

For questions or more information
contact us at
info@thewildrosepress.com.

The Wild Rose Press, Inc.
www.thewildrosepress.com

Stay current with The Wild Rose Press, Inc.

Like us on Facebook

https://www.facebook.com/TheWildRosePress

And Follow us on Twitter
https://twitter.com/WildRosePress

www.ingramcontent.com/pod-product-compliance
Lightning Source LLC
Chambersburg PA
CBHW060528260626
47161CB00003B/809